**Here's what critics are saying about
Gemma Halliday's Wine & Dine Mysteries:**

"I rank *A Sip Before Dying* as one of my favorite fun reads.
I say to Gemma Halliday, well done. She wrote a mystery
that encompassed suspense flavored with romantic notions,
while giving us a heroine to make us smile."
—*The Book Breeze Magazine*

"Gemma Halliday's signature well-written story filled with
wonderful characters is just what I expected. All in all, this
is the beginning of a great cozy series no one should miss!"
—*Kings River Life Magazine*

"I've always enjoyed the writing style and comfortable tone
of Gemma novels and this one fits in perfectly. From the
first page, the author pulled me in…when all was said and
done, I enjoyed this delightfully engaging tale and I can't
wait to spend more time with Emmy, Ava and their
friends."
—*Dru's Book Musings*

"This is a great cozy mystery, and I highly recommend it!"
—*Book Review Crew*

"I could not put *A Sip Before Dying* by Gemma Halliday
down. Once I started reading it, I was hooked!!"
—*Cozy Mystery Book Reviews*

BOOKS BY GEMMA HALLIDAY

High Heels Mysteries
Spying in High Heels
Killer in High Heels
Undercover in High Heels
Christmas in High Heels
(short story)
Alibi in High Heels
Mayhem in High Heels
Honeymoon in High Heels
(short story)
Sweetheart in High Heels
(short story)
Fearless in High Heels
Danger in High Heels
Homicide in High Heels
Deadly in High Heels
Suspect in High Heels
Peril in High Heels
Jeopardy in High Heels

Wine & Dine Mysteries
A Sip Before Dying
Chocolate Covered Death
Victim in the Vineyard
Marriage, Merlot & Murder
Death in Wine Country
Fashion, Rosé & Foul Play
Witness at the Winery

Hollywood Headlines Mysteries
Hollywood Scandals
Hollywood Secrets
Hollywood Confessions
Hollywood Holiday
(short story)
Hollywood Deception

Marty Hudson Mysteries
Sherlock Holmes and the Case of the Brash Blonde
Sherlock Holmes and the Case of the Disappearing Diva
Sherlock Holmes and the Case of the Wealthy Widow

Tahoe Tessie Mysteries
Luck Be A Lady
Hey Big Spender
Baby It's Cold Outside
(holiday short story)

Jamie Bond Mysteries
Unbreakable Bond
Secret Bond
Bond Bombshell
(short story)
Lethal Bond
Dangerous Bond
Bond Ambition
(short story)
Fatal Bond
Deadly Bond

Hartley Grace Featherstone Mysteries
Deadly Cool
Social Suicide
Wicked Games

Other Works
Play Dead
Viva Las Vegas
A High Heels Haunting
Watching You (short story)
Confessions of a Bombshell Bandit (short story)

FASHION, ROSÉ & FOUL PLAY

a Wine & Dine mystery

GEMMA HALLIDAY

Dedicated to Susie, my partner in crime.

CHAPTER ONE

"Flash me some teeth," I said, aiming my camera at my best friend, Ava Barnett. Usually she was the one playing photographer for me, snapping pictures at events I attended or hosted to help promote my winery, Oak Valley Vineyards. Tonight, however, I'd pulled out my trusty old camera bag, and it was all about her and the amazing jewelry she made at her jewelry boutique, Silver Girl.

She tossed her blonde hair and gave me a bright smile as she held up her wrist, displaying a silver charm bracelet with tiny gemstone accents. Then she pursed her lips, making a duck face and goofing with the camera in a way that had me laughing behind it.

"You're a natural born model," I told her, snapping a couple more pics.

"Shh." She put her finger to her lips. "Don't say that too loudly around here. Someone might wrangle me into a skimpy dress."

The two of us were in the Grand Ballroom of the local golf club, the Sonoma Links, which had been transformed into a makeshift backstage area for a charity fashion show being hosted there that evening. The air was electric with pre-show energy—hairdressers, makeup artists, designers, and models buzzing in all directions to make sure every button, zipper, accessory, frill, curl, and eyelash was positioned perfectly. The event featured fashions from two notable San Francisco designers who were showcasing several pieces from their latest collections, which would then be auctioned off with all proceeds going to help local children's charities. Thanks to Ava's father being a longstanding club member, she'd also gotten a key spot in the show—loaning all of the jewelry that the models would be accessorizing their custom outfits with. It was a huge opportunity for her, one that meant mass exposure to the type of clientele that would put her store on the map—country club members with deep pockets and addictions to shiny things.

"At least you could *fit* into one of the skimpy dresses," I noted, watching a particularly short red outfit walk by us on a long legged creature who was at least three sizes smaller than I.

"Please," she said, waving me off as she smoothed imaginary wrinkles from her vintage-inspired outfit. Black, salmon, and complimentary green lengths of fabric formed the skirt, while the black halter-type top did its best to contain her ample chest. "You know we're the same size."

Which might technically be true—both of us owning wardrobes in size eight. Though Ava's eight was more of an athletic, lithe shape that spoke to her love of outdoors, while mine was more of a soft, comfortable eight that spoke to my training as a chef…and regular enjoyment of the fruits of my own labor. Plus, her padding was up top, while mine tended to drift lower. Case in point—the little black dress I had on for the occasion, which was fitting just a little more snuggly than I would have liked in the hips. And waist. And bust. Might be time to concede a size ten soon?

"Oh, get a picture of the earrings Jada is wearing, would you?" Ava asked, pointing behind me.

I spun, glancing in the direction she indicated, spotting the tall, slim, dark haired model, Jada Devereux. Her skin was a warm tan, and her stunning blue eyes were pale and wide, giving her an unexpected exotic look that was captivating in person. Her long, shiny hair was sleeked back from her face to showcase the dangling silver earrings accented with small crystals that caught the light with her every movement.

Beside her I noticed Carl Costello, one of the designers being featured that night, using a roller to whisk away stray lint from her skintight navy jumpsuit. Like his model, he was also dressed in navy—in a turtleneck sweater and rhinestone studded blazer paired with white leather pants that clung to his stocky legs. Costello had been a fashion icon for years, his classic designs and chic silhouettes gracing runways from Paris to Milan as well as major department stores around the country. While his style was a bit more formal than my own—and a bit pricier than my meager bank account would allow—he had an uncanny knack for flattering a woman's shape.

Once he seemed satisfied that his subject was lint free, he gave Jada a wink and an affectionate pat on the cheek, having to lift just slightly on his tiptoes to do so.

"Mr. Costello, do you mind if we snap a picture?" I asked as Ava and I approached the pair.

Costello turned his attention from his model, a bright smile taking over his round features as he spotted Ava. "Of course, my dahlings. Ava, these earrings are to die for. Très magnifique!"

"Thank you," Ava said humbly. "I'm just glad I could find a piece to accent your jumpsuit."

"Well, that you did! She looks stunning, doesn't she?" he asked, standing back and admiring Jada as if she were a work of art.

Jada smiled softly, expertly turning her head to just the right angle to show off the earrings.

"She does," I had to admit. Though, I had a feeling the model would look stunning in a paper bag. I shot off a couple of up-close pictures of the earrings. "Do you mind if I grab one with you and Ava as well?"

He waved his hands in dramatic fashion. "Yes, yes, of course. Quickly, though, babies. I've got to track down Gia."

"Track her down?" Ava asked, moving to pose next to Jada. "Is she missing?" Her blonde eyebrow drew down in concern.

Concern I understood, as Gia Monroe was the show's closer, slated to wear the highlight of Ava's jewelry collection—a heavy, hand forged silver chain ending in a teardrop pendant holding a large, princess cut emerald. It was one of the most extravagant and expensive pieces Ava had ever made, having created it just for the occasion. Usually her designs ran more toward boho chic than gem encrusted, but knowing the type of crowd that would be in attendance that day and the type of exposure her designs would get, she'd gone all out. A hundred thousand dollars all out, to be exact, just to purchase the green gem itself. An investment she was hoping to make back and then some with the sale of the necklace, as well as the demand for more that she hoped the show would generate.

"No, no," Costello said, waving off her concern as he stepped to the other side of Jada and draped an arm around her middle. "I'm sure she's probably just holed up in her dressing room."

"Sipping champagne," Jada added, speaking up for the first time.

Costello laughed. "Yes, well, that's Gia. Champagne and caviar all the way, right? Smile, dahlings!" He showed off a row of sparkling white veneers, and I quickly snapped off a few shots of the trio.

As soon as I was finished, Costello turned back to Jada. "Quick, kisses for luck, babies, and I'm off." He dropped air kisses on either side of the ladies' cheeks before giving me a little wave and going off in search of his champagne sipping starlet.

Jada watched after him for a moment before giving us a nod and smile and fading into the sea of humanity bustling backstage.

"Do you think I should check on Gia too?" Ava asked, biting her bottom lip.

"I'm sure she's fine," I said. "But if it would make you feel better, it wouldn't hurt to get a picture or two of you with the necklace before the show."

Only, before we had a chance to follow in Costello's footsteps, a woman hailed Ava from across the room. "Yoo-hoo! Silver Girl!"

The voice belonged to the other designer being featured that day, Daisy Dot. She was tall, almost as slim as her models, and sported wild frizzy hair that was colored in alternating pink and blue stripes, reminding me of cotton candy. Her outfit was a clash of bright, bold prints sewn in a seemingly random pattern that somehow all worked together—much like the outfits her models were wearing. Where Costello's esthetic was sleek and classic, Daisy Dot's was loud and exuberant in such a way that you couldn't help but smile when you looked at it.

While Daisy was old enough that a swath of white hair mingled with the pink and blue, she was new to the fashion scene, having emerged as a breakout star on the hit reality TV competition show, *On the Runway*. I knew because I'd watched every episode of her season and, like the rest of the viewing public, had fallen in love with her big personality and quirky designs. I tried not to be star struck as she made her way through the increasingly chaotic backstage area toward us.

"You—you're the jewelry woman, right? Silver Girl?" she asked, reaching Ava's side.

My best friend nodded. "Yes, Ava Barnett. It's a pleasure to work with you, Ms. Dot."

Daisy threw her head back and laughed. "Daisy, please. And the pleasure is all mine. I love discovering emerging artists." She turned her attention to me. "Are you a jeweler as well?"

"No," I said, shaking my head. "I'm just here to support Ava."

"This is Emmy Oak," Ava said, properly introducing me. "She runs Oak Valley Vineyards. It's a winery just outside of town."

"A winery! Now you're speaking my language," Daisy said with a wink. "Don't suppose you smuggled any of your wares backstage? I could really go for a glass of rosé right about now."

I laughed. "No, sorry. But I'm sure there will be plenty of refreshments at the reception after the show."

She shrugged. "I suppose I'll live until then."

"Though, if you're in town for the weekend, please do feel free to stop by the winery," I offered. "I'd be happy to give you a personal tour."

"Oh, honey, that's an offer I can't pass up." She winked again before turning to Ava. "Listen, Silver Girl, would you mind having a look at the necklace Amanda is wearing? I don't think it's lying quite right."

"Of course," Ava agreed, following as Daisy led the way to where her models were starting to line up for the show.

"I have to say, I'm a huge fan," I told Daisy as we approached her model, Amanda, a redhead wearing a large, hand forged silver collar. "I watched you on *On the Runway*."

"Well, thank you." Daisy did an exaggerated bow. "I try my best to infuse a little fun into fashion." She glanced over to where two of Costello's models stood in tailored pantsuits. "A lot more fun than that snoozefest Boring-ello, huh?" She chuckled at her own joke.

Luckily, I was saved from answering, as she turned her attention to her model, directing Ava to make some small adjustments to the clasp on the necklace in question.

I hung back, letting Ava do her thing, enjoying the front row seat to the beautiful, one-of-a-kind creations around me. By the time Ava had the necklace lying across the model's clavicle just how Daisy had envisioned, I could see the rest of the models lining up as well—Jada in her navy jumpsuit beside two other tall women in sleek skirts and well-constructed blazers, clearly walking for Costello. Several of Daisy's colorfully clad ladies were also in line, the makeup and hair teams having shifted from their stations to last looks before the ladies emerged onto the outdoor runway.

I did not, however, see Gia and the emerald necklace among them yet. I could see the frown on Ava's face as she moved down the line, checking the jewelry on each model, clearly noticing the same absence.

"I'll go make sure Costello found her," I assured her, stowing my camera in its small black bag for safety.

Ava nodded. "Thanks," she said as I stepped away.

The weather this time of year was perfect for an outdoor show, and the Links had set up a long runway down the south lawn, leading from the large Grand Ballroom that had been converted to the staging area, through the several dozen wooden folding chairs set out for eager audience members. Off the interior of the ballroom, I found what looked like a smaller storeroom, now converted to a private dressing room with the name *Gia Monroe* taped to the outside.

I moved my hand to knock but stopped as I heard voices on the other side.

Raised ones.

I paused, not sure if I should intrude.

"…you know what that means," yelled one voice—clearly female and presumably Gia's.

"…dare threaten me?" came the reply. Male. And a voice I recognized, having just heard it earlier. Costello.

I felt a frown form. *Threaten* was a big word. Despite not initially meaning to eavesdrop, I leaned forward, straining to hear the reply. Unfortunately, through the thick wooden door, I was only able to make out snippets of it.

"...big talk," Gia yelled. "...old man!"

Whatever they were arguing about, it was getting heated. The volume of Costello's response rose so high that I made out every word.

"Careful what you wish for, *dahling*. It might be your last!"

I was trying to interpret the meaning behind that when the door in front of me was suddenly flung open, Costello charging out so furiously that he almost plowed right into me.

I stepped to the side to avoid a collision, but he barely acknowledged my presence, his pudgy face red, his jaw tense, as he stalked toward the rest of the models.

I waited until he was clear before peeking into the dressing room through the open doorway.

If she'd been affected by the exchange with the designer, Gia didn't show it, calmly perched on the edge of a tall chair, long legs crossed one over the other in a flowing, floor length silver gown with a slit so high you could almost see her lady bits. In her hand she held a slim champagne flute, and on her lips sat a smirk of satisfaction. Whatever the exchange between the two had been about, she clearly felt she'd had the last word.

Though, all of that felt secondary as I spied the large, sparkling emerald necklace clasped around her neck, safe and sound and ready to dazzle the jewelry buying elite of Sonoma Valley.

"Uh, Gia?" I asked.

She turned a pair of bored brown eyes my way. "Yes?"

"Everyone else is lining up for the show now."

She gave a small shrug of her slim shoulders. "So?"

"So, maybe you should join them...?" I trailed off, feeling very out of my element.

She gave a small laugh. "Sweetie, I don't know who you are, but the show will start when *I* get there."

With that, she slipped off her perch, gracefully crossed the few feet to the door, and slammed it in my face.

Well, that went well.

I tried not to take it personally as I retraced my steps back to the staging area, where Ava was just finishing adjustments on a pair of bracelets around the wrist of a beautifully androgynous model in a tutu and halter top.

"Is Gia coming?" Ava asked, the frown still etched on her face.

I nodded. "She's dressed, and the necklace looks stunning," I assured her.

She smiled, some of the worry easing out of her. "Good. She had me nervous."

Me too. But I didn't voice that. "She's a professional," I said instead. "I'm sure the show will go off without a hitch."

I glanced up, noting the stage manager was signaling for the ladies to get in position to walk. "We should probably go find our seats."

Ava nodded, wishing the model in the tutu good luck. Then she slipped her arm into the crook of my own as I hoisted my camera bag onto my shoulder and we made our way back through the ballroom. We stepped out a side door and inconspicuously joined the growing crowd assembling outside to watch the show.

The Links Club had done a great job creating a fashion week atmosphere. The wooden planks that had been constructed for the runway were polished and gleaming beneath the lights erected for the event. Club patrons chatted excitedly to one another as they took their seats, trading in their usual tennis skirts and polo shirts for cocktail dresses and slacks.

As we took our seats, the music began to pulse, signaling the start of the show. All chatter subsided, all eyes on the large curtain erected at the head of the runway. I could feel the audience's collective anticipation as they leaned forward to catch sight of the designs…and hopefully mentally calculate their bids for the outfits afterwards.

The air buzzed with excitement, and murmurs of approval washed through the crowd the moment the curtain separated. One by one, the models strutted down the runway, fierce expressions on their faces. Costello's clean lines and tailored cuts were the picture of elegance, and I saw several heads nodding their approval. In contrast, Daisy's models looked flirty, fun, and casual, causing smiles to ripple through the audience.

In addition to Daisy's funky prints, her current line featured a diamond shaped cutout in the back of each outfit as a signature look that tied her wacky collection together. She had also paired each outfit with long, elegant gloves and a wide brimmed felt hat—adding to the eclectic vibe. If I didn't know better, I'd say that Daisy's collection was almost mocking Costello's—taking a jab at traditional sophistication.

Either way, the effect of the juxtaposition of their styles was lively and entertaining, offering something for every taste. I held Ava's hand as I watched several women point out the jewelry to their companions. I hoped they were making notes to purchase after the show.

The whole spectacle was over much too soon, ending with Gia, bursting through the curtain right on cue. I let out a sigh of relief as she sashayed onto the runway in a long, flowing gown that billowed beautifully behind her. I heard a collective gasp from the crowd, followed by applause. At least some of which I hoped were for the stunning necklace showcased in the scooped neck design of the dress. I had to admit, the way the light reflected off the emerald was almost magical.

I lifted my camera, taking several pictures that I knew Ava could use on her social media pages to draw in clients not in attendance at the actual event.

"She looks gorgeous," I whispered to my friend.

Ava squeezed my hand, her eyes not on the runway but on the crowd's reaction. "Let's hope they all think so too."

"They will," I promised. I gave her a grin and squeezed back.

As the show came to a close, all of the models joined Gia on the stage, and Costello and Daisy both made the walk down the runway to thunderous applause.

"Thank you all so much for coming to support such a worthy cause," Costello said into a microphone as he reached the end of the runway. "We hope you've enjoyed the look at our latest collections and will bid generously in the auction to follow the reception."

More applause followed as Costello did a deep bow and Daisy curtsied.

"And," Costello added, straightening up again, "we would both like to thank Ava Barnett of Silver Girl for the loan of the magnificent jewelry you've seen our models wearing today, all of which will be available for sale in her shop downtown and online." He blew a kiss in Ava's direction, and I felt her relax beside me for the first time that day.

She smiled and waved as the eyes of the crowd went her way.

"Advertising doesn't get better than that," I mumbled to her.

"Let's just hope the sales follow," she said. But the smile on her face looked much more optimistic.

As the designers and models left the stage, we waited a few minutes for the crowd to thin out. Guests slowly rose from their seats, making their way toward the lounge where a cocktail reception preceded the live auction. If there were two things the Links Club set enjoyed, it was spending money and drinking. Tonight I hoped they indulged in both.

I hoisted my bag onto my shoulder, and we followed the crowd to the brightly lit lounge, where servers in the blue polos bearing the club logo were already circulating the room with trays of red and white wine. I snagged a couple glasses of white from a passing waiter, handing one to Ava as we made our way through the crowd.

"This is well deserved," I told her. "Cheers to a great show."

She took the glass, clinking gently against mine. "Thank you. I couldn't have done it without you."

"You could have," I argued. "But it wouldn't have been nearly as much fun."

She laughed. "Agreed," she said, taking a sip from her glass. "Let me go collect the jewelry and get it in the safe, and then we can really celebrate."

"I'll help," I offered, following her toward the hallway that led to the Grand Ballroom.

The mood backstage was even more celebratory than the one in the lounge, the collective breath everyone had been holding now exhaled on a successful finish. We passed a few models heading toward the lounge—changed from their designer duds into street wear. I didn't see Daisy or Costello anywhere and assumed they were likely in the lounge chatting up their designs pre-bidding. Several of the crew seemed to have dispersed already as well, a couple makeup artists cleaning up brushes and models lingering as they changed into lower heels.

The Silver Girl jewelry the models had shed was laid out on a low table near the back wall. Ava made quick work of putting each piece back into the velvet lined box she'd brought it in and checking it off her inventory list. A few were still unaccounted for as we began, but they trickled in as she packed pieces away until almost every velvet lined box was full.

"Just one piece left," Ava finally said, looking up from her list. "Gia's emerald."

I glanced across the room to the closed dressing room door bearing her name. "Well, she took her time getting ready. Maybe she's just as slow undressing."

Ava picked up the last box, a large, square one. "Think we should rush her? I'd really feel better once this is all locked up in the club safe."

"It is *your* necklace," I pointed out.

Ava nodded, and I followed her to the starlet's dressing room door, where Ava rapped sharply. "Gia?" she called.

No response. We waited a beat, but I heard nothing on the other side of the door to indicate that she'd heard us.

Ava tried again. "Gia? It's Ava Barnett—the jewelry designer? I need to lock up the emerald necklace now."

Still nothing from the other side of the door.

Ava pursed her lips together. "Maybe she's not in there?"

I glanced around the largely empty backstage area. "Where else would she be?" I asked.

"You don't think she'd wear the necklace to the reception, would she?" Ava asked.

I shook my head. "She'd know better." As much as Gia had struck me as a diva, she had seemed like a professional on the runway. I couldn't imagine her walking out with someone else's jewelry like that.

"Gia?" Ava tried one last time, accompanied by another knock at the door. When no answer resulted, she put a hand on the knob and twisted it.

She glanced at me. "Unlocked." She pushed the door open.

"Gia, are you—"

But that was as far as she got before her voice froze in her throat, catching and turning into a strangled sort of gasp.

One I echoed as I spied Gia.

She lay faceup on the floor, her long legs crumpled under her at an odd angle, her big brown eyes open and staring at the ceiling, mouth frozen in a grimace of horror as the heavy chain she'd been so artfully wearing earlier sat tightly tangled around her neck.

It was clear why Gia hadn't answered our knock.

Gia Monroe was dead.

CHAPTER TWO

The next few hours went by in slow motion, every minute feeling like it lasted a horrible eternity. Somehow Ava and I had found our voices, our initial shocked gasps turning into screams that were just as reflexive but loud enough to bring the remaining few people left backstage running toward us. Someone had checked Gia for a nonexistent pulse, someone had called 9-1-1, and someone had helped Ava and me to a pair of chairs at a makeup station, where my legs had given out and I'd crumpled into a pile, trying to block out the imagine of Gia's dead body that I feared would haunt me forever.

The two of us had huddled there, holding hands and trying not to let nausea take over, as we'd waited for the authorities to arrive. Which hadn't taken long. A dead body at the most exclusive club in town had the police moving pretty quickly. Uniformed officers were soon swarming the Links, corralling models, guests, and staff alike into small groups to question them.

Ava and I were separated as officers took our statements, her telling her tale to a young guy in a uniform that was at least a size too big for him and me to a large woman with a brusque manner who jotted down everything I said into an electronic tablet.

I was just getting to the part where we'd opened Gia's dressing room door when I spotted a familiar face among the growing number of law enforcement.

Detective Christopher Grant of the Sonoma County Sheriff's Violent Crimes Investigations Unit.

His presence shouldn't have come as a surprise—a dead body definitely qualified as a violent crime—but at seeing him, a jumble of emotions hit my stomach, making me feel queasy all over again.

Detective Grant and I had a history that had begun shortly after I'd moved back home to take over Oak Valley Vineyards last year. We'd first met over a dead body in my wine cellar, though more recently our paths had crossed for more personal than professional reasons. In fact, the last time I'd seen him, he'd been half undressed on my sofa and I'd been having fantasies about uncovering the other half. Just when I'd suggested a change of venue to the bedroom, his phone had pinged with an emergency downtown, which had ended those particular fantasies. That had been a couple of weeks ago, and while I wouldn't say I'd mind a repeat, I was never sure how hot or cold things were running with Grant. I knew him well enough to know he lived for the job and everything else was secondary—not a role I was sure I'd enjoy being in long term.

But a girl could still fantasize.

Grant's dark eyes met mine across the room, his jaw tensing beneath the day's worth of stubble that seemed to perpetually cling there. In two quick strides, his long, denim encased legs crossed the distance between us, and he was at my side.

"Emmy," he said, his voice strained as if making an effort to remain neutral. "You okay?"

I nodded, biting my lip to keep the bubble of tears at bay.

"Ms. Oak and the woman over there"—the officer nodded toward Ava—"were the ones who discovered the victim."

Grant's eyes cut to the dressing room door, where several CSI had converged. "How long ago was this?"

The officer consulted her tablet again. "First responder arrived at the scene at seven forty-five."

Grant nodded. "Thank you, Officer Cross. I'll take it from here."

She looked dubious for a moment, but considering he outranked her, she turned her tablet off and walked away, joining another uniformed officer who was talking to Costello and his model, Jada, near the exit.

Grant waited until she was out of earshot before taking a step closer, invading my personal space.

Not that I minded. His warm, familiar presence felt like a beacon of safety in the midst of chaos.

"You really okay?" he said, his voice lower now, more intimate.

Those tears threatened again, but I sucked them down for his benefit, forcing a smile as I nodded again. "I will be."

The corner of his mouth quirked up in a smile, though it was laced with more sympathy than humor. "Good. Can you tell me what happened?"

I sucked in a long breath, trying to filter emotion out of the memory as I relayed the events once again, starting with Ava's jewelry being showcased on the runway and ending with us knocking on Gia's door and finding her body.

Grant listened with his stoic Cop Face in place, though when my voice faltered at the part where we spied Gia with Ava's necklace wrapped tightly around her throat, he reached out and took one of my hands in his.

"She couldn't have been there very long," I finished. "We only waited a few minutes after the show ended to gather up the jewelry."

Grant let his eyes rove the room, and I could see the little hazel flecks in them dancing in a frenzy as he assessed the scene. "According to the stage manager, Gia went straight from the stage to her dressing room."

I glanced at the room where I could see CSI dusting the doorjamb for fingerprints. "Do they know how she died yet?" I asked, halfway hoping he said allergic reaction to champagne or something equally accidental.

Grant didn't answer right away, as if assessing how much to share given my tentative hold on my emotions. But he must have believed the tough façade I was trying to front, as he finally nodded again. "Victim appears to have died of asphyxiation. The ME found ligature marks on her neck consistent with the size and shape of the silver chain she was wearing."

"She was strangled with Ava's necklace?" I asked, trying not to picture it.

"We'll know more after a formal autopsy. But, yeah, it appears that way." He paused, and I could see him holding something back.

"What?" I asked.

He cleared his throat, his eyes going to a spot over my head.

"Grant," I said. "What is it?"

"Witnesses said the necklace contained a large emerald stone. Is that correct?"

"Yes," I said slowly, not sure where he was going with this.

"Did Ava have it insured?"

"Insure—" His meaning hit me. "Oh no. Don't tell me…"

"It's gone."

I felt my heart sink into my stomach. "Gone? What do you mean, gone!?"

"I mean, the gem is missing from the pendant."

"Are you sure? Maybe it just fell out. There must have been a struggle, right?"

Grant gave me a look like I was being naïve, but to his credit he didn't voice the thought. "CSI has been over the room. There's no sign of it."

"Does Ava know?"

He shook his head. "Not yet. I take it the stone was valuable."

"Yeah. At least a hundred grand valuable."

His eyebrows went up into his hairline. "That's quite a necklace."

"Ava made it especially for the show. She wanted to wow the Links set," I said, glancing to my friend. This was going to devastate her. Like most small business owners, I knew Ava's profit margins were small. It wasn't like she had ample funds to cover this sort of loss.

"What time did you say you knocked on Gia's door?" Grant asked, pulling a worn notebook and pen from the pocket of his blazer, clearly preferring the old-school style of note taking.

I tried to think back. "I'm not totally sure. I know that after the show, we waited a minute for the crowd to thin out. Then we stopped at the lounge to grab a glass of wine. Once we came backstage again, Ava cataloged all the jewelry on the back table, but it didn't take her very long. It couldn't have been more than half an hour after the show ended."

"And who had access to this area?" he asked, gesturing around him.

"Well, the models, of course. The designers—Daisy Dot and Carl Costello." I nodded toward the exit, where Daisy had joined Costello and Jada as officers took down all of their statements. "And there were makeup artist and hairdressers and a bunch of club employees working to manage the show." I paused. "But it wasn't like anyone was checking credentials at the doors. It was just a charity show."

"No security?" he asked, eyes going to me.

I shook my head. "Just the regular club security guards, I guess." Which had seemed like enough at the time. The Links was a members-only club with a hefty price tag and a staff of gatekeepers whose sole job was to keep out the riffraff. As I well knew—having been that riffraff trying to get in on occasion myself. "You don't think a *club member* killed Gia for the necklace, do you?" I asked.

"I wouldn't want to speculate on who. But I think we're looking at a pretty clear case of a robbery gone wrong."

I shook my head. "Look, I know a hundred grand is a lot of money in my world, but I'd bet half the women in that audience were wearing that much themselves. Have you seen some of those rocks?" I asked, wiggling my own bare left ring finger.

Grant grinned. "I have."

"I can't see one of them committing murder for that little."

Grant didn't concede my point, but he didn't argue it either. "You didn't notice anyone backstage who seemed out of place?"

I shook my head. "I mean, there were a lot of people here. It was busy. A little chaotic."

"What about at the runway show? Anyone seem to pay particular interest to Gia or the necklace?"

I thought a moment, but really, that had been the point of the necklace. "Everyone did." I shrugged. "Sorry. But it was the finale piece. It was supposed to get everyone's attention."

"Well, it certainly got someone's," Grant mumbled, putting his notebook back in his pocket.

I felt my gaze darting around the backstage area again, suspicion suddenly filling me as my eyes went from one person to the next. "You don't think the killer is still here, do you?"

"Not likely," Grant said. "If they were after the gem, I doubt they'd stick around. We're checking everyone for any sign of it before they're cleared to go just in case, but my guess is whoever did this had a clear exit strategy."

Which should have made me feel better, but it was little comfort, given the situation.

"I'm going to be tied up here for a bit," Grant said, some of the cop slipping from his tone, his eyes softening. "You want me to have an officer drive you home?"

I shook my head, trying to put on that brave face again. "No. I came with Ava. We'll be okay getting back on our own."

While I could sense hesitation in his warm brown eyes, he nodded. "Okay. Call me if you need anything."

"I will," I promised.

He gave my hand one last comforting squeeze before he turned and melted into the crowd of law enforcement surrounding the crime scene.

* * *

An hour later, Ava and I were settled on the worn sofa in my living room, our heels kicked into a discarded pile beside my camera bag, an open bottle of Pinot Noir on the table between us, and two slices of Flourless Chocolate Cake with Mocha Whipped Cream from the local bakery, The Chocolate Bar, on paper plates. Though, the comfort food wasn't entirely doing its job, Ava's face having been etched into a permanent frown ever since she'd found out that her emerald was not only missing but also likely the reason a woman had been murdered.

"You know it's not your fault," I said for about the hundredth time since we'd pulled up to the winery.

Ava nodded. "If only we'd put the necklace away sooner. I should have gone after that piece first."

I shook my head. "If someone was really after the gem, there's nothing you could have done differently."

"I could have stuck to cubic zirconia," she said, regret thick in her voice as she sipped at her wine. Her cake had gone largely untouched, I noticed. A sign of just how upset she was.

"I'm sure Grant will figure this all out," I said.

Ava nodded. "Poor Gia. To think someone was strangling her while we were sipping wine and celebrating." She shook her head, clearly feeling guilt weigh heavily.

"You have to stop doing this," I told her. Usually my friend was the optimism trying to cheer my realist's approach. I hated seeing her this way. "It's not your fault."

She shook her head. "My necklace was the murder weapon, and my gem was the motive."

"Assuming the gem was the target," I countered.

She frowned. "What do you mean?"

I almost hesitated to voice the doubt that had been creeping into my mind on the ride home. "Well, I overheard Gia arguing with someone. Just before the show."

"Who?" she asked, shifting her legs underneath her to face me.

"Carl Costello."

The frown deepened. "Why would she be arguing with him? She was his star."

I shrugged. "I don't know," I said honestly. "I didn't hear the whole thing. But he accused her of threatening him. Then he said something about being careful what she wished for, as it could be her last."

Ava raised an eyebrow at me. "That sounds ominous. You know, considering that it probably *was* her last."

That had been my thought too. "It's probably a coincidence, right?"

Ava shrugged. "I don't know. I kinda liked Costello. You know, in that endearing gay uncle kind of way."

"Me too," I admitted. While my interaction with him had been brief, he'd seemed lively and charming. Unlike the brief interaction I'd had with Gia.

Though I tamped that thought down, not wanting to think ill of the dead. Heck, for all I knew, maybe she got nervous before shows and her diva-like behavior had really been a cover for stage fright.

"Well, not to seem calloused about the woman's death," Ava said, letting out a long sigh. "But I honestly don't know what I'm going to do if Grant doesn't find that emerald."

"I'm guessing you didn't have it insured?"

She shook her head. "There didn't seem much point. I mean, I only planned to have it in my possession for a couple of months. I was hoping it would sell after the show."

"And you had a lot of money tied up in it, didn't you?"

She nodded, and I could see tears forming behind her eyes. "I had to take out a loan to buy it."

"Oh honey," I said. That was something she hadn't shared with me before.

She sniffed. "I know, it was a gamble. But I figured it was a short term thing—I could float the loan for just a couple of months to buy the gem and create the necklace. Once it sold, the profits would pay back the loan in full plus be enough that I could hire someone on to expand the shop hours like I've been wanting to."

I almost hesitated to ask, but… "What did you use for collateral for the loan?"

She sucked in a deep breath. "Silver Girl," she said on an exhale.

"The shop?"

She nodded, those tears spilling over her lashes now. "I could lose everything, Emmy. There's no way I can pay back that loan without the gem. The interest alone will eat me alive."

"It's going to be okay," I said, reaching out and wrapping her in a hug.

I knew exactly what that fear in her eyes felt like. Ever since I'd moved back home to take over running our struggling little winery, I lived with the fear that I might lose everything my family had spent generations building.

"We'll figure this out," I told her, trying to exude more confidence than I felt. "We'll think of something."

Even if I had no idea what that something would be.

* * *

Morning broke through my bedroom curtains much too early the next day, the bright sunshine and cheerily chirpy birds in direct contrast to my mood. It possibly had to do with the fact I'd been up until the early morning hours trying to console Ava. Or possibly it was due to the several glasses of Pinot we'd both consumed when the consoling had been unsuccessful. Either way, I practically had to drag myself out of bed into a hot shower by sheer force of will, adding an extra layer of mascara to compensate for the sleep I didn't get. I shoved myself into a pair of jeans and a simple white T-shirt before making my way downstairs.

Ava had beaten me to the coffee, putting the one appliance in my tiny kitchen—a stainless steel coffee maker—to good use. Generally I took the bulk of my meals in the large commercial kitchen attached to the winery. It was better equipped, always well stocked thanks to my house manager, Conchita, and much more comfortable to cook in than the cubby hole in my small cottage at the back of the property.

"Hey," Ava said by way of greeting, her eyes on her phone as she leaned against the counter.

"Hey, yourself. Sleep okay?" I asked, knowing that my guest room faced the sunrise—probably why Ava had beaten me to the kitchen.

She nodded, setting her phone down. "Well enough." She shot me a smile. "Thanks for letting me stay here last night."

"Like I was gonna let you drive home after the barrel of wine we consumed," I joked, pulling a mug down from the cupboard and pouring myself a cup of coffee.

"Grant just left me a message," she said, glancing to her phone on the counter again.

"Oh?" I tried to tamp down the flare of giddiness that his name produced in my empty belly.

"He said they've finished processing the backstage area and I could come pick up my jewelry anytime." She paused. "Minus the murder weapon, of course."

I put a hand on her arm. "I'm sorry."

She shook her head, obviously doing her best to pull out some cheerfulness. "It's okay. I'm sure he'll find whoever did this soon."

"And the emerald along with them," I added.

"Right." She smiled, though it was shaky at best.

"Want me to come to the club with you?" I offered.

"Would you?" she asked, clasping her hands in front of her in a pleading motion. "Honestly, I would not turn down the moral support."

"Of course," I offered, taking a sip from my cup. It was hot enough that it almost burned my tongue, but the acrid beans served as a much needed wake up call to my brain. "Just let me get one cup in me first."

"Ditto." Ava grinned. "And maybe I could bum a couple of aspirins to go with it?"

*   *   *

Once we were fully caffeinated and had enough painkillers in our systems to combat the mild Pinot hangover, we hopped into my Jeep and headed back to the Sonoma Links. A short drive later we were pulling up the winding drive that was much like my own at Oak Valley. Though, while Oak Valley sported mature oak trees, rustic gravel, and wildflowers that had been planted in accordance with Mother Nature's blueprint, the Links entrance was lined with carefully manicured cypress trees, lines of bright non-native annuals, and a sprawling expanse of lawn that shimmered an impressive green color year round, despite the threat of drought.

We handed my Jeep over to the valet at the entrance, and I was glad I'd added a pink floral scarf and kitten heel sandals to my T-shirt to at least have a prayer of fitting in among the rich and idle on a sunny summer morning. I gave our names to the woman in the blue club polo shirt at the desk, who, with a few clicks of her keyboard, ascertained that we were approved to enter, giving us a warm smile that I knew was reserved for members and their guests.

Our heels clacked against the polished marble floor as we wound our way through the club, passing the lounge, which was largely empty at this time of day, except for a couple of early morning Scotch drinkers getting a jump on the day before their first round of golf. The outdoor terrace, however, was brimming with brunch-time life. Men in checked shorts and golf shirts chatted beside the green, and ladies in tennis shirts and sundresses with wide brimmed hats sipped mimosas. They were all laughing, chatting, drinking, and generally carrying on as usual. There was no indication that anything out of the ordinary had happened there the day before. The upper crust were quick to bounce back from a little thing like murder.

As we entered the Grand Ballroom, only a couple of uniformed officers still lingered. Crime scene tape had been erected across the doorway to Gia's dressing room, but the rest of the room looked as if it was in the throes of being transformed from backstage at a fashion show to a club room once again. The makeup artist stations were empty, chairs being folded and put away along a far wall by a couple of club employees. I spied Daisy's assistant zipping garment bags shut and a couple of young men carefully packing away the shoes and handbags Costello's models had worn.

Ava's jewelry was once again laid out on the back table, though several pieces had been taken from their boxes. Apparently the police had wanted to inventory what was there themselves. I didn't blame them. It would have been a very convenient end to the search for the emerald if Ava had just misplaced it in another box. Unfortunately, she was much too thorough to have done that.

"Let's get this over with," she said, and I could tell by the pale color of her cheeks as she averted her eyes from the dressing room that she was as uncomfortable being there as I was.

"I'll help," I added, handing her one velvet lined box after another as she carefully cataloged and replaced accessories in them.

We'd almost gotten them all boxed up again and back into her large storage bin to transport home, when a familiar voice piped up from the other side of the room.

"No, no, no! You cannot fold that. It must be laid flat or you'll ruin the integrity of the garment." Costello shook his head at one of the young men we'd seen earlier, taking a large black cape from the man's hands. "Just—get these other boxes in the van. I'll take care of the rest."

"Poor Costello," Ava said, sympathy in her eyes. "Do you think we should go pay our respects?"

Personally, I didn't think Costello looked like a man who was grieving. He'd dressed today in another pair of white leather pants with shimmering rhinestones on the back pockets and a hot pink shirt that billowed around his portly frame in a cascade of ruffles. If his outfit were any louder, it would be shouting.

But, people grieved in all different sorts of ways, so I nodded and followed Ava's lead as she set the storage bin down and approached the designer.

"Mr. Costello," she said softly.

He spun to face us, his eyelashes fluttering for a beat before recognition set in. "Oh, Ava. Hello, my dear. And…"

"Emmy," I supplied.

"Yes, yes, of course." He shook his head in apology. "We met before the show."

"We're so sorry for your loss," Ava said, taking one of his hands in both of hers.

At the reference to Gia, his expression changed, all emotions draining from it as if wiped clean. "Thank you. Yes, such a tragic loss."

"I can't imagine what you must be going through," Ava added, genuine sympathy in her eyes.

"It's…shocking. Hard to believe it's real." He attempted a smile, but it came off as more of a grimace. "Such a waste. All that beauty taken too quickly."

"You and Gia were close?" I asked, my mind going to the argument I'd witnessed.

He sighed deeply. "As close as anyone can get to a beautiful creature like Gia, I suppose."

"Oh?" I said. "Was she difficult to get close to?"

But he waved me off with a laugh. "Oh, don't get me wrong. Gia could be a pussycat when she wanted to be. But, like all successful people in this business, she had her eccentricities."

"Had you worked with her for long?" Ava asked.

Costello nodded. "A couple of years." He gave us a sad smile. "She was my star. She closed every show."

"She was stunning," I agreed.

He turned to fiddle with the sleeve of one of the jackets on the rack. "Yes, well, thankfully beauty is not a rare gift in my line of work."

"I only had the chance to meet her briefly," Ava added. "At the fittings the week before the show. But she seemed—" Ava paused, and I could see her mentally searching for a complimentary thing to say. It was a long pause. "—very professional."

"Yes, well, I suppose she had her moments..." He let that thought trail off. Clearly everyone was having a hard time speaking well of the dead woman.

"Did Gia normally have her own dressing room?" I asked, thinking hers was the only name I'd seen on a private room.

"Oh yes," Costello said with a laugh. "She insisted on it. One that had to be stocked with champagne and Belgian chocolates." He shook his head.

"She sounds like she could be demanding," I noted.

Costello turned his attention to the hem of the jacket on the rack again. "Well, can't we all? But as my boyfriend Fabio says, to get the best prices for your designs, you have to hire the best. And, as I'm sure you know, Gia was the best."

Actually, I didn't know that. I got the impression that she'd *thought* she was the best, but I'd seen a lot of beautiful women on the stage the previous day.

"The police asked if we saw anyone hanging around backstage," Ava said. "You know, anyone who wasn't supposed to be here. You didn't see anyone like that, did you?"

Costello shook his head. "Goodness me, no. But then, I was running around like a madman, wasn't I? Always am before a show. Barely had a moment to breathe, let alone notice anyone else."

"I think we were all a little preoccupied." Ava frowned, and I could see her veering into guilt riddled waters again.

"Did you see Gia after the show?" I asked.

"After?" I might have imagined it, but I thought his voice rose just the slightest on that word. "No." He shook his head vigorously. "I did not see her."

"Did you go to the lounge?" I asked. I didn't recall having seen him there, but it had been crowded.

"Wh-what?" He blinked at me as if not understanding the question.

"After the show. Did you go straight to the lounge for the reception or did you come backstage?"

His eyes narrowed, and I noticed for the first time that they were rimmed in soft, nude eyeshadow. "The police asked me that too. Though, I can't imagine why everyone wants to know. Surely no one thinks *I* stole that necklace and did poor Gia in."

Actually, the thought had crossed my mind.

"Of course not," Ava said, quickly jumping in. "We're just wondering if you saw anyone heading backstage. Or noticed anything out of place."

"No." The word was laced with finality. "I was with Fabio, my boyfriend. We were celebrating a successful show. Together," he emphasized.

"That's so important," Ava said, putting a hand on his arm. "You know, to have someone you can lean on at a difficult time like this."

Her sympathy softened his expression some. "Yes, well, Fabio is a doll. Love of my life."

I noticed that he hadn't actually answered my question about where he and the love of his life had been, exactly. "So you and Fabio went straight to the lounge to celebrate?" I asked.

"We were actually celebrating privately, if you must know. In one of the cabanas by the pool." He gave me a pointed look, like if I had to ask exactly what sort of celebrating they were doing together, I was terribly naïve.

"So I guess you didn't see Gia at all after the show, then," Ava surmised.

"No," Costello confirmed. "Like I said, I did not." He fiddled with the button on the sleeve of the jacket hanging on the rack in front of him.

"Were you avoiding her because of your argument?" I asked, watching for a reaction.

His fingers froze, and his gaze slowly rose to meet mine. "I'm sorry. Argument?"

I licked my lips, feeling distinctly intrusive. "I, uh, couldn't help but overhear the raised voices. You and Gia just before the show yesterday."

He blinked at me, and for a moment I thought he was going to deny it. But then he spread his arms wide in a theatrical motion. "Oh that. It was nothing."

I'd overheard him accuse her of threatening him, which had not felt like nothing at the time. "What was it about?" I pressed.

"This is a high stress business, and people argue all the time."

I wasn't sure, but he seemed to be avoiding my questions.

But before I could say anything in response, he continued. "Listen, Gia was a very opinionated person. She argued with people all the time. In fact, I heard her arguing with Hughie over the phone just before I went into her dressing room."

"Hughie?" Ava asked.

Costello brushed stray lint off his sweater. "Hughie Smart. Gia's agent. From Smart Models?"

Being that I was a few inches too short and more than a few pounds too heavy to qualify as a model, I'd never heard the name.

"Anyway, confrontation was just Gia's way," he said, still trying to make light of it all.

"What was Gia arguing with her agent over?" Ava asked.

Costello let out a humorless laugh. "Well, she only threatened to fire him."

"Fire him?" Ava echoed. "Why?"

He shrugged. "Search me, dahlings. Gia's business was Gia's business." His eyes went to a spot behind us. "Uh, Joey, let's get the rest of these bags into the van quickly, huh?" He turned his attention back to us. "Sorry, ladies, if you'll excuse me."

He didn't wait for an answer before brushing past us to grab an armload of garment bags and shove them at his young assistant.

CHAPTER THREE

Since we were at the Links anyway and we'd both skipped breakfast, Ava and I found an empty table on the terrace and ordered a couple plates of the brunch special, a Roasted Tomato Frittata. In deference to the mild headache still pounding out a memory of last night's overindulgence, I ordered more coffee in lieu of a mimosa. Ava went for an herbal tea, and as soon as the server arrived with them both, Ava turned to me.

"So what do you think of Costello's story?"

"Story?" I asked, sipping my coffee.

"About Gia threatening to fire her agent?"

I shrugged. "I think it was a good diversion from answering our questions about why *he'd* argued with Gia."

"You caught that too, huh?" Ava nodded, blowing off her hot tea. "You know, I'm starting to wonder if maybe you weren't right last night."

"Right about?" I asked.

"About maybe Gia being the killer's target and not the necklace."

I sipped my coffee. While I *had* been the one to float that idea last night, it had been born out of trying to alleviate Ava's guilt rather than any real evidence. And in the light of day, I wasn't as sure it held much merit. "If that was the case, then why take the emerald?"

"I don't know. Maybe they just panicked? Grabbed it because it was there? Or maybe they took it to throw the police off. I mean, they're out there looking for a random thief, right? Not someone who might have had a grudge against Gia."

I nodded. "Actually, you're right," I agreed. "That would be a pretty effective misdirect."

"Exactly!" Ava said, some of the light I normally associated with my best friend returning to her eyes. "And, if Costello is telling the truth, Gia had heated arguments with two separate people before she died. Doesn't sound like she was very well liked."

"I think that's a fair assumption," I said, thinking of my one and only interaction with her. "*If* Costello is to be believed."

"Easy enough to find out." Ava set her teacup down and pulled her phone from her purse, swiping open a search engine.

"What are you doing?" I asked as she did some typing and more swiping.

"Calling Hughie Smart."

I paused, coffee cup midway to my mouth. "You're just going to call him up and ask if he murdered Gia?"

Ava gave me a playful *get real* look. "No! But I am going to casually ask if he possibly had a disagreement with her coincidentally right before she died." She set the phone on the table as it began to ring on the other end.

"Ava, I'm not sure this is a—"

But that was as far as I got before a voice answered, "Good morning. Smart Models, this is Kelly speaking. How may I direct your call?"

"Hughie Smart, please," Ava said in an upbeat tone. She shot me a smile.

"May I ask who is calling?"

"Uh, yes, this is"—Ava glanced my way again—"Ava Barnett, head of special promotional projects at Oak Valley Vineyards."

I set my coffee down on the table with a clang and shot her a look.

Ava did an innocent palms-up thing before forging ahead. "We're looking to hire a model for our latest social media campaign."

"I see. Well, I can certainly set something up for you to look over our talent list."

"Actually, I was hoping to discuss it with Mr. Smart directly," Ava told her.

"Oh, well, I'm afraid that Mr. Smart is out of the office at the moment."

Ava's face fell. "He is?"

"I'm sorry. May I take a message?" she asked.

"Uh, sure. Can you please have him call me as soon as he gets in?" she asked, rattling off her phone number to the woman.

"Of course. I'll give Mr. Smart the message as soon as he returns."

Ava thanked the woman and hung up, looking dejected. "So much for that."

I shook my head as our food arrived. "Special promotional projects, huh?"

She shrugged as she picked up her fork and stabbed a blistery tomato. "Hey, it's not like Oak Valley *couldn't* use the marketing."

She had me there.

* * *

After we'd fully gorged ourselves on the sweet, savory, and creamy frittata, I drove Ava to Silver Girl, where I helped her open up the shop and unload all of the jewelry the models had worn in the show, returning the pieces to her glass cases. While the square footage of the store itself wasn't vast, Ava made the most of the space she had, with several long L-shaped cases displaying her wares around the room, as well as hanging racks on the walls. I could feel her anxiety as we carefully placed all of the pieces that had been showcased on the runway back on display. Ava had worked hard over the past few years to grow her jewelry business from an online Etsy shop to a physical location in the heart of downtown, and I knew it would break her heart to lose it all.

I was just wondering how many of her smaller pieces she'd have to sell in order to recoup the loss of the emerald, when the bell over the glass front doors dinged and a young couple walked in, hand-in-hand. They were dressed in casual khakis and T-shirts, looking like typical weekend Wine Country tourists— her in comfortable sandals and him pushing a pair of mirrored aviator glasses up on his head.

Ava straightened from the case of silver grapevine themed pendants she'd been arranging and put a sunny smile on her face. "Welcome to Silver Girl," she told the couple. "Can I help you find anything?"

"We're just looking," said the woman, a brunette with her hair pulled up into a fashionable messy knot.

"Well, if you have any questions, please let me know," Ava offered, stepping behind the counter to allow the couple space to browse.

I busied myself putting the velvet boxes away, shelving them in her small storage closet behind the register. I could see Ava keeping a keen eye on her potential customers as they did a slow tour of the store, eyeing each piece of jewelry before moving on to the next. I hated to burst Ava's bubble, but they looked more like window shoppers than actual buyers.

Once they'd done a full circuit, Ava approached the pair again. "Find anything that interests you? I'd be happy to pull something out for you to try on."

The brunette looked at her companion, then urged him on with a soft elbow to his ribs.

He cleared his throat, addressing Ava. "To be honest, we wanted to see...well, you know."

A small frown formed between Ava's blonde eyebrows. "Sorry, is there something particular you're looking for?"

"Uh...yes. I mean, we were hoping to get a look at *the piece*." He said the last words on a mock whisper, leaning in toward Ava.

Who was still frowning, clearly trying to grasp their meaning.

"We're enthusiasts," the woman added, looping her arm through her man's. "It's how we met."

"Enthusiasts?" Ava asked.

"True crime enthusiasts," the man clarified.

Ava went pale.

The brunette nodded. "We were hoping to see the murder necklace. Maybe even...try it on?" She looked practically giddy at the idea.

Ava's frown turned into a downright scowl. I could see several scathing responses going through her head as her eyes began to blaze.

Before she voiced any, I jumped in. "As true crime buffs, I'm sure you realize that particular piece is still in police custody. It's evidence."

The brunette huffed and took another shot at the man's ribs. "I told you it wouldn't be here!"

"Okay, okay, you told me." He sent her an annoyed look before returning his attention to Ava. "You don't by chance have any other jewelry that was worn by the dead woman, do you? You know, like the earrings she had on when she was strangled?"

"No!" The word was forceful enough that the couple took a physical step backward.

"What about a replica? Like, maybe another piece *like* the murder necklace?" the woman asked.

"Uh, maybe you better come back another time," I offered, ushering them toward the door.

"Any idea when the necklace will be released from police custody?" the woman asked as I herded her out.

"Will you be putting it on display then?" the man added.

"Should we leave our number?" the woman persisted.

Ava's icy glare should have said it all.

"Have a nice day," I told them before shutting the glass door behind them and flipping the *Open* sign to *Closed*.

I watched them walk down the sidewalk, the woman giving the man's ribs one last jab, before I spun around to face Ava.

She was shaking her head, the expression on her face a mix of anger and defeat. "Did you hear them?" She sighed, falling onto a stool behind the register. "The murder necklace? Is that what Silver Girl is going to be known for now?"

"I'm sure no one else is calling it that," I told her.

She sent me a look. "Clearly you did not see Bradley Wu's column in the *Sonoma Index-Tribune* today?"

Oh boy. I had not. But I knew Bradley Wu was a syndicated columnist who covered the Sonoma food scene and, more recently, local news. He had a sharp tongue, a thing for flowery language, and a witty style that could either be laugh-out-loud entertaining or cringe-worthy, depending on if you were the object of his column or not. "What did Bradley say?"

"He said my 'deadly designer necklace' was an ironic commentary on the 'suffocating trappings of our beauty-obsessed society.'"

I cringed. "At least he called it designer?" I offered, trying to find a silver lining.

She shook her head. "Obviously it was enough to excite the morbid types like them." She inclined her head toward the door. "That necklace was supposed to put me on the map as a local designer. Not as the creator of murder weapons," she moaned.

"*They* are not your client base," I pointed out. "I'm sure the women at the Links are remembering how beautiful the design was and not what happened to it after the show."

"Fat lot of good that does if I can't sell it," she mumbled.

"Need me to make a chocolate run?" I asked, shooting her a sympathetic smile.

Ava grinned back. "I don't think my waistline can take much more cake." She paused. "But thanks for the thought. And thanks for jumping in to keep me from telling those two where they could shove their enthusiasm."

"Cheer up," I told her. "What do they say—all publicity is good publicity?"

"I'll believe that when I see it," Ava said, staring out at the empty shop.

"Maybe you can use some of the photos I took last night to drum up some business," I suggested. I pulled my phone from my purse. I'd uploaded the pictures from my camera to my cloud drive before going to bed the night before, but I'd not yet had a chance to look through them.

"Maybe," Ava said, glancing over as I pulled them up.

A few seconds later I had several dozen thumbnails on my screen of Ava posing with the designers and models on the runaway and close-ups of various pieces of jewelry.

"What about this one?" I asked, pulling up the photo we'd taken of Ava and Costello's model, Jada, with the sparkling crystal earrings.

Ava nodded. "It's nice. I could post it on social media."

"I'm sure it would sell those earrings."

"Maybe." I could see Ava's mood improving slightly at the thought of a sale.

I scrolled some more, seeing a few photos I'd taken earlier of the models putting on their accessories, trying to capture the behind-the-scenes feel. I paused on one of Gia, a pang of sadness hitting me. She was in her finale gown, makeup not yet done, as Costello helped her into the necklace. I scrolled through a few more that I'd taken of the same scene—one closer on Ava's handmade creation and a couple wider shots, encompassing the chaos of backstage. I noticed Jada in the background of the wider shot, having her hair curled by one of the stylists. The corner of Daisy Dot's colorful outfit was caught moving off frame, and a couple of guys I didn't recognize stood behind Gia—likely crew or wardrobe assistants.

I moved past a few more photos—one of Daisy's models showing off silver bangles, a couple of Costello's other ladies in ornate pendants, several of the models being transformed by hair and makeup. We had another of Gia in that series, having thick eyeliner artfully applied in wings in the same vivid green color as her gem. Again I felt my heart clench for her. She had been strikingly beautiful, and as Costello had said, it seemed like such a waste that she'd been taken so young.

"Is that the same guy?"

"Hmm?" I pulled myself out of my own thoughts as Ava stabbed a finger at my phone.

"That guy. In the baseball cap." She gestured to a man in the background, standing off to the side of the makeup table. "Didn't I see him in another picture with Gia?"

"I don't know," I answered truthfully. I scrolled back a few to the series of her getting dressed.

"There!" Ava stopped me at the wide shot of Costello putting the necklace on the model. She pointed to one of the two men I'd noticed in the background earlier. "Look, he's behind Jada. Doesn't it look like he's watching Gia?"

His body *was* facing the model. I used my thumb and forefinger to zoom in on the man. He looked tall—taller than most of the models—and he was dressed in a pair of nondescript jeans and a white T-shirt advertising a soft drink. I could see dark hair peeking out underneath a baseball cap, which bore the logo of the San Francisco Giants. His head was angled so that most of his face was shadowed from the camera. All I could really make out was a prominent chin with a deep cleft in it that reminded me of Chevy Chase.

"It does look like the same guy," I agreed. "Probably one of the crew?"

But Ava frowned. "Weren't the crew all Links employees? They'd be wearing the blue polo shirts, right?"

"Maybe he was one of the designers' assistants?" I offered instead.

"Maybe." She scrolled through the next few pictures on my phone. "But he certainly isn't dressed like someone who works in fashion."

I laughed. "That point, I concede."

"Look, there he is again," she said, stopping at a picture of Gia stepping out onto the runway. Sure enough, the guy was standing just off to the side, clearly focusing his attention on the model.

"Is he in any other photos?" I asked, scrolling through more, this time focusing on the background. After looking at another half dozen, it didn't appear he was present.

"He only seemed to show up around Gia," Ava noted.

"Maybe he was a friend of hers?" I offered.

"Or a boyfriend!" Ava said, perking up. She reached behind the counter and grabbed her laptop, quickly pulling up a social media website. "Isn't it always the boyfriend whodunit?" she asked.

"Only when it's not the butler," I joked as I watched her type Gia's name into a search.

She shot me a look. "Laugh all you want, but as I'm sure those 'enthusiasts' would tell you, 60% of crimes are committed by a *supposed* loved one."

"Where did you hear that statistic?"

"*Dateline*," she said. "And Keith Morrison would not lie."

I stifled a snicker. "So, did Gia have a tall, dark, and baseball cap clad man in her life?" I asked, leaning closer to see her screen over her shoulder.

"Well, according to this site, she is not in a relationship." She pointed to the little status icon. "But it could have been new."

"Or old," I said. "Maybe he was an ex-boyfriend."

"Ooo, I like that. Exes are much more dangerous."

"Though why she'd invite an ex to her show, I don't know," I mumbled, second-guessing that.

"Wow, she's got a ton of followers." She pointed to a number that had several more zeroes than Oak Valley's social media sites did.

"Looks like she was pretty active on there."

"And took a lot of selfies," Ava noted, going through her photo album on the site.

"Well, she *was* a model," I pointed out.

"Apparently a well-paid one. Look, she's on a yacht in this one. A private jet to Europe," she said, scrolling through to another photo. "And it looks like she drives a Ferrari. A new one, too." She stopped at a photo of Gia dangling the keys to a fire engine red sports car outside a dealership.

"Wow." I suddenly wished I were about five inches taller and twenty pounds lighter. I was so in the wrong business.

"Seriously, wow," Ava said. She scrolled to the next photo—one of Gia and a couple of other long-legged models posing for a photo shoot on a beach.

"Wait—look at that guy in the background!" I pointed to a guy wearing a pair of sunglasses standing behind Gia, partially obscured by a sand dune.

Ava squinted at the man. "Is that Baseball Cap Guy?"

"Hard to tell," I admitted. "No hat, but he seems tall enough. And he's got that same dark hair and cleft chin."

Ava scrolled through a few more pictures. In almost all of them, Gia was posing alone or with other female models and friends. I noted Jada in a couple of them, and one or two were professional photos of her on the runway. Nothing in any of the pictures hinted at an indication of a relationship with anyone—

no romantic dinners, no Valentine's photos, no cute kissing selfies.

But I noticed the same tall, dark haired man in the background of at least four of them.

"It's weird," I said. "This guy always seems to be hanging back from the action, you know? Gia seems to be mostly ignoring him."

"Or maybe she didn't know he was there!" Ava said, putting a hand on my arm.

"What do you mean?"

"I mean, Gia was gorgeous, posted all about her life on social media. Maybe this guy wasn't a friend at all. Maybe Gia Monroe had a stalker!"

I glanced down at the man who never seemed to be quite facing the camera. I had to admit, it was not a bad theory. "All the photos with him do seem to be in public places."

Ava nodded. "Look—two at runway shows. That one at the beach photo shoot. This one looks like it's some sort of car show."

"So you think this guy found out Gia was doing the charity show at the Links and somehow snuck in to stalk her?" I asked. I knew from personal experience how hard it was to break into the club.

"Or who knows—maybe he knew someone who knew someone who got him in. The point is, he was *there*."

"And apparently a lot of other places that Gia was," I mused.

"Maybe he decided to take things from stalking to something more violent. It's possible he snuck backstage and, in some obsessed fan moment, attacked her."

It sounded entirely possible. "I wonder if Gia knew about him," I said. "I mean, you think maybe she noticed him hanging around a few times?"

Ava glanced at the array of Gia's selfies. "I don't know." She pointed to one photo of Jada and Gia with their arms wrapped around each other, posing at some red carpet event. "But it looks like Jada and Gia were close. Maybe she'd know?"

CHAPTER FOUR

———

Twenty minutes later, Ava and I parked my Jeep in the lot behind the Sonoma Valley Inn, where the models and designers were staying the weekend. As we made our way through the lobby and past the bar, it looked largely deserted, the weekend guests already out on winery tours or enjoying the perfectly sunny weather of the mild summer we were having this year.

A middle-aged woman with a soft face and pleasant smile sat behind the check-in counter. "May I help you?" she asked as we approached.

"Yes, we were hoping to speak to one of your guests. Jada Devereux. Do you know what room she's in?" Ava asked.

"Oh, I'm sorry," the woman—whose nametag read Judy—said. "We can't give out room numbers of our guests. You know, for security reasons."

"Oh." Ava frowned and sent me a look.

"But I could call up to her room and let her know you're here," Judy offered.

"Could you?" Ava asked, perking up. "Oh, that would be great."

Judy sent her a pleasant smile again, picking up an old corded style phone from behind the desk. "Happy to. And who may I say is waiting for her?"

"Ava Barnett, from Silver Girl jewelry."

Judy nodded then typed in a number from her computer screen. After a short beat, we heard her mumble something into the phone before hanging up.

She shook her head. "Sorry, she wasn't in. I left a message."

Ava let out a long sigh. "Thanks."

She looked so dejected that even Judy seemed to feel a little bad, as she asked, "Is Jada by any chance one of the models in town for that fashion show?"

"Yes," I answered.

Judy's eyes darted from one side to the other. "Look, I don't know if *your* model was with them, but I did just see a group of them go to the pool." She pointed down a hallway to our right. "It's just out the back."

"Judy, you are a peach," Ava said, giving the woman a winning smile before she quickly grabbed me by the arm and steered me down the hallway.

It ended in a glass double door leading to an outdoor courtyard. We pushed through, revealing a crystal blue pool at the courtyard's center. Lounge chairs surrounded it, and a large rock waterfall at one end provided some shade and a breathtaking cascade of shimmering water. A couple of families sat near the shallow end, enjoying the break from the heat with their children, and near the decorative waterfall I spied four slim women in bikinis, soaking up the sun's rays.

Luck was with us. The exotic looking Jada sat on the farthest lounger, her chair pulled a bit away from the rest of the girls, her head down, as if she were napping.

"Jada?" Ava said as we approached.

The model flipped over onto her back and propped herself up on one arm. "Yeah?"

"Hi. Ava. From the fashion show?" she supplied. "And my friend, Emmy."

Jada pushed her sunglasses up onto her head. "Sure. I remember you." Up close I could see that her eyes were red-rimmed and puffy. I felt my heart go out to her. I wasn't sure how close she and Gia had been, but even the thought of losing Ava made my chest clench.

"I'm so sorry for your loss," I told her, honestly meaning it.

Her eyes misted, and she sniffed loudly. "Thanks."

"How are you holding up?" Ava asked, gingerly sitting on the edge of an empty lounger beside her.

Jada shrugged her bare shoulders, shifting to a seated position. "It is what it is, you know?" She sucked in a deep breath, letting it out on a sigh. "The police asked us to stay in town for the weekend." She glanced over at the other models, who were largely ignoring our private conversation as they looked at something on the middle woman's phone. "But I guess it's better to grieve together than alone, right?"

The other three women didn't look to be particularly grieving to me. In fact, if I didn't know better, I'd say they were three single ladies enjoying a couple of cocktails and some sun, as laughter erupted from the group at some private joke.

"I got the impression that you and Gia were close?" Ava asked.

Jada nodded. "I guess so. I mean, Gia was kind of a hard person to really get close to. But we were roommates when we first started out." Her eyes took on a faraway look, as if she was remembering happier times.

"When was that?" I asked.

"A couple years ago, I guess." She blinked her attention back to the present. "We were both new at Smart Models."

"Hughie Smart is your agent too?" Ava asked.

Jada nodded. "I introduced Gia to him. I introduced her to Carl, too." She frowned, and I wondered if she was feeling some ill-placed guilt—as if somehow that introduction had led to her friend's demise.

"Carl Costello?" I clarified.

"Yes," she said on another deep sigh. "Hughie had booked me for a photo shoot, and one of the other models didn't show. I called Gia to see if she could fill in. The rest, as they say, is history."

I wondered if there was some jealously on Jada's part that she'd been Costello's model first but Gia had become his star.

As if reading my mind, Jada added, "Turns out, Gia had the perfect look for Carl's esthetic. She closed all his shows."

"It sounds like you all worked together a lot."

"Mm-hmm," she said. She shielded her eyes from the sun as she turned to me. "Why is it you want to know about Gia?"

"Actually, we were wondering if Gia ever mentioned someone to you," Ava said, shifting on the lounger. "Someone who might have been getting a little too close to her for comfort."

Jada frowned, her line-free forehead pulling her eyebrows down. "What do you mean?"

"Did Gia ever mention anything about a guy following her? Or giving her maybe too much attention?" I asked.

"Gia was beautiful. Lots of guys gave her attention."

"We were thinking more along the lines of stalker type attention," Ava said.

"Stalker?" Jada's face registered surprise.

I nodded. "We noticed the same guy hanging around in the background in quite a few pictures of her."

Ava grabbed her phone from her purse, pulling up one of the photos from Gia's social media pages that we'd found earlier. She zoomed in on Baseball Cap Guy and turned the screen to face Jada.

Jada leaned forward, eyes scanning the picture. "I-I don't know. I mean, Gia never mentioned anything like that to me." She squinted at the man. "Hard to see his face."

"I know," Ava said. "He's kind of hidden in all of them." She scrolled through two more photos, but Jada just shook her head.

"Sorry. I don't recognize him."

"You sure Gia never mentioned anything about someone following her or maybe being a little overly friendly?" I pressed.

"If this guy really was stalking her, she didn't mention it to me." She lifted her eyes from the phone, gaze going from Ava to me. "You don't think this guy had anything to do with her death, do you?"

"It's possible," I admitted. "We know he was at the fashion show."

"Are you sure?" she asked.

"Positive." I pulled up one of the photos from backstage. "I took this just before the show."

As Jada glanced at the picture, something flashed behind her eyes, though I couldn't quite read the emotion before it was just as quickly gone. If I had to guess, though, I'd say it was fear.

The idea of a man stalking models backstage at a fashion show wasn't exactly a comforting one.

"This was taken with your camera?" she asked me.

I nodded. "I didn't notice him at the time. It was just when we were scrolling through some photos for publicity shots today that we found this."

"You didn't see him backstage?" Ava pressed.

Jada licked her lips, a frown of concern still on her face. "No. But, I mean, everything was kind of hectic. It always is before a show. Lots of people involved and close quarters."

"What about after the show?" I asked. "Did you and Gia leave the runway together?"

She pried her eyes from the image of Baseball Cap Guy on my phone and leaned back in her lounger again. "No. I mean, yes, we all exited the stage at the same time, but Gia had her own dressing room." She paused. "As I guess you know. Anyway, she went straight to it and closed the door. The rest of us changed in the main room." The hint of resentment in her voice again made me wonder if she hadn't harbored a bit of jealousy over Gia's rise to private dressing room status over her.

"And you didn't notice anything out of the ordinary?" Ava asked. "Maybe see anyone approach Gia's dressing room?"

But Jada shook her head. "The police asked me the same thing. But I didn't really pay attention. Just too many bodies all packed into the same place, you know?"

I nodded. I knew. I'd felt much the same way.

"Plus," she went on, "Hughie wanted me to get to the reception as quickly as possible so I could mingle with potential clients. Wineries book a lot of print ads. He practically shoved me out the door as soon as I was dressed."

"Wait—shoved you out the door?" I shot Ava a look. "Hughie Smart was *at* the fashion show?" His receptionist had failed to mention that Hughie was "out of the office" in Sonoma.

Jada nodded again. "Yeah. He likes to be at the shows of his bigger clients like Costello. Why?"

Because according to Costello, Gia had fired him just before she'd been found dead.

"I was actually hoping to talk to him," I said instead.

"Emmy is thinking of doing some social media ads for her winery," Ava said quickly, going with her previous cover story.

"Oh?" Jada asked, perking up at the idea of a potential job.

I nodded, feeling like a heel for deceiving her. Especially while she was mourning the loss of her friend. "You don't happen to know if Hughie is still in town, do you?"

She nodded. "Like I said, the police told us we all had to stay another day."

"He has a room here?" I asked, glancing up at the hotel building in the background.

But Jada shook her head. "No, he's staying at some bed and breakfast. The View something."

"The Valley View?" Ava asked.

Jada smiled. "Yeah, that's it. You know it?"

"My mom is friends with the owner," Ava confirmed.

"Guess Sonoma is a smaller town than San Francisco," Jada said with a shrug.

I wasn't sure if that was said as a statement of fact or a subtle put-down, but either way it seemed to be Jada's final word, as she pulled her sunglasses down over her eyes again and leaned her head back down on the lounger. "Tell Hughie I said hi," she added.

"Sure," I promised halfheartedly as we left the model to her sunbathing-slash-grieving.

Ava waited until we were through the lobby and back outside the hotel again before pulling her phone out and dialing another number.

"Calling the Valley View?" I asked, leading the way back to my Jeep.

She nodded. "Janet Kim runs the place. She plays tennis with my mom on Tuesdays." She put the phone to her ear, and I could vaguely hear the sound of it ringing as we slipped inside my car and I cranked on the air conditioning.

I'd just gotten the vents pointed correctly at us for maximum cooling as someone on the other end of the call picked up.

"Hi, Janet, it's Celia's daughter, Ava." She paused a moment, and I heard the sound of a voice responding, though it was too faint to make out the words. "Oh, thank you. Yes, the fashion show was lovely." More pausing. "It *is* tragic how it ended."

She glanced at me across the car interior, shaking her head in a way that I could tell she was mentally cursing Bradley Wu and his well-read column for spreading the news like a California wildfire.

"I appreciate that, Janet," Ava said. "Listen, I was calling to see if I could speak to one of the guests you have there this weekend. Hughie Smart?"

I didn't have to hear the answer to know the response was not positive. Ava's smile dropped, and her shoulders sagged. "Oh, he's not in." Janet said something. Then Ava added, "Sure, that would be great. Can you ask him to call me when he does? It's kind of urgent. You have my number?"

Janet must have, as Ava nodded. "Perfect. Thank you, Janet."

She hung up and put the phone back in her purse. "Well, hopefully he calls back," she said as I pulled out of the parking lot and headed back to Silver Girl.

"I wonder if Hughie knew about Gia's stalker?" I mused as I navigated the light traffic through downtown.

"You think she told her agent?"

I shrugged. "I guess it depends on how close they were. Or if she thought Stalker Guy was a threat."

"*If* Gia even knew," Ava added, looking out the window at the passing storefronts—a charming mix of old California mission style buildings and modern coffee shops and art galleries. "If Stalker Guy was stealthy enough at blending into the background, it's possible she hadn't even noticed he was following her yet."

That was a scary thought for any woman. That a stranger could be cataloguing your every move without you even knowing.

"Don't you think she would have noticed him lurking in her photos like we did?"

Ava shrugged. "Depends on how closely she was inspecting them. I know when I look at selfies, I'm usually focused on myself." Ava paused. "And I'm not even a model."

I grinned. "Good point."

A few minutes later, we pulled up in front of Ava's shop and I parked at the curb. We were both getting out of my Jeep when I noticed a couple of women standing beside the front window where Ava's Silver Girl logo had been hand-painted. A younger one posed beneath the logo, and an older one took her photo with a small camera.

"Can I help you?" Ava asked as we approached.

The older woman started, looking embarrassed. "Uh, no. We were just taking a couple of pictures."

"Well, I'm the owner," Ava said, giving them a wide smile. "I was just about to open up the shop again, if you'd like to take a look inside."

"Ohmigosh," the younger one gushed. "Are you the one who made the murder necklace?"

Ava's smiled faded, her jaw clenching.

"Uh, on second thought, we're closed right now," I told the two women. "Sorry, you'll have to come back another time."

The younger girl's face fell, but the older woman must have picked up on the proverbial steam starting to come out of Ava's ears, as she ushered the other one away. "Come on. We'll come back later," she promised.

"Please don't," Ava mumbled under her breath. Though, I was pretty sure both women were out of earshot by then.

Hopefully.

"Do you need me to stay with you?" I asked her, resisting the urge to check my watch. While I would never abandon her in a time of need, I did have inventory reports and a harvest budget patiently awaiting my attention back at the winery.

"No," Ava said, taking a deep breath and letting some of the tension release from her jaw. "I'm fine. I'll just…shoo the looky-loos along and hope some of the Links ladies-who-lunch come by." She gave me a smile that wasn't totally believable.

"You sure?" I hedged.

She nodded. "Positive. I'm fine. Go make some wine or something." This time her smile was more genuine.

I returned it, giving her arm a quick squeeze. "Okay, but call me if you need anything. Or if you hear back from Hughie," I added.

"Will do," she promised as I got back into my Jeep.

I waited until she'd unlocked the doors to Silver Girl and turned the sign back around to *Open* before I pulled away from the curb.

* * *

Oak Valley Vineyards was located in the hills above the valley, about twenty minutes outside of the bustling downtown. It was just under ten acres of lush vineyards and majestic oak trees that had been in my family for generations. My ancestors had planted the first Pinot Noir vines on the land, and our family had reaped the rewards ever since. Over the years, generations had added to the property—more varietals of grapes, the long, low winery buildings in the Spanish revival style that housed our tasting rooms, offices, and kitchen, and the tiled outdoor courtyards where we hosted private parties and weddings. But the one constant at Oak Valley was a sense of peace I always felt as I approached. A sense of home.

I let that familiar, comforting feeling wash over me as I pulled up the oak tree–lined drive, inhaling the warm scents of blooming lavender and grapes ripening in the sun. I parked in the gravel parking lot in front of our main building. It was sparsely populated, being a bit early for the happy hour crowd, though I was glad to see at least a few cars other than those of my small staff. Every sale counted.

I locked my Jeep and made my way inside, popping my head into the tasting room first. A couple of the tables had groups of three and four people, sipping wine and laughing amiably. An older couple in Bermuda shorts and Hawaiian style shirts sipped at one end of the long polished bar, and I spied my sommelier, Jean Luc, opening a Petite Sirah for a woman at the other end.

Jean Luc had been born and raised in Bordeaux, France, knew everything there was to know about wine, and with his tall, thin frame and long black mustache to rival any vaudevillian villain was a spectacle that kept the tourists coming back for more.

This afternoon, however, it was the woman he was pouring for who caught my attention. I immediately recognized her pink and blue cotton candy hair and technicolor outfit, comprised of a long skirt in a floral print, a hot pink T-shirt, and lime green feather boa.

Fashion designer, Daisy Dot.

CHAPTER FIVE

"Ah, here eez Emmy now!" Jean Luc said, gesturing toward me with flourish as I approached the pair.

Daisy Dot turned toward me, her face breaking into a smile that I suspected had at least a little bit to do with the nearly empty wineglass on the bar in front of her. "Well, what good timing. I was just telling your sommelier, here, that I decided I'd take you up on that offer of a tour of your winery." She gestured to Jean Luc, who was preening at the correct usage of his title. Jean Luc much preferred the term sommelier to wine steward. Then again, he preferred the French term for anything.

"Of course," I agreed. "I'd be happy to show you around."

"Jean Luc was such a dear, he's already let me sample several of your wines. I believe this Petite Sirah is my favorite." She picked up her glass and downed the last dribble of wine from the bottom.

"We only do it in small runs, but it is very popular," I told her.

"Only in small runs, huh? Well, then I'll have to order at least a case of it."

My opinion of her was looking up. "We'll be sure to set one aside for you," I told her, nodding toward Jean Luc.

"Zee mademoiselle's glass, she seems to be a bit light, no?" Jean said, holding up the bottle. "Another pour for zee *jolie femme*?" While Jean Luc had been living in the California for years, his French accent remained as thick as ever. Sometimes, I wondered if it was on purpose.

However, the customers seemed to eat it up, which was currently illustrated by the way Daisy was grinning ear to ear.

"Please, my good man!" Daisy set her glass on the bar.

Jean Luc filled it again. Then once finished, he gave her an elegant bow before moving on to refill the glasses of the Hawaiian shirt clad couple.

Daisy took a generous sip from her glass. Or gulp, depending on how liberally you wanted to measure. "Well, this makes being forced to stay in town an extra night a little more palatable," she said, licking a stray droplet off her lips.

"I assume the police asked you to stay as well?" I asked.

She nodded, shrugging her shoulders in a way that made her boa look as if it had come to life. "Ridiculous. As if I'd have anything to do with that bore Costello or his models. I mean, his designs put one to sleep, no?"

"You do have very different esthetics," I said, choosing my words carefully.

"Ha!" She let out a bark of laughter. "That's putting it mildly, my dear." She paused to watch Jean Luc as he moved to the next table. "He's cute. Single?"

"Very," I said. As far as I knew, Jean Luc's one and only love was wine.

"Interesting." She waggled her eyebrows up and down at me, and I noticed they, too, were dyed pink.

"Did you know Gia well?" I asked, changing the subject.

"Hmm?" She pried her eyes from my sommelier, turning her attention back to me. "Oh, Gia? Uh, yes. I mean, the San Francisco fashion scene isn't like New York. We're a close-knit community."

"So you worked with her?"

She shrugged. "I'm sure I've worked with most of Hughie's models at one point or another."

I wasn't sure if she was being purposely evasive or just didn't care. "Costello mentioned Gia being difficult to work with."

"Did he?" She laughed again. "Well, that's hilarious. I mean, a crab apple like Costello calling *someone else* a diva."

"I get the feeling you don't like Costello much," I said, watching her take another generous sip from her glass.

"Well then, *that* would make *you* one perceptive little lady," she told me. "No. I don't like Costello. In fact, I loathe the man."

Those were pretty strong words. "Any particular reason?" I couldn't help asking.

"Besides his stifling, awful garments?" she said, getting in another dig. "Yes. He has no ethics whatsoever. He's so intimidated by a strong female designer who celebrates a woman's body like I do that he's tried to sabotage me."

"Sabotage?" Another strong word. "Really?" I asked.

She nodded vigorously, the boa slipping off one shoulder to droop onto the empty barstool beside her. "Yes, really! He stole from me!"

I frowned. "What did he steal?" I asked, wondering how much of that was reality and how much was the Petite Sirah talking.

"Ruby earrings."

Now she had my attention. That sounded very much like a missing emerald. "Go on," I prompted.

Not that she needed much prompting. She seemed more than eager to share, leaning in toward me as if relaying some delicious gossip. "It was at the spring show. At the Palace of Fine Arts? Costello was there purely as a spectator, but *I* was unveiling my line. Big deal. All the top buyers were there." She paused. Sipping again.

"What happened?"

"Well, I had these large gemstone earrings made for each of my models. Heart shaped, a good two inches across each. You see, they corresponded with the months—twelve girls, twelve gems, each one dressed in an outfit that represented their month's color. It was all thematically coordinated."

"It sounds very beautiful."

"Well it *would* have been, if my July had had her ruby earrings! They went missing right before the show."

"And you think Costello stole them?"

She nodded. "Yes! Deliberately to sabotage me. My July had to walk down the runway with *bare* ears! Ruined the entire show." She sniffed indignantly before reaching for her glass, which was rapidly being depleted.

"What makes you think Costello was behind the theft?"

"Well, who else would do it?" she asked, looking at me like that was a silly question. "It's not like the Bloomingdale's buyer has anything personal against me, right?"

"I mean, what makes you think they weren't taken for their monetary value by someone wanting to steal the gems?" I clarified.

"Oh." She cleared her throat. "Well, they wouldn't have returned the jewelry, now, would they?"

"Wait—are you saying the earrings were returned?"

"Yes. Didn't I say that? As my assistant was putting everything away after the show, there were the ruby earrings— right where they were supposed to be with all the other sets. So, there you have it! Costello must have taken them deliberately to ruin my show." Having clearly proven her point in her mind, she downed the rest of her Sirah and set the glass on the bar with a definitive clunk.

I blinked at her, trying to process what she'd told me. While at first I'd thought maybe her rubies and Ava's emerald were connected, the more she talked the more I wondered if maybe she hadn't just misplaced the earrings herself. While quirky and eccentric were hallmarks of creativity, I wasn't sure they always lent themselves to organization. At least, if the way she'd just told that story was any indication.

"You're sure the earrings weren't just misplaced temporarily?" I asked. "Maybe put away in the wrong case?"

She scoffed. "No, they were not. It was intentional sabotage, I tell you. That man has had it in for me ever since I won designer of the year at the San Francisco Fashion Awards and he got bubkus." She grinned. "Which shows how much creativity his old lady styles have—bubkus." She giggled.

While his pieces weren't necessarily on the cutting edge, I didn't think they were terrible and found myself defending them. "His finale gown was lovely," I said.

"Yes, well, Gia could have made anything look lovely." She paused. "Poor thing," Daisy's eyes misted and she shook her head. "She was so beautiful. What a terrible waste."

A sentiment I'd had myself.

"Of course, it does fill me with some glee that Costello now has several pieces to refit." She tried to get Jean Luc's attention to refill her empty glass, but he didn't see her. Or very effectively pretended not to.

"Oh?" I asked her, moving behind the bar to refill her glass myself.

"Uh, yes. Well, as you know, Gia was his closer in almost every show he did. His big finale pieces are all tailored to her measurements. And that man does like to tailor pieces within an inch of their life," she added, watching me pull a bottle of wine from behind the counter and pour a generous helping into her glass.

"Surely he can find another model of her size?" I asked.

"Size? Yes. Specific measurements? Oh no." She wagged her index finger at me with one hand, reaching for the glass with the other. "Unlike your off-the-racks stuff, the clothes that walk a runway are custom fitted. Every seam! I'm sure Costello is just itching to get back to The City to start tearing his finale gowns apart." She giggled again, sounding more like a vindictive teen than a woman old enough to be sporting white hair.

It occurred to me that maybe Daisy wasn't just tipsy on Sirah but possibly a little toward the unbalanced end of eccentric as well. A woman had been strangled to death, and she was giggling about how inconvenient outfit alterations would be. I wasn't sure if Costello had really had anything to do with the ruby earrings that had gone missing, but in Daisy's mind it was clear the two were locked in a serious feud.

I suddenly wondered just how far Daisy would go to get back at Costello. As far as killing his signature model?

"Did you go backstage with your models after the show?" I asked in what I hoped was a casual tone.

"Hmm?" Daisy asked, clearly lost in her own thoughts again. "What was that?"

"I wondered if you accompanied your models backstage after the fashion show at the Links? Or did you go directly to the reception?"

"Oh no," she said, shaking her head. "No, I went with the models. I can't relax until I know my garments are all tucked away neatly."

"So you were backstage?" I clarified.

She nodded, sipping again. "Mm-hmm. I helped Amanda get out of her jumper, then made sure that Marcus had all the gloves and hats collected. Diana got her zipper caught in her hair taking off her dress, and *that* took a while to get undone."

I wasn't sure if it was intentional, but she was ticking off names as if giving me the list of people who could alibi her out. I followed her narrative, mentally trying to pinpoint exactly where she might have been when Gia had died.

"Anyway, it was almost as chaotic after the show as it was before." She waved her hand in the air. "Trust me, I got to that rosé in the lounge as soon as I could."

"When was that?" I asked.

"When?"

"Yes. What time?"

"Well, I...I don't wear a watch." She held up her bony wrist, which was adorned with a few jelly bracelets from the 1980s but no timepiece. "But I'm sure Fabio could tell you."

"Fabio?" I asked, trying to place the name.

"Costello's little boy toy. He was the first person I saw at the reception. Poor thing. Sitting all alone. If I had a treat that tasty, I certainly wouldn't leave him to his own devices. Not among the country club set, if you know what I mean." She cackled at her joke, even though I was hazy on the exact punch line.

"Are you saying you spotted Costello's boyfriend alone at the reception?" I clarified. "Costello wasn't with him?"

"Yes." She blinked at me. "Why?"

Because Costello had sworn he was with Fabio when Gia was murdered.

"No reason," I lied. I gave her big smile, refilling her drink.

* * *

By the time I'd given Daisy Dot a quick tour of the grounds, including the south vineyard, where we had picnic tables set up for outdoor events during these mild summer months, and The Cave, our cellar where our old vintages were stored, she was looking distinctly unsteady on her feet and, by her own admission, ready for a nap. I politely suggested she call an Uber and helped her into the back of the beige sedan before waving her off down the winding drive with the backdrop of a brilliant sunset behind her.

Not that she seemed awake enough to appreciate it. Her head slumped on the seat cushions the moment she got inside the car. Luckily, she had purchased her case of wine before the Sirah had gotten the best of her, and once her Uber's taillights were a thing of the past, I made my way to the large barn that had been converted to house our storage and bottling facility to see about getting it delivered to her hotel.

As I entered, I found my winery manager, Eddie Bliss, leaning casually against a barrel, chatting with Jean Luc.

Eddie had come to work for me after a long career as a househusband to his partner, Curtis, and his actual managerial skills had left something to be desired. In fact, what Eddie had known about the wine business, I could fit into a thimble. A small one. For mice. But his perpetually cheerful countenance seemed to make up for what he lacked in actual knowledge, at least as far as customers were concerned. And to his credit, he was willing to work for what I could afford to pay—which was not much.

Jean Luc grabbed a bottle of Pinot Noir from the shelf behind Eddie, muttering something half in French and half in English.

"That's a very nice way to insult me." Eddie laughed, causing his pudgy face to light up. Eddie was a shade over 5'6" tall, his ears were two sizes too big for his face, and he was dressed today in herringbone shorts, complete with white linen shirt and Italian leather boat shoes.

"Excusez-*moi*," Jean Luc replied. "But you are mistaken once again, *mon amie*. France eez, in fact, zee best place in the world for an 'oliday."

"I'm sure France is all well and good," Eddie countered. "But America has a lot to offer. Hawaii, the Grand Canyon, Niagara Falls."

"An island, a hole in the ground, and some water." Jean Luc shook his head. "Zey cannot rival zee French Riviera and zee Eiffel Tower."

"A big metal pole?" Eddie teased.

"A big metal..." Jean Luc's mouth opened and closed with indignation. His cheeks were starting to flush when he caught sight of me. "Emmy, tells zees man why zee Eiffel Tower eez a modern marvel!"

I put my hands up in the surrender position. "Sorry, boys. I'm not getting involved." Plus, since I could barely afford a trip to the Vegas version of the Eiffel Tower, let alone the French Riviera, I was hardly qualified to argue.

"I thought you were off today, Eddie," I commented, turning my attention to him.

"Actually, I have a meeting with an influencer off-site." He stood as tall as his stout frame would allow, straightening his shirt that was presently testing the laws of physics across his plump belly.

I cocked an eyebrow. "An influencer?"

"You know, those people online who are so amazing that everyone wants to be them and wear what they wear and go where they go—"

"Like France!" Jean Luc cut in.

But Eddie ignored him. "—and they earn zillions of dollars documenting it all on social media."

My other eyebrow cocked. "Zillions?"

He waved me off. "Depends on how many followers they have."

I shook my head. "Okay, I know what an influencer is," I told him. "What I don't know is why you are meeting one."

"Aurora Dawn is in town, and I want to take her a couple of bottles of our wares in the hope she'll send a few Insta posts into the world of the uninfluenced."

While his lingo might be slightly off kilter, the idea wasn't half bad. "It might not hurt to expand our online presence a little."

"Honey, Aurora could expand it a lot," Eddie told me.

"I was just giving 'im a bottle of Pinot Noir for her," explained Jean Luc.

"Good idea. Why not take along a bottle of the Petit Sirah as well?" I said, nodding toward an open case. "Daisy Dot seemed to like that one."

"The designer?" Eddie asked, his eyes lighting up. "Was she here?"

"You just missed her," Jean Luc said with a sniff. "Lucky you."

"Oh." Eddie's face fell. "Speaking of which, I heard what happened at the fashion show. How's Ava holding up?"

"She's okay," I said, stretching the truth a little. I quickly filled him in on the broad strokes of the last twenty-four hours.

"Poor thing." Eddie shook his head when I was done. "I assume Grant is involved?"

"He is. And I'm sure he'll clear it all up in no time," I said with more confidence than I felt.

"Does that mean that he'll be around here just a bit more often?" he asked with a glint in his eye.

"I don't see why he would. The murder didn't take place here." Thank goodness. We'd already been down that road. More than once.

Eddie's chest deflated like I'd popped his favorite balloon. "Well, that's just disappointing."

Jean Luc shook his head and moved to a case of wine bottles that had just been labeled. He returned with a bottle of Chardonnay and a bottle of Petite Sirah.

"If zee influencer eez not impressed with zeez, then she doesn't know her wine," he commented, handing the bottles to Eddie.

"I'm sure she'll love them," Eddie remarked, tucking the bottles under his arm.

I was about to tell him to keep the bottles cool, when Jean Luc beat me to it. He huffed, snatching the bottles back, and then stepped away, muttering something about finding a bag.

"Tell her to make sure that our label is facing the camera," I instructed Eddie.

He tutted. "I cannot tell a woman with over half a million followers how to take a photo."

"Half a million?" I turned, calling to Jean Luc over my shoulder. "Maybe you should throw in a bottle of Zin too."

"We don't have zat many bottles," he yelled back.

"Even better. If it's in high demand, you can up the price." Eddie grinned.

I had to admit, he might be catching on to this winery manager thing after all.

I left Eddie to Jean Luc's capable hands as he bagged up the wines for Eddie's influencer and readied Daisy's case of Petite Sirah for delivery, and I made my way across the meadow to the main buildings that housed my office.

I'd only just sat down behind my computer when a text buzzed in on my phone. I checked the readout. Grant.

Busy tonight?

I was glad I was alone in my office so no one saw the goofy grin I could feel spreading across my cheeks as I typed back a reply.

Not particularly. Why?

I didn't have to wait long for his response to buzz in.

Dinner?

I glanced at my computer screen—dark. As it had been all day. I'd fully meant to put some time in on the inventory reports for this month and start working on the budget for the upcoming harvesting season, but somehow the day had gotten away from me. Besides, I did have to eat eventually.

What did you have in mind?

Meet me at The Vine? Half hour?

I looked down at my jeans and plain T-shirt. Definitely not dinner date with a hot cop attire.

Give me 45 min.

CHAPTER SIX

———

Forty-eight minutes later (but who was counting), I walked into The Vine, a quaint restaurant just outside of downtown with a menu catering toward seasonal California cuisine and an atmosphere that was just swanky enough to bring a casual dinner into romantic date territory. I'd settled on a pair of black skinny dress pants and a cream colored, off-the-shoulder top in a light fabric that skimmed my curves in a flattering way. Black strappy heels gave me a few extra inches and a boost of confidence, and I'd completed the ensemble with simple silver teardrop earrings, which had been a gift from Ava, and an extra swipe of eyeliner and mascara. I was hoping the overall effect was chic without looking like I'd put *too* much effort into it.

Grant had beaten me to the restaurant and was sitting at a table near the window, sipping something dark and probably alcoholic from a short glass. He caught my eye as I entered, waving me over to bypass the hostess stand.

"Hey," he said, rising from his seat to plant a quick peck on my cheek. "Glad you could meet on short notice."

"Me too," I told him, trying to keep the blush from my face at the touch of his lips on my skin. I cleared my throat as he pulled a chair out for me. "Busy day?"

He chuckled. "Aren't they all?" He signaled the server over, who immediately took my drink order. I settled on a glass of Sauvignon Blanc, and Grant ordered another Scotch on the rocks.

"Must have been a *very* busy day," I noted, gesturing to his nearly empty glass.

He gave me a grin. "Let's just say I've been schooled in the world of fashion far more than I ever wanted to be."

My turn to chuckle. "I take it you spent some time with Carl Costello and Daisy Dot?"

He nodded. "And several models and a handful of makeup artists. I'm pretty sure I had it pointed out to me at least three times that cowboy boots are *so* last season." He gestured to the worn leather pair on his feet.

"Well, I could have told you that," I joked.

The server arrived with our drinks, and we paused our conversation for a moment while he took our orders. I went with the Sea Bass with Lemon Herb Sauce, and Grant ordered the bacon wrapped filet mignon. Then the server took our menus, and we both thanked him before I turned my attention back to my date.

Date. Looking across the table at Grant's dark eyes, sexy way-past-five o'clock shadow, and thick dark hair starting to curl just a little at the ends above his broad shoulders, I felt my stomach flutter at the word. Not that I was a total novice in the romance department, but it had been a while since my hormones had gotten so worked up over a guy. I wasn't sure if I liked it or feared it.

I cleared my throat, shoving those thoughts aside as I took my first sip of wine. "So, I'm guessing you didn't make a whole lot of headway into finding Gia's killer?"

He shrugged, setting his glass down. "I didn't make an arrest today, if that's what you're asking."

"Get any steps closer to one?" I asked, knowing I had to tread lightly. While Grant might joke about his day with me, I knew sharing details of an ongoing investigation was something he seldom enjoyed. I nonchalantly swirled my white wine in my glass, taking another small sip. It was light and fruity, less oaky than our Chardonnay but still bright and vibrant.

"We're still interviewing witnesses."

"Learn anything interesting?" I asked.

He shook his head. "Nothing you probably couldn't find out from googling Gia's name."

"Such as?"

He sighed. But considering he knew I was good with Google, he relented. "She was twenty-three, lived alone, no significant other and no family in the area, at least no one she was close with. Apparently she liked to live the good life—the very good life, if her credit card statements are any indication. Her favorite hobby seemed to be spending money."

I nodded. I'd gotten that impression from her social media too. "I'm guessing no one you talked to saw her after the show?"

He shook his head. "From what I can gather, she went right to her dressing room and was alone."

Until her killer attacked her.

I tried not to picture her lying on her dressing room floor. "There were a lot of people backstage. It's hard to believe no one saw her killer go into her dressing room."

He shrugged. "Apparently there was a lot going on. Everyone was focused on getting to the reception."

I thought about that. "You know, everyone I've talked to seems to say the same thing—there were so many people backstage that they didn't notice any one person in particular."

He lifted an eyebrow my way. "Everyone *you've* talked to?"

I shrugged. "We girls like to chat." I shot him an innocent grin.

"Uh-huh." He wasn't buying it, but the little hazel flecks in his eyes were dancing with amusement. Which I took as a good sign.

"Anyway, it's possible someone saw something, but they just don't *know* they did."

He nodded. "That's exactly why we've been conducting multiple interviews. Hoping to jog some memory loose."

"But no luck so far?"

He shook his head.

"CSI come back with anything useful?" I asked.

He gave me a dubious look, like he wasn't sure he should be sharing.

"Come on," I prompted. "You invited me to dinner the day after a woman was murdered with my best friend's necklace. Did you really think we were gonna chitchat about the weather?"

He laughed in earnest that time, the low, rumbling sound causing another flutter in my stomach that had nothing to do with the wine. "Fair enough." He ran a hand over his stubbled jaw. "But I honestly don't know a whole lot more than I did yesterday."

"You guys find any fingerprints?" I asked, hoping the killer had left some.

He nodded. "Forensics analyzed the murder weapon, and only the victim's and Ava's prints came back as a match."

"Which makes sense. It was Ava's necklace. I'm sure she handled it plenty that day."

He nodded. "Sure," he agreed as a server stopped by with a basket of bread and a tray of dipping oils.

I waited until he'd walked away again before continuing. "So, you think the killer wore gloves?"

Grant shrugged, grabbing a slice of sourdough bread and dipping it into the pool of rosemary infused olive oil on his plate. "That's one theory."

I pursed my lips, following his lead and tearing off a bit of bread. "You know, Daisy's models all wore gloves."

"She didn't mention that." He popped his bread into his mouth and chewed thoughtfully.

"They did," I added. "Of course, that doesn't mean one of her models did it. All the accessories were out in the open after the show. Once the models changed, anyone could have grabbed a pair."

"Or brought their own," Grant pointed out. "If someone planned to steal the necklace ahead of time, they would have come prepared."

"So you're still going with the robbery gone wrong?" I asked, nibbling my bread.

Grant nodded, then paused. He cocked his head, giving me a side eye. "Is there some reason we shouldn't?" he asked.

I let out a big breath. "Honestly? I don't know. I do know that Gia was not well liked."

"That much I gathered, too," he admitted. "Everyone we talked to seemed to struggle to say something nice about her."

"I only met her once, but I had much the same impression," I told him.

"So you think this could have been personal?" Grant asked.

I wasn't sure if he was taking my idea seriously or just humoring me. I tried to read the expression in his dark eyes, but those gold flecks were giving nothing away now. "I think it could have been. There was someone backstage that day who…well, we think might have been following Gia specifically."

"We?" he asked, jumping on the word.

"Ava and I."

"Oh no." He let out a *tsk* of air and shook his head. "Please don't tell me you two are playing Nancy Drew again?"

"Excuse me, I take offense to that," I said, giving him a look of mock anger, puffing my chest out. "We are grown women. If anything, we're Charlie's Angels."

He grinned and gave my puffed cleavage a healthy appraisal. "Point taken."

I hated the way my hormones got all giddy with that look. "Thank you," I mumbled, covering my hot flash with another sip of wine.

"Okay, tell me about this someone backstage," he said, thankfully seemingly oblivious to my discomfort as he dragged another slice of bread through oil.

"Well, we noticed this guy in the background of a couple of the photos I took at the show." I set my wineglass down and grabbed my phone from my purse, pulling up the shot again. "He also appears in a few of the photos on Gia's social media pages. But always off to the side. Always kind of hidden in the background. Like, maybe she didn't even know he was there."

I passed my phone across the table to him, and he frowned as he assessed Stalker Guy.

"Can't see much of his face here."

"Yeah, that's kind of a theme. He's usually wearing a hat or sunglasses. Almost like he doesn't want to be recognized."

Grant sent me another dubious look across the table. "Or because he lives in sunny California?"

I rolled my eyes and held my hand out for my phone to be returned. Grant gave it back, but the teasing glint still remained.

"Look, the guy was backstage the day Gia was killed. And I don't think he was associated with the show."

"Well, I can say he's not one of the witnesses I've interviewed so far," Grant conceded.

"So don't you think it's possible he was stalking Gia?"

"Stalking is a strong word," he cautioned. "This guy could have just been a friend of Gia's. Or one of the other models. Or it could even be a coincidence he was in the same place at the same time as Gia more than once."

"Kind of a big coincidence, right?" I asked, swirling my wine in my glass again.

Grant shrugged. "They happen more often than you'd think."

"So you're not even going to look into this guy?"

Grant blew out a big breath, his eyes going to the phone in my hand again. "I guess I could see if Gia ever filed for a restraining order or made a complaint."

I tried to stifle my grin. No one liked a gloater.

"But," he added, "it's entirely possible this guy is just some fan or friend."

I nodded. "Sure. Totally possible."

He shot me a look over the rim of his glass like he didn't believe I thought that for a second.

Luckily, our food arrived then, and we both dug in with gusto. I realized I hadn't eaten since the brunch at the Links, and while the hectic pace of the day had kept hunger at bay, I was famished now as I inhaled the scents of garlic, thyme, and oregano. My sea bass flaked delicately onto my fork, and I savored the velvety texture of the cauliflower purée artfully arranged beneath it, thinking the bright tang of the lemon and the lusciously buttery sauce were a match made in culinary heaven. I closed my eyes and may have even moaned a little.

"How's the fish?" Grant asked.

I opened my eyes to find him watching me, a look that was part amusement and part heat on his face—bedroom eyes dark and hooded, mouth cocked in a half grin.

I willed the blush rising up my neck to halt before it clashed with my mauve lipstick.

"Uh, it's good. Great," I said, forcing a light tone into my voice. "How's the steak?"

"Delightful." He stabbed a bite with his fork and popped it into his mouth, still grinning.

"So," I said, eyes going to my plate in an attempt to regain my composure. "All these witnesses you interviewed. I'm guessing no one saw a guy with an emerald size bulge in his pocket making for the door after the show, huh?"

He swallowed before answering. "Wouldn't that be nice?" He grinned. "No, and the security tapes at the front didn't show anything obvious either. Whoever took it probably simply put it in their pocket and walked out."

"Before you arrived," I noted. "You said officers were checking everyone before they left."

He nodded, lifting his fork to his mouth again. "We did. It was not on anyone who left the Links after law enforcement arrived."

I thought about that, shoving the herbaceous sauce around on my plate. I'd noted Costello backstage with Jada while police had been questioning witnesses. I remembered seeing Daisy as well. Of course, the recently fired Hughie Smart had been absent from the whole scene. I also hadn't seen Stalker Guy. Had he slipped away before the police had arrived? Possibly with a hundred-thousand-dollar emerald in his pocket?

"I know what you're thinking," Grant said.

"Huh?" I looked up to find his eyes on me.

"You're mentally going through who you saw backstage and who you didn't."

I wasn't sure if I loved or hated that he knew me so well.

I opened my mouth to protest, but he didn't give me the chance.

"Don't." His voice held a note of command in it. "Emmy, I know you and Ava like to play detective—"

"I wouldn't say *like*."

"—but if Gia was killed for that gem, whoever did this is ruthless. And I don't want you anywhere near them."

While my first instinct was to be offended at the insinuation that I'd intentionally put myself in harm's way by *playing* anything, the genuine emotion in his eyes melted me a little.

"Promise you'll leave this to the authorities."

Before the strong, independent woman in me could talk me out of it, I found myself nodding.

To his credit, there seemed to be a bit of surprise mixed with the relief in his eyes. "Good."

I licked my lips. "If you'll promise me one thing in return."

He cocked his head to the side again, looking wary. "What's that?"

"Find whoever did this and find that emerald for Ava. She's in real trouble without it."

His expression softened. "I'm guessing that means she did not have it insured."

I shook my head. "She only expected to have it in her possession for a short time. She was hoping the showcase at the Links would sell it."

He nodded in agreement. "Several people did mention to me today how pretty the necklace was. From how popular it sounds, I don't think she was wrong."

Which should have made her feel better, but somehow I thought it would just rub salt into the wound now.

"I'll do my absolute best, Emmy," he said, and he reached across the table to take one of my hands in his.

It was warm and softer than I might have thought, his thumb caressing my fingers in a comforting way that sent tingles running up my spine.

I was just about to start fantasizing about *dessert* when ringing erupted from his hip.

He pulled his hand back quickly, grabbing his phone to silence it before it disturbed the other patrons in the restaurant.

"Yeah?" he answered, putting it to his ear.

I was too far away to hear the person on the other end, but from the way Grant's expression went from relaxed to tense as he listened, I assumed it wasn't great news.

"Got it," he said, his tone clipped. "I'll be right there." He stabbed the phone off, shoving it back into his pocket.

"Work?" I guessed. Sadly, this wasn't the first time my fantasies of Grant à la mode had been rudely dashed by the Sonoma County Sheriff's Office.

He nodded, signaling the server for the check. "Sorry. Looks like I've got to go."

"Is it Gia's case?" I held my breath, hoping something had broken.

But he shook his head. "No. Break-in at an antique shop on 1st Street." He gave me small smile. "Sorry to bail on you."

I shook my head, forcing a smile of my own. "It's okay. We can pick up where we left off another time."

He paused as he reached for his wallet, shooting me a look that was pure heat. "I look forward to that."

Oh boy. There was no containing the blush this time, as it swept clear up to my hairline.

CHAPTER SEVEN

———

Sleep was a fitful battle that night, and as soon as the first rays of pale sunlight peeked in my windows, I conceded defeat and threw myself into a hot shower. I tossed on a simple pair of jeans, a blue cable knit sweater that my mom had bought me for my last birthday, and a pair of sturdy boots, only pausing long enough for a cup of coffee before heading out to inspect the vines.

The air held a chill this early, despite the late summer month, and I could see morning dew glistening off the grapes like diamonds as it caught the light. I inhaled the scents of damp earth and cool moss as I traversed the rows of plants that were as familiar to me as my own skin. I'd been walking this vineyard since I was a kid, had grown up among the lush acreage that comprised our land, and I felt more at home here than anywhere else in the world. It was amazing to me that I'd ever thought I could leave this place.

I remembered my father telling me as a young child that all this would one day be mine—the legacy that generations had left me. He'd passed away as I'd been entering my angsty teen years, and the anger and regret had pushed me to leave, wanting to create my own legacy on my own terms.

I shook my head, feeling a smile tug at my lips at the memory. While I didn't regret the culinary training I'd gotten when I'd left home, the priorities that had driven my youth were ones I was glad to leave behind in my rebellious years. Of course, what was really important in life had come crashing down on me with startling clarity the moment I'd gotten word my mom was sick.

While Oak Valley had once been a thriving little operation, after my father had passed away, the corporate giants of the region had moved in, outpricing little family run wineries like ours and pushing us to the brink of bankruptcy. A brink that had been all that much harder to navigate away from as my mother's mind had started to go, letting figures and facts and even memories slip through its fingers more and more often.

Early onset dementia had been the eventual diagnosis. I'd hardly been able to believe it at the time. She'd only been in her fifties, and even now I was still grappling with the unfairness of it all.

When she'd been diagnosed, I'd been cultivating a burgeoning culinary career on the LA foodie scene. One that I'd abandoned to come home and take over operations of the winery—even though my knowledge of the grapes was rusty and my skill at running a business nonexistent. But I'd learned, worked hard, and somehow managed to keep our ten acres of home afloat thus far. I was grateful that I'd been able to come home and reconnect with my roots.

Metaphorically and literally, I thought with another smile as I bent down to pull a weed from the base of a Zinfandel vine.

"Is that my Emmy?"

I looked up to find Hector sauntering toward me, his face crinkled up into a wide smile.

Hector Villareal had been the vineyard manager on the property since I was a child and was as much a fixture there as the shady oak trees. He knew more about grapes than any man I'd ever met, and his love of the outdoors was apparent not only in his skill at coaxing the robust, full flavors from our fruit but also in the dark tan and weather worn appearance of his skin. Despite his network of wrinkles, his smile was infectious and not only removed years from his face but also warmed my heart. I'd been the flower girl at Hector's wedding to Conchita, who now served as our house manager, and they were more like family to me than employees.

Some days, they almost seemed like the only family I had left.

"Hi, Hector," I told him, straightening to join him on the next row over.

"What are you doing up so early?" he teased.

I grinned and shrugged. "Couldn't sleep. Thought I'd come check up on you out here."

He scoffed, but it held more humor than anger. "I should be checking up on *you*. How's the budget coming for harvest this year?"

I groaned and rolled my eyes. "Please. Don't ruin a perfectly good morning with spreadsheet talk."

He laughed, the sound washing over me like a warm, familiar blanket in the crisp air. "Fair enough."

"They're looking pretty good this year, aren't they?" I asked, tipping my chin toward the Zin grapes.

He nodded. "Yes, they are." He lifted one of the vines, and I could see the rich purple color deepening and the stem starting to turn from green to brown. "They're almost ready."

I carefully fingered a couple and popped one particularly plump one into my mouth. "I hope they'll get a little sweeter."

Hector nodded. "They will." He looked up at a large oak tree offering its branches as shade. "I'll wait until the birds tell us it's time."

I glanced up, hearing a couple of faint chirps but not seeing much activity. I knew Hector relied as much on modern machinery and science as he did Mother Nature and the tried and true methods of past generations of farmers. Increased bird activity in the vineyard was a sure sign the grapes were ready— when the birds wanted to eat them, they were perfect for human consumption too.

"How are the Chardonnay grapes coming along?" I asked, gesturing to our right where the south pasture lay.

He shrugged, gazing out onto the horizon. "We might be a little light this year."

"How light?"

"I wouldn't worry about it, but you might want to label your runs limited edition this year."

"'Limited edition'? Have you been talking marketing with Eddie?"

He laughed out loud. "Yeah, he mentioned something the other day about some lady online. Sunrise or something?"

"Dawn. Aurora Dawn. Apparently she has a lot of followers on Instagram."

He shook his head. "Well, I don't know anything about that, but as long as they drink Oak Valley wine while they do their internet typing, I'll be happy."

"That makes two of us," I agreed as we came to the end of the row. "Any other good news about this year's crop?" I almost hesitated to ask. "How are the Pinot Noir grapes?"

"Good, good." He nodded, eyes on the ground as we walked. "Had the motion sensor lights go on last night over there though."

"Oh no," I said, knowing that was not good. Normally they were triggered when large animals got into the vineyard— like deer. While most people thought of deer as cute, innocent creatures, they were the biggest pests we'd had to contend with yet, eating our profits right off the vines before we'd even had a chance to harvest.

"You think it's deer?" I confirmed.

"Most likely," he responded.

"Any idea how they're getting in?"

He pointed to an area just east of where we were standing. "The fencing over there needs to be reinforced. And we could use some additional barriers up on the ridge."

I felt my stomach clench. This was not good news. Fencing was pricey. Correction—*good* fencing was pricey. But I knew the cost of not putting a fence up could be even higher if the deer damaged the vines. "Don't suppose you can do a few repairs with what we have?"

Hector shot me a look. "I'll do what I can. For now," he added.

"Okay, okay. I'll see if Schultz can help me find a magical pot of gold somewhere in our books." Gene Schultz was my accountant, and if there was anyone who hated expensive news more than I did, it was Schultz.

Hector smiled and gave me a clap on the back. "You're doing great, kid. Your dad would be proud."

That comment unexpectedly choked me up, and it was all I could do to nod and give Hector a watery smile before I headed back to the main winery building.

I almost had my emotions in check again by the time I'd poured a second cup of coffee from the main kitchen and said good morning to Conchita, who was elbows deep in pie dough. I snitched a couple of cinnamon-sugar apple slices from her bowl of filling before she chased me out and I settled myself behind my computer screen in my small office.

Luckily, spreadsheets sucked any emotion right out of me, and I spent the next couple of hours with mind numbing numbers as I did, as promised, work on the harvest budget. Problem was, as much as I worked at trimming it down, our expenses still outweighed our assets. As per usual.

I was just wondering if vintage wine could be used as collateral for a small business loan, when my phone rang out from my desktop beside me, jarring me from the unpleasant task.

Seeing Ava's name come up on the screen, I swiped the call on. "Hey, Ava."

"Finish up whatever you're doing. I'm on my way to pick you up," my best friend said, a note of command in her voice.

"Good morning to you too."

She laughed. "Good morning, Emmy. Now, grab your purse and meet me out front." In the background I could hear her radio playing a country station and the sounds of cars passing by her windows.

"Where are we going?" I asked, glancing up at my computer screen. But it wasn't as if I needed much excuse to table that task. I quickly hit *Save* and closed my files.

"Janet called me. Hughie Smart is at the Valley View B&B."

I raised my eyebrow at the phone. "And you're headed there?"

"*We're* headed there. I'll be out front in ten."

I opened my mouth to ask more, but I realized she'd already disconnected, apparently having issued her decree and hung up before I could say no.

Not, honestly, that I would have. I was almost as curious as Ava to hear what Hughie Smart had to say about his dead model.

I had just enough time to change from my sweater and boots into a soft pink sleeveless blouse and a pair of wedge sandals before Ava pulled into my gravel-lined parking lot in her baby—a vintage 1970s olive green convertible Pontiac GTO. Some people had pets—Ava had her GTO. Being that it was top-down weather, Ava had pulled her hair back into a ponytail, and a white tank top nicely displayed her tanned shoulders atop a paisley printed skirt in shades of turquoise and pale blue.

"Ready?" she asked, leaning across the car to open her passenger side door.

"Barely, but yes," I agreed, slipping into the seat. "Have you talked to Hughie yet?"

She shook her head as she pulled back down the driveway. "No, but Janet said he just finished breakfast and looked like he'd be there for a while. Perfect time to ambush him."

"Ambush makes me nervous," I said, remembering Grant's warning from the night before about not upsetting potential murderers.

Ava shot me a grin. "Okay, let's go with quietly catch him off guard with our polite questions."

I rolled my eyes, but I was pretty sure that my hair flying around my face covered it.

"Did you just roll your eyes at me?" Ava asked.

"Just drive," I mumbled.

* * *

The Valley View Bed & Breakfast was located only a few minutes south of Oak Valley Vineyards, nestled in a small residential neighborhood of older homes and stately Victorians. The outside of the building was painted a cheery yellow and sported a large wraparound porch outfitted with inviting rocking chairs and a bench swing. Several cars lined the street in front of it, and we had to park two doors down on the opposite side of the street.

I followed Ava to the carved wooden front door, propped open to catch the morning breeze before the midday temperatures rose too high. Like most older buildings in the area, this one didn't appear to be upgraded with AC.

Beyond the door, the foyer had been outfitted with a small check-in desk, manned by an older woman in a blousy, floral printed dress that almost felt period to the house itself.

"Can I help you—" she started. Then she focused on Ava, and a bright smile hit her soft features. "Oh, Ava. So nice to see you, dear."

"Hi, Janet," Ava said, giving the woman a couple of air kisses and a hug. "This is my friend, Emmy."

"Nice to meet you," I told her, shaking a proffered hand.

"He still here?" Ava asked.

Janet nodded. "He's on the back porch. Said his room was too stuffy and he needed to make some calls." She shrugged and pointed down a short hallway.

"Thanks!" Ava gave the older woman a wave before heading in the direction she'd indicated.

Down the small hallway was a screen door that led to another wooden porch, this one looking out over a garden blooming with colorful roses, snap dragons, and tall sunflowers. To our right sat a wrought iron table and chairs, and beside it a man pacing back and forth as he yelled into a phone.

Hughie Smart stood about six feet tall, with a slight build and skin that looked like he'd invested heavily in spray tanning. A short sleeved black silk shirt hung loosely on his frame, and his hair color looked dyed to match. His phone was glued to his ear, and I could hear him barking at whoever was on the other end.

"No, that's not the price we agreed on," he said. "No, it does *not* include travel time."

Ava and I stood awkwardly to the side, waiting for him to finish.

He must have noticed us, as he told the person on the other end, "Look, I'll have Maureen send over new contracts, but I've got to go." He paused only long enough for the person on the other end to respond before stabbing his phone off and turning an expectant expression our way.

"Uh, Mr. Smart?"

"Yes," he said, looking past us as if the answer to who we were and why we were bothering him might be there.

"My name is Ava Barnett. I left you a message yesterday?" She stepped forward and offer a hand in greeting.

He shook it, apprehension still in his gaze. "Did you? Sorry, I, uh, haven't called in for my messages this morning."

"Yes, well, I'm in charge of special promotional projects at Oak Valley Vineyards," she said, forging ahead with the same lie she'd concocted the day before. "And this is the owner of Oak Valley, Emmy Oak."

I gave him a little wave. While Ava was quick with a cover story, I was a terrible liar. I figured the less I said the better.

"Anyway," Ava went on. "We wanted to talk to you about possibly hiring models for a social media campaign."

"Oh?" His face broke into a welcoming smile. "Well, then, why don't you have a seat?"

"Thank you," Ava said.

Hughie gallantly pulled out chairs for Ava and me at the table before settling opposite us. "So, what sort of ads are you looking to shoot?" he asked.

"What sort?" Ava gave me a hesitant look. Apparently she hadn't worked the story out that far yet. "Uh, just some photos of people enjoying our wine, maybe? You know, to entice weekenders our way?"

Hughie nodded. "Sure. Sure. I have several young ladies who would fit the bill. I assume you're looking for more character models than fashion?"

"Is there a difference?" I asked.

Hughie gave me a patronizing smile. "Fashion models are generally a certain weight, height, body type. They have a certain look that lends itself to runway. Our character models are more like just average people, like you and me. But, you know, better looking." He shot me a wide smile, showing off a row of veneers that could blind a person from space.

"I see," I said, trying not to take offense to being just an average person.

"Uh, actually, we were interested in a couple of specific models," Ava said, shooting me a sidelong glance. "Ones we saw walk in the show this weekend at the Links."

At the mention of the tragic event, Hughie's smile fell, veneers hiding again behind his thin lips. "You were at the show, then?"

I nodded. "Yes, Ava was actually showing her jewelry there."

His eyes shot to Ava. "I thought you said you worked at a winery?"

Oops. See what I meant about not being good with lies?

"I do," Ava said, covering quickly. "I, uh, just design jewelry part time. On the side. It's a hobby." She matched his shark-like smile with one of her own. Even if her teeth were just "average person" white.

"Huh." Hughie didn't look totally convinced. But he didn't throw us out either, so I forged ahead.

"You were at the charity show as well, weren't you?" I asked. I tried to keep the note of accusation out of my voice, but it must have crept in, as the previously welcoming look in his eyes was still tempered with a healthy dose of suspicion as he turned my way.

"I had two models walking the show. Why shouldn't I be there?"

"One of those models was Gia Monroe?"

He nodded. "She was," he said hesitantly, as if not sure what he was admitting to.

"I'm so sorry for your loss." Ava reached out and put one of her dainty hands over his unnaturally orange ones.

The gesture of sympathy must have caught him off guard, as he stammered, "Uh, th-thank you."

"Had she been with you long?" I asked.

"A couple years," he said. "But she booked out a lot. She was popular."

"Costello seemed to like her look," I said, feeling him out.

Hughie nodded. "Yes, he used her quite often."

"Even though she could be difficult to work with."

"Who said that?" he asked hotly.

Costello. Jada. Pretty much everyone I'd talked to. But, instead I went with "Just an impression I got."

He made a sort of noncommittal grunt in the back of his throat. "Gia was a professional. She was in high demand."

"What was *your* relationship with Gia like?" Ava asked.

Hughie's eyes turned on her. "Excuse me?"

"I mean, it's such a tragedy. Were you close?" she asked, still going for the sympathy angle.

"She worked for me." His words were clipped, and I feared we were losing him.

"Wasn't it more like *you* worked for *her*?" I asked. "I mean, at least until she fired you."

"Fired me!?" Hughie shot up from his seat, his voice booming across the small yard. "Who told you that?"

"Is it true?" I pressed.

"No!" he said emphatically. "Gia wouldn't dare fire me."

That was an interesting word choice. "Or else…?"

His eyes narrowed, and I could see a red angry flush tinting his orange skin. "I don't know what you're implying. It is a horrible tragedy that Gia was killed. But it had nothing to do with me."

"Of course not," Ava said, trying to soothe him. "That's not what she meant at all."

"No?" Hughie sputtered. "Her meaning seemed pretty clear to me."

I licked my lips. This was going downhill fast. "I didn't mean to accuse you. I just happened to talk to…someone," I hedged, not wanting to point a finger directly in Costello's direction, "who said they overheard Gia and you on the phone."

"When?" he asked, his eyes sharp.

"Backstage at the Links. Right before the showcase."

But Hughie shook his head. "No. Gia didn't call me before the show."

"Are you sure?"

"Positive. And if anyone told you otherwise, they're a liar!" He stabbed a finger at me for emphasis.

To be perfectly honest, I wasn't entirely sure Costello hadn't been lying about what he'd heard. Especially since I *had* actually caught him in another lie the day before—about having been with his boyfriend when Gia was killed.

"Are you saying Gia did not fire you before she walked in the show?" Ava asked.

"Of course not! Gia wouldn't fire me. I *made* her into who she was. Without me, she'd still be doing catalogs." He narrowed his eyes, gaze going from me to Ava. "You're not trying to insinuate that I'd *kill* Gia over her firing me?"

I shrugged. "You did say she got booked a lot."

Hughie laughed, but it sounded hollow and filled with more anger than mirth. "Oh, that's rich. Look, yes, Gia was popular, but she was hardly a supermodel. The fifteen percent commission I made on her thousand dollars a show rate is nothing worth *killing* over."

Well, when he put it that way, it did sound like thin motive.

"Besides, the police think Gia was killed by some thief," he went on, turning a pair of hard eyes on Ava. "So if anyone at this table is to blame for her death, it's certainly not me."

Ava's cheeks went pale.

"That's not fair!" I protested. "There's no way Ava could have known someone would steal that gem."

I didn't think Hughie really believed there was either, but the smug smile on his face said his comment had had the intended reaction—shift the blame and put someone else in the hot seat. "Well, let's just say I'm not going to risk putting any more of my models in harm's way by taking your winery on as a client." He crossed his arms over his chest.

"Come on, let's go," I said, grabbing Ava by the arm and pulling her from the table. I'd had enough of Hughie Smart and his not-so-smart remarks.

Ava complied, not seeming to be able to find her voice again until we were clear of the B&B and back in her car.

"I'm so sorry about that guy," I told her, sliding into the passenger seat beside her. "He's a jerk. He was just trying to rile us up."

Ava took an unsteady breath. "Well, it worked."

"Ava." I put a hand on her arm.

She attempted a weak smile in response. "It's okay. I know it's not my fault Gia died."

"No, it's not," I said definitively. "It's whoever killed her that's at fault."

"I know," she said again. "At least, I know it in my head. My heart is a little harder to convince."

"Well, maybe this will help," I said, turning so I was facing her. "Hughie was right about one thing—the person who said he overheard Gia fire Hughie is a liar. Carl Costello."

Ava raised an eyebrow my way. "You really think Hughie was telling the truth?"

"About that?" I shook my head. "I don't know. But I caught Costello in another lie last night." I quickly filled her in on Daisy Dot's visit to my tasting room and her offhand comment about having seen Fabio alone at the reception when Costello had distinctly said he and his boyfriend had been in a private cabana by the pool at the time.

When I was done, Ava's soft blonde eyebrows were drawn down in a frown. "You really think Costello intentionally lied about his alibi?"

"You saw how adamant he was about the fact that he and Fabio were together."

She nodded. "Well, if he lied about his whereabouts and he lied about Gia arguing with someone else, I'd be curious to know what else he's lying about." I could see the previous guilt being replaced by a determined light in her eyes again. "I say we find him and interrogate him right now!"

"I don't know…"

"Emmy! You said yourself that you overheard him threatening Gia."

"I did. And all of Costello's lies probably do warrant a little chat with him."

Ava opened her mouth to say something, but I ran right over her.

"But *just* a *chat*," I emphasized. "Just a calm, friendly chat."

Ava grinned. "Sure. I can do friendly." She sent me a wide grin with teeth and everything, as if to illustrate her point.

I shook my head, a tiny voice inside me—which coincidentally sounded a lot like Grant—telling me this was a bad idea. However, Ava's nearly diabolic grin was better than the sadness and guilt I'd seen a few minutes ago. So I reluctantly stowed my doubts away as Ava put the car into gear and pulled away from the curb, heading toward downtown and the Sonoma Valley Inn.

CHAPTER EIGHT

———

Fifteen minutes later we were back in the lobby of the hotel asking Judy at the front desk to ring for Carl Costello's room. Luckily, unlike on our previous visit, this time our intended guest did pick up and cleared Judy to send us up to his room. Which turned out to be the penthouse suite. I wasn't sure if Costello was worried about security or image, but he'd certainly made sure he had the best of what Wine Country had to offer in the accommodations department.

As soon as we reached the penthouse, Ava and I stepped out into a foyer that practically oozed luxury with every fiber of its flocked wallpaper and grain of inlaid wood flooring. Two crystal chandeliers hung from the cathedral ceilings, and an ebony side table was adorned with a large vase sporting a bouquet of fresh flowers that was larger than some of Costello's models.

"Wow," Ava said, clearly having much the same reaction I was. "I wonder what this place costs per night."

"I have a feeling that if you have to ask, you can't afford it," I mumbled, knocking on the polished wood door that led to the suite.

We waited. And waited. I was beginning to think our knock had gone unnoticed, when I heard the sound of the lock being thrown on the other side and the door opened to reveal a young man with warm tanned skin, dark hair, dark eyes, and chiseled features, from his strong jaw to his defined shirtless abs. His broad chest tapered into a perfect *V* at the waistband of his jeans, slung low enough that I felt a blush creep into my cheeks and had to purposely drag my eyes up to meet his.

"Uh, hi. We were looking for Carl Costello," I told the man.

"Carl's here." He gave me a bored look and stepped aside.

"Thanks," Ava said. I noticed she'd yet to be able to pull her gaze upward. If she wasn't careful, she'd start drooling any second.

We followed the man into a large main room that featured floor to ceiling windows, showing off a spectacular view of rolling hillsides and flooding the space with natural light. In case that wasn't enough illumination, three more crystal chandeliers hung from the ceiling, shimmering like diamonds against the inlaid ceiling. At least, I assumed they were *like* diamonds and not the actual gems, but from the upscale finishes, gilt framed artwork, and marble accents around the room, I didn't put anything past the decorator. White leather couches with royal blue pillows provided the perfect place to sit back and relax after a stressful day of doing whatever type of work allowed you to afford such luxurious accommodations.

"Carl!" The young man's voice cut through my gawking as he yelled toward the open door at our left. "Visitors!"

A beat later, Costello appeared, bedazzled in a purple velour sweat suit that was hovering precariously on the border between gawdy and fashionable. "Hello, my dahlings," he said, descending upon us with air kisses all around. "I hope you don't think me rude, but I've only got a moment for a quick chat. It's been a trying few days, and Fabio and I really must relax and decompress."

My eyes flitted to the young man.

Costello must have seen the gesture, as he added, "Oh, you've met Fabio, haven't you?"

"Uh, not formally," Ava answered. She stuck a hand his way. "Ava Barnett."

Fabio stepped forward and lifted her hand to his lips for a gentle kiss accompanied by some serious smoldering eye action.

Ava giggled.

"Isn't he lovely?" Costello draped an arm around Fabio's shoulders. "He's Puerto Rican. They know how to grow them there, right ladies?" Costello purred.

Fabio offered a placating smile before stepping out of the embrace. "Drink?" he asked us as he moved to a tall glass wet bar along the back wall.

"No thank you," I answered automatically. I had a strict(ish) policy never to drink before noon. You know, unless it was a *really* bad day.

Ava shook her head as well. "How are you holding up?" she asked Costello.

He sighed dramatically. "Oh, my, as well as one can, I suppose." He gestured for us to sit on a leather sofa before dropping into the one opposite with another sigh.

"Are the police still asking you to stay in Sonoma?" Ava asked.

Costello shook his head. "No, we'll be heading home today." He turned to Fabio, who was pouring himself a generous glass of something clear. "Honey, a gin and tonic, please, with just a scooch of fresh lime?"

Fabio gave him the same placid smile before grabbing a fresh glass from behind the bar.

"Anyway," Costello went on. "Hopefully we can get back to our normal lives and put all this unpleasantness behind us soon."

"I doubt any of this will really be behind us until Gia's killer is found," Ava noted.

It might have been my imagination, but I thought I saw Costello squirm a little at the word killer.

"Yes, well, I'm sure the police are hard at work on that," he mumbled. "Anyway, it's just all been so stressful, you know? I mean, a show on its own is difficult enough, but given the tragedy…" He trailed off, shaking his head and clucking his tongue as Fabio handed him his drink. "Thank you, dahling," Costello told the younger man. He patted the sofa beside him, and Fabio complied, taking a seat.

"I can imagine it's been difficult," Ava told him.

Costello turned to his boyfriend. "I'm so very lucky that Fabio has been such a comfort. So fortunate he's here with me."

"Yes," I said, feeling an opening. "You mentioned that Fabio was with you after the fashion show as well, right?"

"Hmm?" Costello asked, sipping his drink. "Oh, yes. Yes, he was. We were inseparable." He scrunched his nose at Fabio in a loving gesture.

Fabio seemed to find a spot on the thick carpeting at his feet suddenly interesting.

"Are you sure you were together the *entire* time?" Ava asked, leaning forward a bit in her seat. "Like from when the show ended to when Gia was found?"

"Well...yes. I mean, yes, of course."

Ava shot me a look. "Because someone said they saw Fabio alone."

Costello blinked at us. Fabio's eyes didn't leave the floor.

"Oh. Well, I-I wasn't with him the entire *day*," Costello amended. "I mean, before the show I was so busy."

"This was after the show," I told him. "While the models were changing. And Gia was in her dressing room."

Costello did some more blinking. Fabio shifted uncomfortably.

I turned my attention to the boy toy. "You were at the reception in the lounge after the show, weren't you?"

Fabio's gaze shifted between Costello and me as he smoothed his hands over the fabric on his thighs. "Well...umm..."

Costello jumped in, seemingly having recovered control over his eyelids, and looped his arm through Fabio's. He patted his bicep in a reassuring manner before turning his attention to me. "Well, of course I meant that Fabio and I were together *later*. I mean, I had to oversee the garments being racked properly, didn't I?"

"How much later?" Ava pressed.

"What? Oh, well, I don't know. Hardly any time at all."

"So you *did* go backstage after the show?" I clarified, shooting Ava a meaningful look.

"Yes. I mean, just for a short smidgeon of time. Before I met up with Fabio. Then we were inseparable. Like I told you."

He'd told me so many different things, I was having a hard time keeping track.

"Did anyone see you racking the garments backstage?" Ava asked.

"W-well, I don't know. I mean, there were people there."

"Like who?" Ava wasn't letting it go.

Costello fanned himself with one hand. "Oh my…well let me think…it was such a stressful day, dahlings." He chuckled nervously. "Uh, well, let's see… Oh! Yes, of course, I did speak with Jada. Yes, I'm sure Jada remembers seeing me."

"Actually, she doesn't," I informed him.

His nervous smile dropped. "She doesn't?"

I shook my head. "She said she didn't remember who was backstage after the show. She didn't mention being with you at all."

"Well, there you have it!" He smiled triumphantly as he settled back into the sofa cushions. "You see, I'm not the only one who can't remember exactly when and where I was or who I was with. It was utter chaos, I tell you. But, I'm sure if you ask Jada if she spoke to me, she'll remember."

I was less sure, but there wasn't much I could do to refute that without Jada present. "What did you do when you left the backstage area?" I asked instead.

"Hmm?" Costello's gaze shifted to me again.

"After you packed up the garments and spoke to Jada?"

"Oh. I, uh, joined Fabio. For our *private* celebration at the poolside cabana. Right, honey?" Costello batted his eyelashes at the man.

"Uh-huh." Fabio didn't sound quite as sure, his dark eyes holding something back as they looked everywhere but at us.

"And what time was that?" I asked.

"I, um…" Fabio looked to Costello.

"He's notoriously terrible with time, aren't you, baby?" Costello patted Fabio's leg. "But, like I said, it was right afterward. Hardly any time at all."

Which really meant nothing. Costello could have easily slipped backstage and into Gia's dressing room in all the chaos after the show, killed her, and just as quickly slipped back out and caught up with Fabio.

And if I had to guess, by the way that Fabio was shifting uncomfortably on the sofa again, he knew it too.

"I'm just curious," Costello asked, picking at a fraying thread on his velour sweatshirt. "But, uh, when did you say it was that Fabio was seen at the reception?"

"She didn't know exactly," I told him honestly.

"She?" Costello said, raising an eyebrow at me. "And who, may I ask, is this she?"

I hesitated to mention a name. But in all fairness, it wasn't as if she'd told it to me in confidence. "Daisy Dot," I said.

Costello laughed out loud, startling Fabio into nearly spilling his drink. "Oh please! You think that woman is a reliable witness to anything? She's as crooked as her deranged sense of style."

"Crooked?" I asked.

He nodded vigorously. "And conniving, and deceitful, and a thief!"

Ava and I shared a look. "That's funny," I said, "because she actually accused *you* of being a thief."

Costello chuckled softly. "Let me guess…she tried to sell you that ruby earring story?"

"Story?" I asked. "So you're saying it's not true? You didn't steal her earrings before her spring show to sabotage her?"

"Well, of course it's not true! What did I tell you? She's delusional. As if I would need to sabotage her. Have you seen her work? The woman practically sabotages herself. No sense of taste whatsoever."

Said the man in the bedazzled velour tracksuit petting his shirtless lover over a morning cocktail.

But, I glossed over that.

"So you didn't take her earrings?" Ava clarified.

"No," he said emphatically. "I did not. She probably misplaced them herself. Have you seen how scatterbrained she is?"

I'll admit, I'd had the same thought myself.

"She, however," Costello went on, "*did* steal from me!"

"What did she steal?" Ava asked, sounding as dubious as I felt.

Costello smirked, crossing one purple clad leg over the other. "I'm sure you noticed those cutouts she did on all of her horrendously over-designed dresses at the Links show?"

While I wasn't sure about the over-designed part, I had noticed the cutouts. I nodded.

"Well, my original designs for my fall line included cutouts in all of my dresses. Diamond shaped ones." He gave me a pointed look.

"Are you saying that Daisy Dot stole her collection's signature look from you?"

Costello touched his index finger to the tip of his nose. "Exactly. Of course, she did it with no regard for the female form whatsoever, whereas mine were artfully placed to highlight my models' curves."

One could argue there was very little curve to a six foot tall, one hundred pound model, but I decided that was beside the point. "Maybe she just had the same idea as you?" I suggested. "Maybe it wasn't a matter of actual theft?"

But Costello scoffed. "Highly doubtful! That woman hasn't had an original idea since she left that vulgar reality show. TV designers. She just can't hack it in the real fashion world." He leaned in as if telling us a little secret. "You know she's staying in a regular suite here." He laughed, and it was suddenly clear why he was staying in the penthouse—for the sole purpose of keeping Daisy Dot out of it.

"That doesn't explain why you lied about Gia wanting to fire Hughie," Ava pointed out.

Costello turned to Ava. "Who said I lied?"

"Hughie Smart. He said Gia never called him before the show."

"Well, then, he's the liar!" Costello said with a lot more indignation than a man just caught lying himself should have.

"It's easy enough for the police to check his phone records," Ava added, and I could see her watching his reaction.

"And, honestly, why would Gia call Hughie to fire him?" I added. "Hughie was at the show. Wouldn't it make more sense to talk to him about that sort of thing in person?"

Costello's gaze went from Ava, to me, and back again. "Well, I-I don't know. But I *do* know I heard Gia on the phone. And she was firing someone. Who else could it have been? I mean, it *sounded* like she was talking to Hughie." He shrugged and sipped from his glass.

"What, exactly, did you overhear her saying?"

Costello frowned. "Well, let me see…she said she'd had enough, that she didn't need him anymore, and that she could do the job on her own from now on." He looked from me to Ava. "I mean, who else could she have been talking to?"

I didn't know. And honestly, I wasn't sure what to believe. It was quite possible he and Hughie were both telling the truth. Yet again, it was also quite possible they were both lying. And more possible still that the call had had nothing at all to do with Gia's death in the first place.

"Now, if there's nothing else you'd like to accuse me of," Costello said, clearly only half joking, "Fabio and I have some packing to do, don't we, dahling?"

He glanced to his own personal romance novel hero, who was still inordinately interested in the floor. If I had to guess, Fabio knew something he was holding back. But I didn't see him sharing in front of his sugar daddy.

"Sorry to have bothered you," Ava mumbled as we made our way back toward the door.

Which, once we cleared the threshold, slammed behind us with a definitive thud followed by the sound of the lock being thrown.

"Well, I doubt Costello will be calling me for accessories for his next show," Ava said as we waited on the elevator.

"I also doubt he was telling us the whole truth. Did you see how Fabio was averting his eyes the whole time?"

Ava nodded. "You caught that too, huh?" She paused. "Though, his eyes were the least noticeable thing about that guy. Ohmigosh, those abs…"

"Down girl. I don't think he bats for your team."

Ava grinned as the elevator arrived and we stepped inside, pressing the button for the lobby. "True, but maybe he has a brother?" she joked.

"Don't make me remind you about what happened the last time you dated a pretty boy," I said, referring to a short-lived relationship she'd had recently with an actor, which had not ended well.

Ava rolled her eyes. "Trust me, I need no reminders of that one. He was enough to make *me* think about batting for the other team."

I couldn't help a laugh as the elevator doors opened and we spilled out into the lobby once again.

Which seemed to be teeming with activity at the late morning hour, some guests checking out, others waiting on cars or party buses for winery tours around the region. I spotted Jada pulling a rolling suitcase into the long checkout line. I was about to suggest we approach her to corroborate Costello's latest attempt at an alibi, when Ava grabbed my arm.

"Emmy!" she hissed, her voice low. "Look!"

I glanced in the direction she indicated, seeing a group of tourists and one family of six trying unsuccessfully to wrangle their young ones away from a rolling luggage cart the kids had apparently commandeered as a ride-on toy.

"I'm sure they'll be okay," I said.

Ava shook her head. "Not the kids on the cart. Over there. By the potted palm tree."

I shifted my gaze slightly to the left and immediately spotted it.

Or, I should say, him.

Tall, dark hair, baseball cap, cleft chin.

Gia's stalker.

CHAPTER NINE

———

The man was wearing jeans and a plain white T-shirt, the same baseball cap on his head with the Giants' logo. He had his phone out, holding it up in front of his face, as if trying to get reception bars as he blended into the background.

"That's him, right?" Ava whispered beside me, still clutching my arm.

I nodded. "Looks like it." As I watched him point his phone toward the check-out line, I realized that he wasn't trying to dial on it…he was snapping pictures. And as he shifted his position to face us, he must have seen us staring back at him on his screen, as his gaze immediately popped up above the device.

His eyes met mine, and I could see sudden realization in them that he'd been spotted.

And he bolted.

He spun quickly, almost knocking into one of the four kids hanging off the luggage cart as he made for the glass front doors.

"Come on!" I grabbed Ava's hand and darted across the lobby after him. Between the kids on the cart and the steady stream of guests moving in and out of the hotel, it took a moment to reach the doors. By the time we got there, he was gone. I whipped my gaze back and forth down the street, looking in all directions for any sign of him.

"There!" Ava said, pulling toward the right, where I could see Stalker Guy weaving through a crowd lingering outside a coffeehouse three doors down.

We jogged after him, the best that two girls in heels could, dodging passersby as we made our way down the sidewalk.

I caught sight of the ball cap as it made a right up ahead. We rounded the corner, and I spied him ducking into an outdoor farmers' market. Ava and I followed, maneuvering around stalls, skirting street performers, and pushing through the ambling sea of people apparently not in a hurry to get anywhere. Unfortunately, as Grant had pointed out at dinner the evening before, a baseball cap was not necessarily an anomaly in California, and several men were sporting them to shield the sun at this time of day. Making it all that much harder to keep our prey in sight as we weaved in and out of the displays of brightly colored seasonal fruits and vegetables, local honey and jarred preserves, and vendors selling handmade tortillas and hot fresh crepes.

"On the left!" Ava exclaimed in an urgent whisper and pointed, as Stalker Guy stepped behind a booth selling five minute neck massages.

We followed suit, but by the time we came up behind the large blue sign promising to "massage your cares away," he was nowhere to be found.

"You see him?" Ava asked, her blonde ponytail whipping her cheeks as she looked left and right.

I bit my lip. "No," I admitted.

Ava leaned against the nearest building as she fought to catch her breath. "We lost him," she moaned.

I put an arm around her, feeling my own breath coming hard—partly due to the adrenaline surge at initially spying him and partly due to the fact that I avoided the gym like the plague. "Sorry," I told her.

She gave me a sympathetic smile. "Well, we tried." She nodded her head toward the next booth over, selling frozen lemonade. "I think we need a couple of those."

I had to agree with her there. While the morning had started out with a chill, now that the sun was high in the sky, the temperatures had risen as well. I felt sweat on the back of my neck from the vigorous impromptu run.

Once we'd both gotten our breathing under control, we grabbed two frozen lemonades, and since it was nearing noon, we added a couple of savory Crepes with Bacon Onion Jam to go with them, taking our lunch to a wooden bench in the shade to enjoy it.

I dug into the light, creamy crepes smothered in rich jam, loving the salty-sweet-tangy combo of the bacon and caramelized onions playing with brown sugar and vinegar in the filling.

"So what do you think he was doing here?" Ava asked around a bite of crepe.

"Stalker Guy?" I clarified.

She nodded. "You think maybe he was at the hotel following another model?"

I shrugged. "I suppose it's possible." I paused. "I did see Jada in the lobby."

Ava stabbed a piece of caramelized onion. "You think he was stalking both Gia *and* Jada?"

"He could have been. You know, it looked like he was taking pictures."

"Of what?" she asked, popping the bite into her mouth.

"Beats me. Models? The lobby? Us?"

Ava paused. "I don't like that last one."

That made two of us. I sipped my lemonade, the smooth icy texture melting in the hot sun. "It does make him seem a bit guilty that he ran away like that," I noted.

"A *lot* guilty," Ava amended, stabbing her fork at me for emphasis. "Most people don't bolt when they've been caught taking photos."

"Unless they're taking pictures of something they shouldn't be."

"Exactly!"

"Even so, I hate to say it, but it's possible he's just guilty of stalking and not actually killing Gia."

"That's depressing," Ava said.

"Sorry." I paused, moving bits of salty bacon around on my plate. "But I still think that Fabio was hiding something for Costello."

"Like a fake alibi?"

I nodded. "Could be. Or maybe stretching one. They *both* seemed a little hazy on time. Costello could have killed Gia backstage over whatever she'd been threatening him with then met up with Fabio much later. Like, right before we found her."

Ava nodded. "Of course, it's also possible Daisy saw Fabio right after the show ended, like Costello said, and then *she* slipped backstage and killed Gia out of some sort of twisted revenge on Costello."

"Or Hughie Smart really *did* care about being fired, and he followed her backstage and killed her."

I sighed. "Let's face it, the only people with real alibis for the entire time are the two of us."

Ava grinned, sipping her lemonade again. "Thank goodness for small favors."

I corralled another piece of crepe onto my fork and nibbled, letting the light pancake melt in my mouth as I stared out at the crowd, growing now as the weekenders grabbed bites of food to sop up all the alcohol they planned to sip that afternoon. "You know, something Hughie said this morning has been bothering me," I told her, mentally replaying our conversation with him.

"What's that?" she asked, sucking up the last of her drink through a paper straw.

"About how much money Gia was making." I set my fork down. "He said her rate was only a thousand dollars a show."

Ava shrugged. "Nice pay for walking across a stage and back."

I nodded. "True," I agreed. "But you saw how many hours of prep went into that two-minute walk. Hair, makeup, accessories. Not to mention the fittings beforehand."

"What's your point?" Ava asked, setting her plastic cup back down on the wooden bench bedside her.

"Well, just that if you break it down, she wasn't getting a huge hourly rate. And I have to assume she wasn't walking in a show every day."

"Probably more like a few a month, if she was lucky," Ava guessed. "At least in the busy season."

"Which means she was possibly making a living at modeling, but considering the cost of living in San Francisco, she wasn't making a whole lot more than that." I paused. "So if she wasn't making the big bucks, how did she finance her big lifestyle?"

Ava cocked her head to the side. "That is a good point. Yachts, sports cars, designer clothes...those all cost a pretty penny."

"Grant said her credit card statements had tons of charges on them."

Ava shrugged. "Maybe she had a side business?"

I nodded. "Like what?"

"I don't know," Ava admitted. "I have a hard time picturing her driving an Uber part time."

I grinned. "Yeah, she didn't strike me as the side hustle type."

"Maybe she had a sugar daddy? Or some family supporting her?"

"Grant said she didn't have any close family. No boyfriend that he knew of either."

"Well, maybe she did some modeling on the side. Jobs she didn't book through Hughie?"

I raised an eyebrow her direction. "That, actually, sounds like a likely possibility." I thought about it a beat. "And a reason for tension between her and her agent," I added.

"Maybe Hughie found out about it, they argued, and Gia decided she didn't need him anymore," Ava said, picking up the theory. "Maybe that's the phone call Costello overheard. Only instead of letting Gia go, Hughie drove to the fashion show and killed her."

"Over the few hundred dollars he'd lose?" I asked, still skeptical about that part.

Ava shrugged. "Maybe it was more out of anger. Bruised ego? Didn't he say he 'made' Gia? Maybe he was angry that she'd been capitalizing on his hard work behind his back?"

I nodded. "I guess that's possible. He did seem like the kind of guy with a short fuse," I mused.

"And maybe he took the emerald," Ava went on, "as some sort of compensation after the fact for the money he'd lost out on? Who knows—he might have even thought it belonged to Gia if he hadn't caught the end of the fashion show."

"Of course, this is all contingent on *if* Gia actually was taking jobs on the side."

"Right." Ava licked the last of her jam off her fork, eyes going to a point above me as she thought about that. "You think Jada might know?"

I wiped my mouth with a napkin. "If Gia was taking side gigs?"

Ava nodded. "They seemed to be friends."

I grabbed my empty paper plate and plastic lemonade cup. "It's certainly worth asking."

* * *

Ten minutes later we were back at the Sonoma Valley Inn, where luckily the check-out lines had apparently been long and the line to have a car brought around even longer, as Jada was still standing just outside the main entrance, at the valet station, toting her rolling suitcase behind her as she sipped from a paper coffee cup.

"Jada?" I called out as we approached her.

She looked up, recognition taking a moment to set in. "Oh. Hi."

"You're checking out?" Ava asked, gesturing to her suitcase.

Jada nodded. "Yeah. Police said we could go home. I guess they have all the statements they need." She shrugged.

"I'm sure it will be nice to return to normal," Ava agreed, giving her a sympathetic smile.

But Jada just shrugged again. "Sure."

"Uh, anyway, I'm glad we caught you before you left," I said.

"Oh?" One of her perfectly sculpted eyebrows lifted. "Is this about that job modeling for your winery ads? Because you'll have to talk to my agent about that."

"You always book through your agent?" Ava asked.

Jada nodded. "Of course. It's in our contracts."

"Gia's too?" I asked. "I mean, Gia's agency contract with Hughie Smart."

Jada frowned. "It's standard for any agency contract." She paused. "Why are you asking about Gia?"

"We noticed that Gia lived a bit of an…expensive lifestyle," I said carefully.

"Gia booked a lot of jobs," Jada said. "She was in high demand."

"Not high enough to finance a Ferrari," Ava said.

Jada paused, letting that one sink in. She shifted her weight in her heels, eyes going past us to the street as if looking for her car to arrive. "I-I guess I just assumed Gia was getting paid more than I was." Her gaze moved from Ava to me. "Wasn't she?"

Honestly? I had no idea. I did know that her daily rate was not in the champagne and caviar realm yet. Gia might have been in high demand in the small San Francisco fashion scene, but she was hardly a Victoria's Secret Angel.

"Did Gia ever mention booking any side jobs? Ones outside what Hughie was finding for her?" I asked.

Jada scoffed. "No. No way." She shook her head. "Hughie would have a fit."

That was kind of the theory we were going on. "Maybe Gia hid it from Hughie?" I offered.

But Jada just shook her head again. "No. Gia was not that stupid. She would have known Hughie would find out. It's a small community, and it would have ruined her reputation. No one wants to work with someone they can't trust."

"You're sure?" I asked.

"Very. Look, Gia might have been a lot of things, but she wasn't stupid."

"What about Costello?" Ava jumped in.

Jada spun to face my friend, her eyes holding a note of suspicion in them. "Carl? What about him?"

"Could he have been paying Gia extra on the side for her work? Above what Hughie paid her?"

"I don't see why he would," she responded, a frown marring her features.

"You know, we were just up in Costello's penthouse earlier this morning," I said.

"Were you?" Her eyes scanned the street again, looking for her vehicle, as if looking for an escape from the uncomfortable conversation about her coworkers.

"Yes," I answered. "We were talking about where he was after the fashion show ended. He said he went backstage. He said he talked to you there."

"Me?" Her gaze whipped back to me, and I could see some emotion flitting across them.

I nodded. "Did he?"

She quickly blinked, turning her face away. "Well, if that's what he said, then it must be true."

"You don't remember?" Ava asked.

Jada shrugged, sipping from her coffee before she answered. "Everyone was everywhere. It was chaotic. I-I don't remember my every move."

I had a feeling Jada remembered a lot more than she was willing to say. She worked for Costello—who was obviously in the market for a new star closer to his shows. I had a strong feeling the emotion I'd seen flitting behind her eyes had been fear. Fear of losing her job if she didn't back up Costello's new alibi.

"How did Costello and Gia get along?" Ava asked, clearly picking up on the same vibe I was.

"Fine," Jada said.

"You never sensed any tension between them?"

"No," Jada said emphatically. "Why would there be? Costello is an artist. I'm sure Gia was honored to close his shows. The man is a creative genius."

While I thought Costello's designs were very tasteful and wearable, creative wasn't the word that immediately sprang to my mind. "You certainly seem to enjoy working for him."

"Of course," Jada shot back. "He understands a woman's body in a way no other designer does. Even if they think they can hack his designs," she added with a note of disdain in her voice.

"Are you talking about Daisy Dot?" I asked, my mind immediately going to Costello's accusation of her stealing his designs.

Jada smirked. "So you've heard the rumor too? I guess it's obvious to everyone she couldn't have come up with those looks herself."

"Costello did mention he thought she'd copied his cutouts."

"Stole," Jada said hotly.

It was clear which designer held her allegiance.

"How do you think she stole them?" Ava asked.

Jada's eyes whipped to Ava. "What?"

"I mean, if Costello hadn't shown them publicly yet, how did she see them?"

"I-I don't know," Jada sputtered, frowning as if she'd never thought of that. Honestly, I hadn't either. "But I do know that woman has had it in for Carl."

"Really?" I asked. "Because she said the same thing about him."

Jada scoffed again, letting out a barking laugh. "Oh, she would. But, no, it's been the other way around. *She* stole *his* looks. And then she accused him of stealing some earrings. She said he was jealous just because Gia walked in her spring show. As if Carl cared who Gia walked for when she wasn't with him."

"Wait, Gia was in Daisy Dot's spring show?" I asked, remembering how vague the woman had been about her working relationship with Gia. "The one with the birthstone theme?"

Jada nodded. "Yes. Didn't I say she booked out a lot? But it's ridiculous to think that Carl would steal some stupid earrings just to get back at Daisy over that." She shook her head. "It's not Carl's style to do something so petty. Besides, they *were* returned, so chances are the woman misplaced them herself. Heck, maybe she even did it on purpose to accuse Carl."

I felt my mental wheels turning, less focused on whether or not Costello or Daisy Dot was the innocent injured party in their rivalry than on the fact that Gia had been at the fashion show where the earrings had gone missing. Apparently walking for Daisy.

"Jada, do you know which model Gia was at that spring show?" I asked. "I mean, which month of the year she was portraying?"

She blinked at me. "Yeah. July, of course. The one who had the missing earrings."

I was about to ask her more, when a dark colored sedan pulled up to the curb and Jada's face relaxed into relief. "That's my car," she said, tossing her paper cup into a nearby trash bin. "I've gotta go."

With that, she clacked her heels the few paces to the curb, where she exchanged a tip for her car keys from a valet and drove off.

Leaving Ava and me standing on the sidewalk watching her.

"What was that about Gia being July?" Ava asked.

"Doesn't it seem like a coincidence to you?" I asked, turning to face her. "That first a pair of ruby earrings that Gia is supposed to wear goes missing and then an emerald she's wearing goes missing too?"

Ava's eyebrows pulled together. "That does seem like a coincidence."

I shook my head. "I think maybe we've been going about this all wrong."

"What do you mean?"

"I mean, maybe the strangling and theft of the emerald aren't related."

Ava shook her head. "Not sure I follow."

"Well, what if Gia wasn't the *victim* of a robbery? What if she was stealing the emerald herself?"

Ava clamped a hand down on my arm. "Ohmigosh. You think Gia was the thief?"

"She had the opportunity. With both the emerald and the ruby earrings."

Ava nodded. "The private dressing room. Didn't Costello say she always insisted on it?"

"It gave her plenty of time to privately steal the jewelry she was wearing once she'd been dressed with it."

"But the earrings weren't really stolen, remember?" Ava said. "They miraculously appeared after the show ended."

"Right." I thought about that a beat. "Okay, how about this: Gia knew ahead of time what pieces she'd be wearing at shows, right? I mean, she knew she'd be wearing your emerald?"

Ava nodded. "We did a fitting the week before the show to make sure I had all the right pieces to go with Costello's outfits."

"What if she has copies made of the gems she knows she'll be wearing? Then when she's at the show and has the piece alone in her dressing room, she takes the real jewel out and swaps in a fake copy."

"Fakes?" I could see Ava mentally putting it all together too. "That's why the earrings reappeared. Gia took them just long enough to extract the rubies and replace them with the fake ones."

I nodded. "She could have easily taken pictures of the gems with her phone at the fittings. She'd know exactly what the fakes should look like."

Ava nodded. "That was her side business. She was stealing from the designers who hired her!"

"By the time anyone figured out the gems were fake, it would be almost impossible to trace where or when they'd been taken."

"*If* they ever figured it out," Ava pointed out. She paused. "The pendant around Gia's neck was empty when she was found. Gia must have been in the process of swapping out the emerald for a fake when she was killed."

I pictured the scene we'd found in the dressing room, this theory painting it in a whole new light: that of a thief being caught in the act of her crime. While no one deserved to die the way Gia had, she suddenly didn't look like the perfectly innocent victim.

"In that case, it wasn't the killer who stole the emerald at all but Gia," Ava went on. "So...where is the emerald now?"

I shrugged. "That is a very good question. If the killer didn't take it..."

Ava's eyes lit up like Christmas. "Then it might still be at the Links!"

CHAPTER TEN

Thirty minutes later, we cruised up to the front of the Links and handed the keys to Ava's GTO over to the valet. The wide glass doors of the exclusive club silently opened with a woosh of cool air that was a welcome relief to the climbing temperatures of the early afternoon. Our heels clacked along the polished marble floors as we made our way across the lobby to the reception counter.

"Good afternoon, and welcome to the Links," a young woman whose nametag read *Cindy* told us. "Guests or members?"

"Hi, Cindy," Ava said, giving her a bright smile. "We're, uh, guests. Ava Barnett."

Cindy gave her a polite smile before turning her attention to a computer screen behind the polished walnut counter. "Ava Barnett," she repeated, typing the name into her system. A beat later, she turned the same pleasant smile back to us. "I'm sorry, but your name is not on our list today."

"It's not." Ava shot me a look. "Uh, I was here with the fashion show the other day."

"Oh." Cindy's smile faltered. "Yes, well, our vendor passes were only good for the event itself. Sorry." She gave us a palms-up and a shrug.

Ava pursed her lips. "Uh, well, I think I might have left something behind."

Cindy frowned again. "Nothing has been turned in to lost and found. But, if you give me a description of the item, I'll have one of our crew double check for it and give you a call if it turns up."

I had a feeling if the crew had found a hundred thousand dollar emerald, Cindy would have known about it by now.

"There's nothing you can do?" I asked, hearing the plea in my voice. "Ava's dad is a long-standing member."

"Has he left a guest pass for her?" Cindy asked.

Reluctantly we both shook our heads.

"Sorry," Cindy repeated. "Our members really value their privacy."

Ava sighed, shooting me a look of desperation.

While I hated to do it, I did know another member of the Links, and being that it was after noon on a Monday, he'd probably be hard at work in his usual capacity in one of the back rooms of the club.

"Um, what about David Allen?" I asked. "Is he by any chance here?"

Cindy hesitated before answering. "I-I'm sorry. I can't give out information about club members who are on premises."

Which I took as a yes.

"Thanks, Cindy," I told her, stepping away from the desk.

"What now?" Ava asked, eyes going to the forbidden zone beyond the lobby where the club rooms sat.

"Now we exploit a precarious friendship," I told her, pulling up David's number on my phone.

I listened to it ring three times on the other end, hoping he didn't have his ringer turned off. Luck was on my side, as on the fourth ring, he answered.

"Emmy Oak, to what do I owe this fine pleasure?"

"Hi, David," I answered. "You at the Links right now?"

"I am. Just finished a game with a couple of investment brokers who should have stuck to the stock market," he said with a chuckle.

David Allen had grown up a trust fund kid of a Silicon Valley mogul, who now spent the bulk of his days card sharking the rich and unsuspecting of Wine Country. Not that he needed the money—he was in it purely for the thrill of the win. And possibly a little for rebellious enjoyment of watching those in high society squirm. When David wasn't bilking the upper crust out of their hardly earned cash, his hobbies included smoking marijuana, painting dark and brooding artwork, playing video games in the guest house on his mother's estate, and hanging around my winery to mooch free drinks.

When I'd first met David, he'd been a suspect in a murder investigation, and while he'd proven himself innocent of that particular crime, I had a feeling there were some shady parts of his past it was best not to ask about—lest I become an accessory after the fact. We had a complicated relationship that I'd hesitate to classify. David had come to my aid on more than one occasion, but I was never quite sure what he expected from me in return for that aid. Or when he'd choose to cash in that favor.

Which made me hesitant to ask for another one.

"I'm glad you're here," I started, "because Ava and I are too. And we need a couple of guest passes."

"This wouldn't have anything to do with the death that occurred here the other day, would it?" he asked. I could hear rustling on the other end, like he was moving.

"Uh, no. Not really," I hedged.

"Wow. You're even a terrible liar over the phone."

I rolled my eyes.

What? Ava mouthed.

I shook my head. "Look, we just need to get into the Grand Ballroom for a minute. Just to check something. We won't cause any trouble."

"That's disappointing. I could go for a little trouble right about now."

"Are you going to get us in or not?"

I heard more movement, like he was shifting the phone. "Ems, you know I'd do anything for you."

Something about the statement caught me off guard, suddenly making me doubly unsure I'd made the right call.

"You in the lobby?" he asked.

I cleared the uncertainty out of my throat. "Uh, yeah."

"I'll call in the passes. Meet me in the lounge."

I was about to respond that we really didn't need to bother him with a meet, but he didn't give me the chance before disconnecting.

"So is he going to do it?" Ava asked, eyes cutting past me to the hallway again.

I nodded. "He said he'd call in passes."

She sighed in relief, her sunny smile returning. "I knew we could count on him."

Ten minutes later, Cindy had happily issued our passes and unnecessarily directed us down the hall and to our right to the lounge. Unnecessarily, because despite our nonmember status, we'd been there on multiple occasions, not the least of which had been for the reception following the fashion show. As on our previous visits, the hallways were filled with the sounds of a calming flute piped in through hidden speakers, the faint scent of lavender from the nearby day spa, and perfectly cool 75 degree air year round.

While I could feel Ava's eagerness in the way her gaze darted toward the hallway to the Grand Ballroom, she followed as I detoured to the lounge, which was a large dark room overlooking the green, filled with a long wooden bar on one side and a baby grand piano on the other, currently being played by a guy in ripped jeans and a black T-shirt, his long dark hair falling into his eyes.

Which was a surprise. I didn't know David Allen played.

Ava went up to him and gave him a hug from behind. "Thank you so much."

David's hands stilled, the music ceasing, as he turned to face us. "Now, would I leave a couple of my favorite damsels in distress?"

Ava curtsied. "Thank you, my white knight."

My eyes twitched to roll again, but considering he *had* done us a favor, I kept them in check.

David's gaze lifted to meet mine. "Emmy." He nodded my way.

"David." I nodded back.

Which earned me a lopsided grin. "Okay, so lay it on me. What are you two girls up to today?"

"Women," I automatically corrected.

His grin widened. "Trust me, I'm aware." I wasn't sure if his look was mocking or flirtatious as it roved my person, but I chose to ignore it either way, focusing on his question instead.

"We wanted to look for something that might have been left behind in Gia's dressing room." I quickly filled him in on our theory of Gia's death and the theft of the necklace, as well as the story of the disappearing-reappearing ruby earrings, and the hope that if we were right, the emerald may still be on the premises.

When I'd finished, David was lightly stroking the piano keys again in thought. "'It is amazing how complete is the delusion that beauty is goodness.'" He paused, attributing his quote. "Tolstoy."

"Well, the Russian was on to something there," Ava agreed. "The more we find out about Gia, the less goodness we see."

"So, you think maybe she was caught in the act, so to speak, and didn't have time to finish swapping her gems?" David asked.

Ava nodded. "We can hope at least."

He shot her a sympathetic look. "The piece was worth a lot, huh?"

She nodded. "It was a bigger gamble than I should have taken."

"Don't say that." He got up from the piano and faced her. "If you want to win big, you have to gamble big."

"Is that what you told the investment brokers?" I teased.

He chuckled, but turned to Ava. "Don't worry, babe. We'll get it back."

Ava's eyes misted as she smiled and nodded.

David pulled her in for a hug.

"Wait—what's with the *we*?" I asked, jumping on the word and breaking up their love fest.

David pulled back. "Oh, I'm sorry—did you have a plan to get into a sealed crime scene without me?"

"Sealed crime scene?" I glanced to Ava. I guess I hadn't thought about that factor.

David nodded. "Cheesy yellow tape covering the doors and everything. Cliché, but what can you do?"

"Okay, so what can *you* do?" I asked.

"Follow me." He gave me a wink and grabbed Ava by the hand, leading us from the lounge and back down the main hallway.

As much as I felt like I was the unsuspecting rat suddenly being led by the pied piano player into territory that no rat should enter, I was already in this deep, so I had little choice but to scurry along behind them.

I tried not to feel like a third wheel as Ava and David mumbled softly to each other, their heads bent together as they walked arm in arm down the hallway. They were huddled a little closer than made me comfortable. I'd suspected lately that David had designs on Ava, a thought that made me nervous, as I knew his bad boy persona was not all for show. But I stowed that worry away as we pushed through the double doors to the Grand Ballroom.

All the remnants of the previous fashion show were gone, leaving in its place a bare shell of a room. The tables that had been used to lay out garments and accessories now had their legs folded in and were leaning against the far wall in neat rows, ready to be stored away. Chairs were stacked on top of each other, tucked into the back corner, and the empty room echoed with the sound of our footsteps on the polished wood floor. The only sign that anything had happened there that weekend was, as David had noted, the clichéd yellow crime scene tape fluttering in the air conditioning across the closed door to what had been Gia's private dressing room.

Ava approached first, gingerly reaching around the plastic barrier and trying the doorknob. "It's locked," she informed us.

Of course it was. It was a crime scene. Again, I felt naïve for not having been prepared for this recovery mission.

"Let me try it," David said, swapping spots with Ava.

She stepped back, and David jiggled the knob with much the same luck.

"See?" she said. "I don't know how we're going to— what are you doing?"

David pulled something from his pocket and inserted it into the keyhole. "I'm picking the lock."

"How do you know how to—" I started. Then I shook my head. "Wait, never mind. Don't tell me. I want plausible deniability."

David grinned, his gaze cutting to me. "Then you better cover your eyes for this."

I almost wanted to comply.

Ava glanced over her shoulder nervously. "We're awfully exposed here," she noted, eyes going around the large, empty room. "Maybe someone should go be a lookout?"

"Lookout? Lock picking? Why do I suddenly feel like I'm in a bad eighties cop show?" I asked, feeling worse and worse about this idea as the seconds ticked by.

David *tsked* between his teeth. "Eighties cop shows are the best. *Miami Vice*?"

"*Cagney & Lacey*," Ava added.

"*Murder She Wrote*," David teased, shooting me a look that clearly said I was supposed to be the Jessica Fletcher style dead body magnet in this scenario.

I threw my hands up in surrender. "Fine! Ava, go be a lookout."

Ava grinned. "Codeword: *Columbo*."

"Codeword?" I asked as she turned away. "Why do we need a codeword?"

"In case anyone comes," she called over her shoulder, jogging toward the hallway to stand guard.

"She's joking, right?" I asked David.

He shrugged. "She's your friend."

"Yeah, but she's your—" I wasn't quite sure what she was to David. I'd witnessed flirtation, and I suspected it might be more. At least on his side. How Ava felt, I hadn't had the courage to ask yet. "—friend too," I finished lamely.

David shot me a funny look, but luckily the lock picking had most of his attention, so he let it go.

"How much longer?" I asked, whispering in the cavernous room.

"Almost there," he said.

"How can you tell?" I bent down, squinting at the knob, which looked exactly the same as it had when we'd first come up with this harebrained scheme.

"It's just a matter of getting all the pins above the shear line. I've got the first one already. A few more to go."

"How long will that take?"

"Patience, my dear." He started whistling the *Jeopardy!* theme song as he worked.

I sighed, staring out at the large, empty, and very exposed room again. "What was that you were playing in the lounge? Bach?"

"Beethoven."

"I didn't know you played the piano," I told him.

"There are a lot of things you don't know about me, Ems," he said, eyes on the keyhole.

"Like you know how to pick locks, for example?"

"Hey, when your family is as good at keeping secrets as mine is, you learn a few choice skills."

He wasn't kidding. The murder I'd once upon a time suspected him of had been his stepfather's. When the truth had finally come out, it had resulted in one member of his family in prison and another fleeing the country. No one put the fun in dysfunctional like David's family. To be honest, I sometimes thought it was a wonder he'd grown up to be as normal as he was.

Well, normalish.

I was about to ask how his mother was doing, when he froze, a triumphant smile on his face. "I think that's it," he said. He put his hand on the knob and slowly twisted.

And the door pushed easily open.

He straightened up and shot me a grin. "Thank you, once again, David."

I couldn't help a laugh. "Thank you, David," I repeated.

He stepped his long legs over the yellow ribbons crisscrossing the doorway, holding them down with a hand for me to do the same. My left foot got caught part of the way over, but I managed to pry it free with a couple of less than graceful hops forward and a lunging landing.

"You okay?" David asked.

"Peachy. Let's find this emerald." I wasn't sure why I was whispering, but somehow in the confines of the murder scene, it felt appropriate.

While I'd gotten a quick look in Gia's dressing room on the previous occasions that I'd been there, Gia herself had been the focus of my attention then. I looked around, taking in the room itself for the first time. It wasn't large—probably used as a small office or conference room on other occasions. A dressing table to my left looked specially placed for the fashion show and held a large mirror above it surrounded by LED lights. A couple of tote bags of personal items sat beneath it, along with a black makeup bag. To my left was a small rolling suitcase, like I'd seen Jada with. Some old filing cabinets stood behind it, and on the far wall were built-in wooden cupboards and drawers.

David started with the built-ins, randomly opening them to reveal extra toilet paper and brown paper towels for the restrooms.

I moved to the vanity, grabbing the tote bag. I wasn't sure if Gia had been inherently messy or if the police had left things in disarray, but all of the contents seemed to have been thrown together in a jumble that had no organization to it. A pair of black flip-flops, a bag of tissues, a charging cord, a couple pens, a pair of novelty socks. No emerald.

And, I noticed, no phone, tablet, or laptop. If Gia had had any electronics on her, the police had already confiscated those.

I looked under the vanity, along the floor behind the door, and behind the bright mirror. Still nothing.

David was making a show of digging through the rolling suitcase, but he'd probably already accepted what I didn't want to admit.

"It's not here," I mumbled.

David glanced up at me. "Looks like your boyfriend has already done a pretty thorough search." He set the suitcase aside. "Not very tidily, I'll add."

"He's not my boyfriend," I said as I plopped down in the chair.

David gave me another funny look before zipping the suitcase shut again. "Whatever you say, Ems."

"But you're right. It looks they've been through everything. If the emerald was in Gia's things, the police would have found it already."

Which, now that I said it out loud, sounded ridiculously obvious.

"Hey, it was worth looking," David said softly. "It was always possible they overlooked something."

Possible. But not likely.

Even though I knew it wasn't my fault, I felt like I'd let Ava down.

I absently grabbed the makeup bag, riffling through its also-not-tidily searched contents. Partly out of a last shred of hope there was something left behind and partly out of at least being able to tell Ava we'd left no stone unturned.

Eyeshadow, liner, lipstick in a dozen or more shades. Even though professional makeup artists had been on hand for the show, it appeared Gia didn't like to leave anything to chance. Or maybe this was just her personal stash—all the important tricks of her trade that made her look as stunning as she had for after parties and meet-and-greets. I noticed several small jars of different types of moisturizers, cover ups, under eye concealers. And one round container that caught my attention.

I reached inside the makeup bag and pulled it out. "Wrinkle cream?"

David looked up from the fruitless searching again. "What?"

"Gia had wrinkle cream in her makeup bag."

"So?" he asked. "Don't all women have that?"

"Maybe over thirty, but Gia was way too young to need this."

"Or maybe she only *looked* way too young," David said, giving me a shrug.

"I don't know," I said. I twisted the top of the container to take a sniff of the stuff.

But as the lid came off in my hand, I froze.

"David!"

"What?" In a second he was at my side, staring down into the container too. "Whoa."

At the bottom of the little plastic jar sat a soft pile of tissues, and nestled in the paper was a sparkling green princess cut emerald.

"Is that—"

But David didn't get to finish the question, as a sound outside the door pulled our attention away from the shiny green gem.

"...*Columbo*!" came Ava's voice.

Accompanied by footsteps.

And a second voice that I knew all too well.

"Ava, what's going on?" Grant asked, his voice loud. Deep. Menacing.

And moving closer to the dressing room door.

CHAPTER ELEVEN

My gaze whipped wildly around the room, looking for an escape route to pop up out of nowhere. File cabinets, vanity, cupboards. Still no magical door to freedom.

"What do we do?" I whispered to David.

His usually sardonic smile was missing, and his eyes actually registered fear. "I dunno." He shrugged. "Hide?"

"Where?" I hissed, hearing Ava try to stall on the other side of the door.

"...uh, tell me again how search warrants work?" I heard her voice asking. "I mean, all I know about them comes from *Columbo!*"

I had to hand it to her, she was really trying.

Not that I thought it was really working.

"Here," David whispered, pulling one of the file cabinets back from the wall. The open space left between them wasn't much, but at least it was dark and in a corner.

I shot one dubious look toward the door again before I shoved the emerald into my pocket, skittered into the corner, and ducked down into a little ball. David pulled a second cabinet away from the wall and hunkered down behind it, next to me.

Close next to me.

So close I could smell the mingling scents of weed and some expensive brand of aftershave coming off his warm body as he pressed against me. The proximity suddenly felt way too intimate. And worse—it had been long enough since a man was pressed up against me that it wasn't entirely unpleasant.

"You're squishing me," I breathed.

"I'm hiding you. Stay still."

"I don't think this is a good—"

That was as far as I got before the sound of the dressing room door opening caused us both to shut up. I clamped my lips together, saying a silent prayer to be at least half as big as I was and twice as quiet.

"—don't know what you're doing here, Ava, but I don't like it," I heard Grant's voice boom in the space as his boots stepped into view through the small crack between the cabinets.

"Doing here?" Ava asked, her voice coming into the room as well, though I couldn't actually see her. "I'm not doing anything." She gave a nervous laugh. "I'm just…meeting a friend here and thought I'd, you know, walk around while I wait."

"Around the empty ballroom?" His voice was a flat monotone—the same one I knew he used when interrogating suspects.

And it seemed to be having much the same effect on Ava, if her nervous giggle was any indication. "Yep! Just, you know, walking. Everywhere. To pass the time. While I wait. For that friend…" She trailed off.

I closed my eyes, cringing. In her defense, the business end of Grant's Cop Stare could fluster anyone.

"So…what are *you* doing here?" Ava asked in a casual tone that sounded anything but, given the circumstances.

"Investigating a murder," came the clipped reply.

"Oh? Any leads?"

"Ava, I think you should go now." Clearly a command, not a suggestion.

"Go?" I heard the hesitation in her voice.

I opened my eyes and peeked between the filing cabinets. She'd stepped into view, and I could see her gaze slowly roving the room as if looking for where David and I could be hiding. I hoped that meant our spot wasn't obvious.

"Yes. Go. Back to the clubrooms."

Ava licked her lips. "Uh, well, I'm not sure my friend is here yet, so why don't I stay *here* and keep you company?"

Grant took a step forward. I had to will myself not to react at the sight of his dark frown and arms crossed over his chest in a combative stance. "This *friend* wouldn't happen to be Emmy, would it?"

"Emmy?" I didn't think Ava's voice could go any higher, but it somehow found a new range. "N-no. Why would you think that?"

"Because where there is trouble, you two seem to have a knack for popping up."

Ava threw her head back and laughed much more loudly than the humor of the moment called for. "Oh, that's a good one. Very funny."

I could tell Grant didn't think there was anything funny about the situation, the storm in his eyes growing.

I was with him on this one. The tiny ball I was scrunched into was no joke. My right foot was starting to go numb, and my nose tickled from the family of dust bunnies living in the corner. Not to mention the fact that I was pretty sure David Allen's hand was on my thigh. I only hoped it was unintentional as he breathed shallowly beside me.

"Alright," Grant finally said. "How about I *walk* you back to the lounge and you can wait for your *friend* there, huh?"

"You want to walk me to the lounge?" Ava repeated. Loudly. As if trying to make sure David and I both heard that Grant was leaving.

"That's what I said," Grant told her, a note of suspicion in his voice.

"Uh, sure, yeah. That sounds lovely. I would love it if you walked me. *TO THE LOUNGE!*"

I heard Ava's heels click along the wood floor, Grant's heavier footsteps falling a beat behind. I waited until they were echoing across the ballroom before I dared to let out the breath I'd been holding.

"That was close," David said.

"Too close." I looked down. "You can take your hand off my leg now."

"Was my hand on your leg?" He gave my knee a squeeze. "Didn't notice."

"You're a terrible liar," I told him, using the file cabinet to push myself back up to a standing position.

"Not as terrible as Ava," David countered. "That was painful to listen to."

"Agreed," I said with a laugh. "Come on, let's get out of here."

*   *   *

We went out a side door, toward the south lawn where the fashion show had taken place, and skirted around the outside of the club to avoid running into Grant as he escorted Ava from the crime scene. David led the way toward the terrace, where we weaved between the tables of golfers enjoying post-game drinks and gossip over cocktails in the shade. Once we finally made our way back into the air-conditioned main building, my heart rate started to return to normal. We found Ava in the lounge— thankfully alone—pacing the length of the bar.

As soon as she spied us, she lunged for me, giving me a tight hug. "Ohmigosh, thank goodness you're okay. I thought for sure he'd catch us."

"He still might," I warned, grabbing her by the arm as we quickly made for the front doors.

"Nice distraction, by the way," David told her, following along with us.

"Thank you." She sent him a smile. "Though, I'm not sure he completely bought it."

"I'm not sure he bought any part of it," I mumbled, unable to keep from looking over my shoulder as we hustled outside and toward the valet station.

Luckily, David had some clout at the club, and Ava's GTO arrived in record time. David gave the guy a big enough tip that I saw just how to earn that sort of speed, before he jumped into Ava's back seat.

"Well, I don't think it matters if Grant bought it or not," David said as soon as Ava pulled away from the curb. "What matters is we succeeded."

Ava's eyes shot to his in the rearview mirror. "What do you mean you succeeded?" She turned to me. "Did you...?"

"We found it." I gave her a triumphant smile.

"Ohmigosh!" She was so happy she swerved a little on the winding drive down toward the main road.

"Whoa, careful, Andretti," David said from the back.

"But you really have the emerald?" Ava asked, clearly having to force her attention back on the road.

"I do." I quickly filled her in on how we'd found the decoy jar of wrinkle cream as we made the trip back to Oak Valley.

By the time we'd arrived at the winery and parked in the gravel lot, Ava was practically vibrating with anticipation. I quickly ushered her and David in through the back door to the kitchen, where I produced the small container from my pocket and set it on the counter.

I noticed Ava's hands were trembling slightly as she unscrewed the top, though if she was feeling anything like I was, some of that was lingering adrenaline at our near miss with law enforcement.

She gasped out loud as she took off the lid and pulled her emerald out. "Emmy, you did it. You found it!" She turned a pair of watery eyes toward me.

"I helped," David protested on the other side of her.

Ava turned her grateful smile to him. "Thank you. My white knight once again."

David bowed at the compliment. "Anytime, mi'lady."

"The cuteness. It burns," I said, only half joking.

Though no one paid me any attention.

"So, I guess this means we were right about Gia," Ava mused, turning the gem over in her hand. "She did take it after all."

I nodded. "It looks like it."

"Do you think the killer knew?" she asked. "I mean, what Gia was up to?"

I shrugged. "I don't know. Honestly? I have no idea how the theft ties in with her death."

"Maybe someone figured out what she was doing, and that's *why* she was killed," David offered. "Didn't you say she'd done this before? Stolen jewelry from another runway?"

"Ruby earrings at Daisy Dot's spring show," I said. "They disappeared long enough for Gia to swap fake gems in place of the real ones."

"So, maybe Daisy Dot figured it out," he went on. "Maybe she realized her rubies were fake and put together what must have happened to them."

"It's possible," I agreed. I moved to the cupboard and pulled down three wineglasses. It was after five, and if there had ever been a day I needed to give my nerves a little Cabernet calming, it was that one. I grabbed a bottle of the red wine from a wooden rack on the counter, quickly uncorking it.

"If Daisy figured out that Gia had robbed her, maybe she confronted her at the Links show," Ava said, picking up the thread. "Maybe Gia denied it and they argued. Or maybe Daisy even saw Gia trying to pull the same thing again with the emerald."

"And she killed Gia out of revenge?" David asked.

"Revenge, anger, preventing another theft," Ava said. "It could have been a heat-of-the-moment attack. It's possible she didn't even realize she'd actually killed Gia until it was too late."

David nodded. "I could see that," he agreed as I handed glasses of wine to both him and Ava. "Thanks," he told me.

I nodded, raising my own glass up in a cheers motion. "To the return of the emerald."

Ava and David raised their glasses in salute before sipping.

Ava took a beat to enjoy the flavor before setting her glass down on the granite counter again. "You know, I think it *could* have been Daisy." She set the emerald down next to her wineglass. "But there are other people who might have been upset at Gia for what she was doing."

"Like her agent, Hughie Smart, for instance," I offered. "Maybe he went backstage to see Gia after the show, saw the empty pendant, and realized she'd stolen the emerald."

"Maybe he even realized she'd taken the rubies too," Ava added.

"And he killed her to what—save face?" David asked.

I shrugged. "Possibly. I mean, she was risking his reputation by stealing from designers. And we don't know how many times she's done this—we only know about two, but it could have been dozens more."

"And don't forget about her stalker," Ava added. "I mean, maybe he had some idolized idea of her, found out she was a thief, and killed her out of some crazed sense of betrayal."

"While we're talking about motive, it sure gives *you* a great one, too," David teased.

"Me?" Ava laughed.

"You catch her trying to steal from you and kill her." He shrugged. "Just saying."

"Yeah, well, Ava has an iron-clad alibi. Me," I added.

David grinned. "Lucky her."

Ava shook her head. "Anyway, I guess it's in the hands of the authorities to figure all that out now." She smiled down at her recovered gem.

I sipped my wine, feeling a small ball of unpleasantness form in my stomach at the mention of authorities. "I hate to say it…" I glanced from Ava to David. "But I think we have to tell Grant we found this."

"Oh, you're on your own there, blondie," David said, putting his hands up in a gesture that said he was backing the heck out of that conversation.

"I mean, we kind of took it from a crime scene," I pointed out, the implication of that settling in now that the rush of finding it was subsiding.

"Oh, no way." Ava shook her head. "I'm not going to feel guilty about taking back what is mine in the first place."

"From a *locked* crime scene," I added.

"You were simply returning stolen property to its rightful owner," Ava argued. "If it's my emerald, you didn't take it. You *returned* it."

"I'm not sure Grant is going to see it that way," I said.

Ava sighed. "Fine. Tell him whatever you have to." She paused. "But I'm not parting with this again!" She pointed to the emerald.

I had a bad feeling it might be evidence, but I didn't voice that as I grabbed my phone and pulled up Grant's number.

David shook his head at me like he thought I was crazy.

It was possible he was right. But I knew this wasn't something I should keep from Grant, even if I *could* keep it from him.

Ava and David sipped in silence while I listened to the phone ring. The tension hung heavy in the air. Finally, four rings in, the call went to voice mail, and I'd admit to feeling just a tiny bit relieved at the reprieve.

"Uh, hi. It's Emmy. Can you please come to the winery when you get this message? It's, um, kinda urgent. Thanks." I hung up, wishing I felt less guilty for having made that call.

"There you are!"

We all turned at the sound of Eddie's voice as he came pushing through the kitchen door in a pair of pressed chinos, a purple silk shirt, and a matching silk ascot. "Well, I've been looking for you all afternoon, Emmy."

"Here I am." I offered a tentative smile and tried to put myself between Eddie and the emerald to block his view. "What's up?"

"I wanted to fill you in on my meeting with Aurora Dawn." He paused, glancing behind me to see Ava and David. "Hi, kids." He gave them a little wave.

David raised his wineglass in greeting. Ava gave a tentative smile, eyes cutting to the emerald on the counter.

"Anyhoo, guess what?" Eddie said.

"Um...what?" I asked.

"She loved it! She said the Zin was nectar of the heavens. Isn't that cute? She totally twitted it to her peeps."

"Tweeted?" Ava supplied.

"Whatever." Eddie waved it off with a grin. "Point is, we're going to go viral." He did a little happy dance, stamping his feet and wiggling his ample hips.

I couldn't help but smile. "That's great. Amazing, really. Nice work."

"Thank you!" Eddie gave an exaggerated bow.

And the lower angle of his eyeline must have been just enough to see past me to the sparkling green jewel sitting out in the open on the kitchen counter, as he froze.

"Oh my goodness gracious. What is that?"

"Uh, what?" I asked.

Eddie straightened and shot me a look. "Emmy Oak, don't you hold out on me. Is that Ava's emerald?"

"Yes," I reluctantly admitted. While I might have wanted to hand it over to the authorities before word got out too widely—and telling Eddie was the equivalent to taking out a billboard on 101—the cat was out of the bag. Or out of the wrinkle cream jar, as it were.

"Where did you find this?" he asked, taking a step closer to pick up the gem.

We quickly gave him the condensed version of events, including our discovering what Gia's real moneymaker was and the theory that she'd been murdered in the act.

When we finished, Eddie was shaking his head. "She had it all. And she needed more." He clucked his tongue. "So sad."

I had to agree.

He picked up the gem and held it up to the light. "Though, I can see how she was tempted. Look at how it sparkles."

"Eddie," Ava said, looking nervous as her eyes followed the gem. "Maybe you should just put it down."

"I mean, I've never actually seen one so big," Eddie said, tossing it from one hand to the other. "Or heavy."

"Eddie," Ava said, warning in her voice. "Let's just set it down on the counter, huh?"

"And it's so expertly cut." Eddie held it up to the light again, squinting one eye. "I'm no jeweler, but that's gotta be what, eight carats? Nine? Fifteen?"

"Twelve. But Eddie, can you please just set it down—"

But Ava didn't get to finish.

I watched it play out before me as if in horrible slow motion.

Eddie spun, his eyes going toward Ava, as his thick fingers fumbled with the gem. It slipped, and he used the other hand to try to catch it.

David's eyes went wide.

Ava gasped.

My heart skipped a beat.

And the gem slowly fell through the air, crashing to the tiled kitchen floor, where it shattered into dozens of tiny green pieces that scattered in all directions.

"No!" Ava cried out, dropping to her knees. "No, no, no, no!"

"I-I'm sorry." Eddie's skin went pale. "I'm so sorry. I didn't mean to..." He trailed off, and I swore he looked like he was going to cry.

I put a hand on his shoulder. "It's not your fault," I mumbled to him, even as my heart broke for Ava, who was carefully trying to gather up the tiny slivers of what had been her future in her hands.

"No, no, no!" she cried again.

I joined her on the floor. "Oh, Ava, I'm so sorry. We'll figure this out." Truthfully, I had no idea how to figure it out. Or fix it.

"Girls, get up," David said from behind us.

I spun around to find his eyes on the shards of emerald. He leaned down to help Ava off the floor. "Come on. It's okay."

"No, it's not okay!" Ava protested, though she did let him help her to a standing position. "You don't understand. I needed that emerald!"

David shook his head. "No you didn't."

"Yes I did!"

"Not *that* emerald."

Ava opened her mouth to protest again, but something in David's tone must have caught her attention the way it did mine.

"What do you mean, not *that* one?" I asked him.

"I mean," he said, his voice calm, "emeralds don't shatter."

Ava frowned, gaze going from me to Eddie to David. "Wh-what?"

"Emeralds are some of the hardest gemstones. They're rated at a 7.5–8 on the Mohs scale."

I blinked at him. Being that I could barely afford costume jewelry, I knew little about precious gems. "So, that means they don't break easily?"

"Correct. It would take some force. If I hit it with a hammer"—he shrugged—"yeah, it would chip. But not shatter like this," he finished, nodding to the floor.

"So you're saying *that* was not actually an emerald." I looked down at the sparkling green slivers on the tiles.

"It was a fake?" Eddie said. I could see the relief flooding through him. "I broke a fake?"

David nodded. Then he cocked his head to Ava. "Sorry, hon."

Ava shook her head. "No. I mean, I-I guess that's good news, right?"

"Then what was this one made of?" I asked, crouching down again to pick up a green shard.

"If I had to guess? Glass," David said.

I stood back up, holding the small piece in my hands. It *had* shattered a lot like a wineglass would.

"It must have been the fake that Gia planned to swap into the necklace after she stole the real one," Eddie surmised.

"So, if Gia still had the fake emerald in her bag, that means she hadn't yet switched them when the killer attacked her," I said.

"Which means the real emerald is still out there somewhere," Eddie added.

Ava sighed deeply. "The killer did take it after all."

We were all silent a moment, contemplating that depressing thought.

David opened another bottle of wine and poured all of us a refill, along with a glass for poor Eddie, who was still shaking. Ava slumped at the counter, looking like the emotional roller coaster had drained her. I grabbed a broom and swept up the mess on the floor.

I was just putting it away, feeling reasonably sure there was no green glass left on the floor that Conchita could step on in the morning, when the sound of tires crunching on gravel outside the window grabbed my attention.

"Now who could that be?" Eddie asked. He glanced at his watch—a Rolex replica his husband Curtis had given him for his birthday. "It's late for wine tasters."

David looked out the window. "Black SUV."

My stomach dropped as I realized I had a pretty good idea who it could be. "Grant," I breathed.

Ava's eyes lifted to meet mine. "You told him to meet you here!"

I did a mental forehead thunk. I'd forgotten all about that. I glanced at the trash can where my very urgent stolen evidence now sat.

"What are you going to tell him?" Ava asked.

I bit my lip. "I don't know."

David set his wineglass down. "When the boyfriend arrives, that's my cue to go." Something in his voice was difficult to read, but considering I was in the middle of a mental meltdown, I didn't try very hard.

"Ava, wanna give me a ride back to my car?" he asked.

Ava shot me a questioning look, clearly asking if she should stay or go.

I nodded. "Go ahead." No sense in both of us getting arrested for tampering with evidence.

Then shattering it.

"What?" Eddie's gaze whipped from one of us to the other, clearly sensing he was left out of the loop on something.

"Nothing. Never mind," I told him. "I'll, uh, fill you in tomorrow."

His pudgy face broke into a smile, and he waggled a finger at me. "You better. I can only imagine what that tall drink of water is doing here so late."

Yeah, not that.

In a matter of minutes, the three had made themselves scarce and I'd stashed their wineglasses in the sink. I was just rinsing out the last one when Grant appeared in the doorway.

He was wearing the same boots, jeans, and blue button up shirt, though the top few buttons were undone now and the sleeves rolled past his elbows. The stubble on his jaw was pronounced, and his hair looked as if he'd run his hands through it several times that day, leaving it tussled and enticing enough that I felt my hormones kick up at the sight of him.

"Hey," he said. Gone was the hard Cop Mode I'd seen earlier at the Links, and in its place was a warmer, softer tone that had me almost melting to a confession right on the spot.

I tried to clear the guilt out of my throat while simultaneously checking the floor for any lingering green sparkles. "Uh, hey yourself. What's up?"

He raised a pair of eyebrows at me. "You tell me. I got a message something was urgent."

"Did I say urgent?" I laughed. It sounded a lot like Ava's had at the club. I gave myself a mental shake. "Uh, sorry. I hope I didn't tear you away from anything."

"No." He shook his head slowly. "I was knocking off for the day anyway." He cocked his head at me. "Was something on your mind?"

I licked my lips. Boy, was it. "Uh, I actually, just..." My brain ran in circles, trying to come up with a plausible lie, gaze roving the kitchen until it settled on the counter near the stove. "Conchita made pie!" I pointed to the pastry she'd been working on that morning, now neatly baked and sitting on a glass plate beside the range.

His eyes followed my gesture, a note of suspicion in them.

"It's Mama Halliday's Apple Pie recipe. I thought you might like some." I sent him a big smile.

He paused, and for a second I thought he could see right through me. Finally, he nodded. "Who would turn down pie?"

I tried not to audibly sigh in relief as I turned my back to him to grab a knife from the butcher block.

"So, what have you been up to today?" Grant asked as he took a seat on one of the tall wooden stools at the counter.

"Up to?" I asked, willing my voice not to raise an octave.

"Yeah. What did you *do* today?" he asked. Still eyeing me.

"Oh. Uh, yeah. I walked the field a bit. Turns out we have deer in the south vineyard. They triggered the motion lights last night," I said, cutting two slices of apple pie and setting them on plates.

"That's trouble."

"Don't I know it." I added a fork to his plate and slid it across the counter to him.

"Then what?"

"Hmm?" I asked, taking a big bite of pie. I was momentarily distracted by the tangy apples and sweet, spicy cinnamon wrapped in flaky crust that held just the slightest hint of nuttiness from the walnut oil—the secret ingredient.

"That all you do today?" Grant asked. "Just walk the fields?"

Why did this feel more like an interrogation than a conversation?

"Uh, no. I…went with Ava to visit a friend. Janet. She runs a B&B nearby." Which was true, if leaving out a few key details.

"Sounds pleasant."

"It was." Okay, that part was an outright lie. Nothing about questioning Hughie Smart at the B&B had been what I'd consider pleasant.

"You visit any other friends today?" he asked, forking a mouthful of tender apples. "At the Links maybe?"

"The Links?" I tried to think fast. Unfortunately nothing came to me. Where was Ava and her amazing story-on-the-spot talents when I needed them? Oh yeah. She'd fled. Lucky her.

"Uh-huh," Grant added. "I ran into Ava there. Said she was waiting for a friend."

I shook my head slowly. "Must have been another friend. I'm not a member of the Links."

"I know." He pinned me with a look.

Oh boy.

"Uh, so how was *your* day?" I asked, turning my back to him as I poured myself another glass of wine. A big one.

"Busy," he said around a bite. He swallowed before continuing. "Had Gia's autopsy this morning."

"Oh?" I poured a glass for Grant as well, setting it in front of him. "How did that go?"

"Fine." He gave me a grin. "Sorry, not sharing."

"Then why bring it up?" I asked, teasing him.

He shook his head at me and took a sip of wine. "Okay, honestly? Nothing came up you don't already know. She died of asphyxiation, bruising consistent with strangulation."

"So, conclusion is she was strangled with the necklace she was wearing?"

He nodded, stabbing more pie with his fork. "Everything supports that theory. We finished up witness statements, so everyone associated with the fashion show headed home. I was just releasing the crime scene as well, gathering up the last of Gia's personal effects, when you called."

I watched as he took another bite. Those personal effects would include the makeup bag that I'd taken the glass gem from. While the CSI might have overlooked the jar of beauty cream at first glance, there was a chance Grant might have found it upon closer inspection and realized what Gia had been up to. Had we not botched that.

"You know, I've been thinking," I said, trying to sound casual and offhand.

Grant's eyes lifted to meet mine. "That's never good," he joked.

I shot him a look. "I've been thinking about Gia's spending habits. I mean, you said she had a lot of charges on her accounts…"

He nodded. "She seemed to enjoy the good life."

"Well, I would imagine a Bay Area model wouldn't be making as much, say, as someone in New York or Paris."

"What do you mean?" he asked around a bite.

What I meant was he should look for Gia's illegal side hustle. But I wasn't sure how to say that without admitting to breaking and entering and theft from a crime scene.

"Well, I guess I was just wondering where Gia was getting all that spending money. I mean, it sounds like she was spending more than she was making."

While I had hoped to gently lead Grant's thinking down the same path Ava and I had traversed to realize what Gia's *real* business was, I was surprised when he answered me with, "No, she was making quite a bit."

I blinked at him. "She was?"

He nodded. "Well, I can't say if it was payments for modeling or something else, but she had a healthy income."

I frowned. "Her agent said she only made about a grand a show. She'd have to be in a lot of shows to make enough to afford a Ferrari."

His bite paused on the way to his mouth. "How do you know what kind of car she drove?"

I rolled my eyes. "She posted a picture of it on social media. Don't you cops go online?" I teased.

He shook his head at me. "Don't you vintners have anything better to do?" he countered.

"Touché."

He gave me a grin before shoving the bite into his mouth.

"But, seriously, was her agent lying?" I pressed.

He swallowed and shook his head. "No, we ran Gia's financials, and we did find several payments around that amount from Smart Models. So chances are that was her going rate."

"But she was making more than that?"

"She was. We found there were other deposits."

"Other deposits?" I asked, leaning my elbows on the counter. "From where?"

"Puerto Rico."

I raised an eyebrow his way. "For?"

"Not sure yet. They were anonymous wire transfers. Maybe payments for some job she did down there."

I frowned. "I don't know. I don't think Gia would do that. I mean, take jobs on the side. Word would get back to Hughie, and it would ruin her reputation in the industry," I said, repeating what Jada had told us earlier.

Grant shrugged. "Well, she was getting paid for something. We found several large deposits to her account."

"And you have no idea who was sending the payments?"

"It's an off-shore bank, and they're being less than forthcoming. Without a whole lot of paperwork to force their records, it doesn't look like they'll cooperate."

"But you can force the paperwork, right?" I asked.

He let out a deep breath, eyeing me. "Not sure there's a real reason to."

Right. I paused. "What about Gia's stalker?" I asked, changing gears. "Did you get a chance to look into him?"

Grant turned his attention back to his dessert. "No stalker." He shoveled more apple pie onto his fork. "Gia never filed any charges against anyone. No restraining orders, no officers called to her residence."

"Nothing?" I couldn't help the note of disappointment in my voice.

Grant shook his head. "Sorry. If the guy was following Gia around, she never told anyone."

"Or never noticed," I mused. "He's good at blending in. I almost didn't notice him today."

"Today?" Suddenly Grant's pie was abandoned and all his attention was on me.

"Uh…"

"Did you see this guy today?" he asked, his eyes pinning me with a look that could scare a confession out of just about anyone.

Me included.

"Yeah," I admitted.

Gone was amiable Maybe-Boyfriend Grant, and in seconds flat he was replaced with Angry Cop Grant. "Where?" he demanded.

"Uh, at the hotel. Where the designers and models were staying."

Grant stood up and let out a couple of swear words. Really good ones.

I felt myself involuntarily taking a step back, coming up against the sink.

"What were you doing there?" he asked, his voice rising in volume like he was chastising a teen who'd broken curfew.

"I-I was just visiting a friend."

"What. Friend."

"Costello?" Though it came out more of a question than an answer.

"Emmy, I told you to leave this alone," he said. Then he punctuated the statement with a couple more colorful words you can't say on television. "You promised to leave this alone."

I cringed. I guess I kinda had. And I hated breaking that promise. "You know I can't turn my back on Ava," I told him in my defense.

"I'm not asking you to turn your back on your friend," he said. "I'm asking you to be smart about this and let me do my job."

I paused. "Wait—did you just say I'm not being smart?"

"What do you call hanging around stalkers?"

"Hey, *he* was hanging around *us*." I paused. "Or maybe Jada."

"You were with Jada too?"

Oops. Did I say that? "Look, this a small town. I run into people."

"How about you try not to *run into* any more of my witnesses, huh?" he said hotly.

I was starting to get a little tired of his overprotective thing. I was a grown woman who had been able to take care of herself just fine for the last twenty-nine(ish) years without his help. "Well, how about *you* do your job and find my friend's emerald," I shot back.

"I'm trying!" he shouted.

"Well, good!" I yelled back.

"Thank you for the pie!" he shouted.

"You're welcome!" I yelled back.

He stood there for a beat, his eyes flashing fire, his breath coming hard enough to make his chest visibly rise and fall. Then he turned and stomped out the door and back to his car.

I listened to his feet fall on the gravel, car door open and shut, the engine of his SUV roar to life. Then I watched the beam of his headlights illuminate the room, arcing away from the parking lot and down toward the oak lined driveway.

Before the anger I'd held back erupted into hot, stupid tears.

CHAPTER TWELVE

———

I awoke the next morning feeling a mixture of guilt and anger, not to mention horror at the puffy eyes staring back at me in the bathroom mirror. After a hot shower, the anger dissipated a little, and with some cooling aloe and a lot of eyeliner, the puffiness was at least manageable. The guilt was another matter.

Grant had gone over the top with his protective routine, he'd been out of line to tell me who I could or could not talk to, and the whole yelling and ordering me around thing had been nowhere in the vicinity of attractive. But he hadn't been totally wrong. I *had* broken a promise to stay out of the whole thing. Of course, it had been made in a moment of romantic lighting and elegant wine, but I was a person who usually held her word in high regard. Plus, there was the fact that I had tampered with his crime scene and not only taken but also destroyed a key piece of evidence that could right now be steering him in the right direction toward Gia's killer.

Assuming the murder was fueled by knowledge of her theft in the first place. Which was not a given.

I tried not to think about how I might have ruined the tentative bond of trust we had, let alone botched his entire investigation. Mostly because it was too depressing to add to the fact that Gia's killer was out there literally getting away with murder, and Ava's emerald was long gone…much like her entire business would be if we didn't find it. And fast.

I threw on a sporty black knit skirt, a pale pink cami tank, and some low heeled sandals before making my way from my cottage toward the kitchen. Where the delicious scents of freshly brewed coffee and sweet cinnamon buns told me I was not the first one up that morning.

In fact, as I entered the kitchen and spotted Eddie, Ava, and my house manager, Conchita, all hovering around the center island, I realized I might well have been the *last* person up.

Conchita spotted me first, her head lifting from their conversation and her face breaking into a soft smile that made me instantly feel better.

Conchita had dark hair shot liberally through with gray, warm brown eyes, and a soft shape that spoke to her love of baking. She'd adopted a mother hen attitude toward me even before my own mother had become unable to fulfill those clucking duties. Not that I totally minded. It was nice to have someone fuss over you now and then. Especially when it came in the form of cinnamon buns. "Good morning, *mía*," she said. "Sleep well?"

Before I could answer, Eddie chimed in, "Oh, honey, I'm hoping the fact you slept in means it was a spicy evening with your detective."

I scoffed as I grabbed a cup of coffee. "Not even close to spicy. Try ice cold."

"Oh." The disappointment in Eddie's voice was endearing. "Sorry, hon."

I shook my head and added cream and sugar. A lot of sugar. "No. It's fine. It could have been worse. I mean, I'm not in jail for obstruction."

"Gee, do you know how to look on the bright side," Ava piped up. I hadn't had enough caffeine yet to tell if she was being sarcastic or sympathetic.

"What happened?" Conchita asked. "I see you had the pie," she pointed out hopefully.

I nodded. "And he thanked me for the pie."

Conchita's smile widened.

"Before he stormed out."

The smile died.

"Ouch," Ava said. She put a hand on my shoulder as I joined the trio at the counter. "Sorry."

I shrugged. "It's okay."

"Did you tell him about the emerald?" Ava asked, her brows drawing down in a frown of concern.

I shook my head. "Maybe I should have." I looked up at all three faces. "*Probably* I should have. I'm pretty sure he knows something is up." I quickly relayed the gist of our conversation from the night before as I dug into a cinnamon bun. Or two. Okay, fine, three. But they were small. By the time I was done, I was licking the last of the sticky gooey goodness off my fingers, and Ava's eyebrows were scrunched down in thought.

"So Gia was receiving large, regular payments from an off-shore account?" she asked, her voice lifting.

"I don't know if Grant said regular," I hedged.

"Emmy, you know what this means, right?" she asked.

I looked from Eddie to Conchita—both faces as blank as my mind was on the subject. I shook my head. "What?"

"Blackmail!" I swear, she looked practically giddy at the thought.

Eddie gave an appropriately scandalized gasp. "Blackmail?"

Ava nodded emphatically. "Why else would someone send her large, untraceable payments?"

"I'm not sure they're totally untraceable either," I added.

But she waved me off, on a roll with this new theory. "And you said they came from a bank in Puerto Rico, right?"

I nodded. "That's what Grant said."

"Fabio is from Puerto Rico!"

"Who?" Conchita asked.

"Carl Costello's young, hot boyfriend." Ava turned to Eddie. "You would adore him. He's delish. Abs you could do your laundry on."

"So you think this boyfriend was being blackmailed by your dead woman?" Conchita asked, trying to catch up.

"It all fits. I mean, let's face it—Gia was no pillar of morality. We already know she was stealing from the designers who hired her."

"True!" Eddie agreed, nodding as he sipped his coffee.

"And it can't be just a coincidence that Gia's getting big sums of money for seemingly nothing from a Puerto Rican bank," Ava reasoned.

Which, when she put it that way, did kind of make sense. "But what would Gia be blackmailing Fabio over?" I asked.

She frowned. Apparently that one stumped her.

"Maybe he knew about her stealing gems?" Conchita offered.

"Which would be a great thing for *him* to blackmail *her* over," Eddie pointed out. "But the money would be going the other way in that case."

"You know, Fabio didn't strike me as independently wealthy. I'm wondering…what if it wasn't Fabio she had something over but Costello?" I said, working it out in my head as the caffeine kicked in.

"Yes!" Ava stabbed a finger at me. "That makes more sense. Didn't you say you overheard Gia and Costello arguing before the show?"

"I did. And she was threatening him with something."

"Maybe the same something she was blackmailing him over," Eddie added. "Maybe she was threatening to make it public if he didn't pay up."

"But he already paid her," Conchita pointed out. "From the Puerto Rican bank."

Eddie shrugged. "Okay, if he didn't pay up *more*."

"Which, maybe he didn't want to do," I said.

"Or couldn't do," Ava added. "Depending on his financial situation."

"And he killed her to keep his secret quiet," I finished.

"Exactly!" Ava said, eyes shining, grin taking over her face, practically bouncing on her toes.

"But what is the secret?" Eddie asked.

"And where is the emerald?" Conchita added.

Ava lowered back to flat feet. "I dunno."

"But maybe Costello does," I pointed out.

"You think he would tell us?" Ava asked, and I could tell she was thinking back to our less than diplomatic last visit to his penthouse hotel room.

I shrugged. "I think it's worth a try."

"I don't know if your detective is going to like this," Conchita said, shaking her head.

I knew he would hate it. But since his status as *my* detective was currently iffy at best, I set that factor aside for the moment. "There's no law against talking to someone."

Conchita gave me a dubious look and mumbled something in Spanish. Having grown up in California, my command of the language was pretty good, but I clearly did not know all the swear words, as the translation of her particular phrase escaped me.

"Conchita!" Eddie said on a gasp. Apparently he was more fluent than I was.

She threw her hands up in surrender. "Okay, fine. I just better get to baking him an *apology* pie now." She shot me a look.

The only way he was getting more pie was if *he* was the one apologizing for treating me like a child.

But I didn't voice that, instead turning to Ava. "Everyone associated with the show was cleared to go home. So, I'm guessing that means Costello is back in San Francisco."

She nodded. "We did the fittings at his studio. I know exactly where it is." She grinned. "Road trip?"

* * *

Carl Costello's studio was housed in a converted crab processing plant that was in a more shabby than chic section of San Francisco, near the wharf. While the outside of the building still bore the historic rusted corrugated metal siding and gray faded logo of a crab wearing a top hat, the interior was as plush as any couture house in Paris. As we pushed through the front doors, gleaming marble floors, a sleek glass reception desk, and a yellow satin covered Louis XV style settee greeted us in the lobby. Costello's blingy hand could be seen in the crystal sconces and gold leaf picture frames on the walls, as well as the photos of the glamorous gowns the frames held.

"Good morning and welcome to the House of Costello. May I help you?" a slim, waifish looking woman behind an enormous glass desk asked.

"Ava Barnett," my friend announced, and I detected just a hint of an upper crust affect in her voice. "Jewelry designer. I'm here to see Carl."

"Do you have an appointment?" the woman asked.

Ava laughed. "Darling, when Ava Barnett shows up, you don't turn her away!"

I stifled a snicker.

But apparently her egotistical third-person reference had the desired effect, as the waifish receptionist hesitated. I could see her checking her mental catalog of who's-who in fashion. "Uh, I suppose I could see if he's free."

"You do that, dahling. Hurry, now, I haven't got all day," Ava said, the accent somewhere between Boston and London.

"Of course. One moment..." The receptionist trailed off, getting up from her desk and disappearing through a pair of double doors to her right.

As soon as she did, Ava let out a sigh. "I'm so glad that worked. I was afraid it was going to be over the top."

I shook my head, letting out the snicker I'd been holding back. "Apparently perfect for the fashion world."

"You think he'll see us?" she asked, uncertainty in her eyes.

"You know what?" I said, making a spur of the moment decision. "Let's not give him the chance to say no."

I grabbed her by the hand and followed in the direction that the receptionist had gone, not waiting for an invitation.

Beyond the double door we found ourselves in an open workspace filled with several seamstresses at sewing machines, some hand beading gowns, and others pinning garments onto dress forms. I had to stop myself from fangirling at the inside peek into a real live fashion studio, as my gaze pinged from one custom outfit to another. A couple of models stood at the far end of the room—one being measured by an assistant and the other wearing a pair of tailored pants and a jacket with strategically placed lapels to cover all the necessary bits. She walked back and forth in front of a pair of large windows with a view of the Bay as the designer himself looked on.

Costello was adorned that day in a pair of tuxedo pants, embellished with shiny sequins all the way down the sides, and a teal shirt that billowed loosely in the sleeves as he gestured to the model. The receptionist we'd seen earlier was whispering to him as he watched his model prance back and forth in his creations.

Though, as soon as the receptionist spied us, she stood up straight.

"You can't be back here," she protested. The look on her face was clearly bewildered at how we'd breached her marvelous security.

Costello turned, and for a brief moment I saw annoyance flash across his features before he pasted on his usual over-the-top flounce. "Well, if it isn't my little Wine Country lovelies. How are you babies?" He dismissed the ineffective receptionist with a wave as he dropped air kisses at Ava and me.

"We're well, thank you," I answered.

"Come to see the master at work?" he asked, gesturing toward the model in the tailored outfit. "Isn't she a doll? I'm in love with this look. Head over heels, in love."

"It's very pretty," Ava said, and I could see her eyeing the jacket with something akin to envy in her eyes.

"But actually, we drove down to talk to you," I added.

The annoyance made a brief reappearance before he could cover it. "Oh? I would have thought we did plenty of talking back in Sonoma."

"We wanted to talk about Fabio," Ava jumped in, tearing her gaze from the outfit. "You mentioned he's from Puerto Rico, correct?"

"Yes, born and raised. But sorry, ladies, he's taken." He laughed. "And, no, I'm terribly sorry to report he does not have a brother." He gave Ava a wink.

"Does he have a bank account?" I asked pointedly.

Costello blinked at me, the jovial smile frozen in place. "A what?"

"An offshore bank account in Puerto Rico, from which he was sending large sums of money?" I shot him a look. "To Gia."

Costello paled beneath his layer of eyeshadow and bronzers. His eyes blinked, tongue darting out to lick his thin lips. "I-I don't know what you're talking about."

"I think you do," Ava said, taking a step closer to the man. "Because I think it's actually *you* who has been using that bank account to send Gia payments. Blackmail payments."

Costello looked about ready to pass out. Or throw up. His gaze darted to the model, now standing idly in front of the large window. "Quiet," he hissed. He took a step close to us, practically whispering. "Someone will hear you, for goodness' sake."

"So it's true?" I asked, my tone lower.

He shook his head and waved his manicured nails in the air. "Shhh." His eyes flickered around the room to the seamstresses and assistants—none of whom were paying us any attention. "Not here." He licked his lips again. "Come. Come."

With one more nervous, over-the-shoulder glance, he ushered us across the workroom floor and into a small private office. Like the lobby, it looked like it had been displaced from an 18th century French palace. Though I did detect a faint fishy scent lingering from the building's days housing crustaceans.

Costello shut the door behind us before daring to speak again. "How could you accuse me of such things! Out in the open! Where anyone could hear you!" Costello collapsed into a white leather chair behind his gold desk and fanned himself.

"So Gia *was* blackmailing you?" I asked, ignoring the theatrics as Ava and I sat in a pair of carved wooden chairs opposite him.

His fanning paused. "Who told you about the Puerto Rican bank?"

"Is it true?" I pressed.

His eyes narrowed, going from Ava to me. Then finally he spat out one word. "Yes."

I could feel Ava vibrating with delight beside me.

"So the payments to her account…those were all you?" she asked.

He nodded. "Gia was bleeding me dry. How could someone so beautiful be so cruel? And to me? I treated her like royalty!" His eyes filled with tears, and I almost felt sorry for him.

That is, if he hadn't killed the model.

"How did it happen?" Ava asked.

He sighed. "At first I thought it would just be a onetime thing. Of course, I was furious she would dare to threaten me. And heartbroken at the betrayal. But, I had the funds, so I paid."

"But it was not a onetime thing," I said.

He shook his head. "No. She"—he took a deep, shuddering breath—"she just kept coming back. The threats growing more and more horrible. I had no idea she could be so terribly unfeeling."

"What were the threats about?" I prompted.

"Well, about telling the world my secret."

"Which is?" I tried again.

His eyes darted around the room that we were clearly alone in. "I-I don't want to say."

Ava gave him a *get real* look. "Look, you can tell us, or you can tell the police."

"Police?" If it was possible, Costello paled even further. "No, no, no. You have this all wrong. I-I didn't do anything illegal. It's not like that!"

"So tell us what it *is* like," I prodded, softening my tone to what I hoped sounded understanding and comforting. "What was she threatening to go public about?"

He sighed again, his shoulders sagging and making his usually larger-than-life personality suddenly seem very small and vulnerable. "My love life."

"Fabio?" I clarified. "Did she know something incriminating about him?"

But Costello shook his head. "No, you see, that's just it. Fabio is all for show. I don't love him." He let out a humorless laugh. "And he surely does not love me."

"I don't understand," I said, meaning it.

"Don't you?" Costello looked from Ava to me. "Babies, my dirty little secret is that I'm straight." He gave us a small smile and a shrug.

"Wait—" Ava said, shaking her head. "The whole scene at the penthouse, your arms around Fabio, all the lovey-dovey stuff?"

"All fake, dahling," he said on a sad sigh. "For your benefit."

"I still don't understand," I said. "Why would you fake being gay?"

"Well, how else was I supposed to get anywhere in the fashion world?"

"Maybe on the merit of your designs?" I mumbled.

Costello scoffed. "Oh dear naïve one." I tried not to be offended as he continued. "I came up in the 90s fashion scene in San Francisco." He gave us a pointed look. "Anyone who had a prayer of getting any attention then had to be beyond flamboyant. So...I was." He twirled his wrists as if to illustrate his point.

"So who exactly is Fabio to you?" Ava asked.

"My straight beard." Costello shrugged again. "Found him on some online hookup site trolling for women. He had a bunch of shirtless photos, and I thought he'd be perfect."

"So, he's straight?" Ava asked. From the lift in her voice, I could tell she was picturing his enticing abs.

I gave her a *down girl* look.

"As an arrow, honey," Costello confirmed. "But really, our arrangement was a win-win for all involved. He gets to live a fabulous lifestyle in penthouses, and all he has to do is make nice with me at public events."

"And Gia found out about this arrangement?" I asked.

Costello clucked his tongue and shook his head. "I don't know how, but yes, she did. She said if I didn't pay up, she'd out me. Tell everyone I'd been living a lie."

"Forgive me for saying this," Ava started, shaking her head, "but do you really think anyone would care now? I mean, it's not the 90s anymore."

"About being a boring, straight, white man?" Costello said. "Maybe not. But about lying? About keeping up the charade and playing gay all these years? Honey, they'd kill me in the press."

He had a point there. Especially with the Daisy Dots of the world, ready to shove him under any oncoming busses.

"I mean," he went on, "can you imagine how offended the gay community would be? Not that I ever meant to offend anyone, but they'd crucify me. And the straight designers would never take me seriously now. I'd be double ostracized! Image is everything in this business, dahlings. No one would ever want a Carl Costello label showing again."

Again, I had to agree there. I couldn't imagine his core audiences proudly brandishing his signature logo handbags if that sort of scandal came out. Let alone paying four figures for them.

"So, you paid Gia off to keep your secret quiet," I said.

Costello nodded. "She asked me to wire the money into her account. I did, and I thought we were done with the matter."

"Only she came back," Ava jumped in.

"She did. Often. And the number for her silence kept going up. It was like, once she realized I'd pay, she just kept pushing and pushing to see how far I'd go."

"Before you cracked," I added.

Costello turned to me, his expression morphing from the teary-eyed victim to a fashion mogul with a little fight left in him after all. "Now, hold on a minute. What do you mean by cracked? *I* had nothing to do with what happened to Gia."

"But you *did* argue with her just before the show at the Links was about to start," I pointed out.

He didn't deny that. He didn't confess to it either, clamping his lips shut.

"What was it I overheard?" I said. "'Careful what you wish for. It might be your last.'"

"That is totally out of context!" he said, popping up from his chair, his previous pale pallor being replaced with two bright, angry red spots on his cheeks.

"So give us the context," Ava told him. "What was the argument about?"

Costello wrung his hands together and began to pace behind his desk. "Fine. Okay. Yes, she was asking for more money, alright? She said she'd go on social media and spill everything—that I was straight, that my relationship with Fabio was a sham, that I'd been lying to my public all this time. And I'd paid blackmail to cover it up."

"How much more did she ask for?" Ava asked.

"Fifty thousand."

I gasped before I could rein it in. "That's a big number."

"Right?!" Costello threw his hands up. "I don't have that kind of money sitting around. I mean, this isn't Milan, dahlings." He gestured around his fishy smelling, gold gilded office. "I-I'm not making what I once was. The fashion market is flooded these days."

And he was old news. Though, none of us voiced that thought.

"You seemed to have enough to rent out a penthouse," Ava pointed out.

But Costello waved her off. "That was for appearances, dahling. I mean, I couldn't very well have all my models going back to their agents saying I stayed in the same type of rooms the models did, now, could I? I'd completely lose their respect. Didn't I say image is everything?"

That point could have been argued, but I let it go. What did I know about the intricacies of the fashion world hierarchy?

"Did you tell Gia that you didn't have the money?" I asked instead.

"Yes. I said it had to stop, that I couldn't keep paying her. She'd had her fun, and it was time to move on."

"I'm guessing she didn't agree with you there," Ava said.

"No." His eyebrows drew down in a frown. "No, she said if I didn't pay her by the end of the day, everyone would know about me."

And then she'd died before she'd had the chance. I couldn't help but notice how convenient that timing was.

Costello must have realized how it looked too, as his voice took on a pleading tone. "I did not harm Gia. I'm telling you, I was nowhere near her when she died!"

"No?" Ava asked. "Because I think you've given several different versions of exactly where you were when she died."

Costello frowned and shook his head, as if unconsciously willing Ava to just stop talking. "I-I don't know what you mean."

Ava shifted forward in her seat. "I mean that after the fashion show, you clearly were not doing some private *celebrating* with Fabio, now, were you?"

"No." He paused, looking distinctly nervous again. "I wasn't with Fabio. But everything else I told you is true."

"Which time?" I asked, giving him a look.

"I-I went backstage for a moment, and then I...I went to meet up with someone. At the pool cabanas. For a private celebration."

The meaning of his words sank in. "You mean you were with a *woman*?"

Costello's eyes went from me to Ava. "Please, please, please, you cannot say a thing to anyone. This would be devastating for me. And Jada... I just can't drag her name through the mud with me."

"Jada?" I couldn't help the lift of surprise in my voice. "Are you saying you and Jada were...*celebrating* together in a private cabana?"

He pursed his lips together and nodded slowly. "We've been seeing each other secretly for the last few months."

I thought back to the way Jada had spoken with such reverence about Costello. And how she'd been so hazy about giving him the alibi he'd claimed. At the time I thought she'd been protecting her job, but it turned out she'd been protecting her man.

I glanced at the fading fashion icon's dyed hair and bedazzled everything, trying to reconcile the image with Jada's exotic beauty. I was hard-pressed to see Jada's side of the attraction, but I supposed love really was blind.

"I know what you're thinking," Costello said, shaking his head.

I bit my lip. I hoped not, because I didn't want to seem unkind.

"But the age difference doesn't matter to either of us."

Oh yeah. There was that too.

"We're truly in love. It started as just a friendship, but the attraction...well, neither of us could deny it after a while. Jada...she understands me like no one ever has before. I tell you, she's an angel on earth."

"So, you really *were* in a private poolside cabana after the show?" I clarified.

Costello nodded. "Yes. I ducked backstage just long enough to see that my assistant was racking the garments. Then I went straight to the cabanas. Jada finished changing and arrived a moment later. And we were together until we heard the police sirens and found out about Gia."

Which was at least half an alibi. Though, I noted that while Jada was changing, that still left Costello alone. We only had his word he was backstage "just long enough" to check up on his assistant and not long enough to check up and *then* slip into Gia's dressing room and eliminate his biggest problem, before joining his secret lover.

And his word was pretty shaky—this was the third alibi he'd given us so far.

CHAPTER THIRTEEN

———

"So do we believe him?" Ava asked once we were back in my Jeep.

I cranked up the AC, adjusting the nearest vent to blow right on my neck. "About being straight and using Fabio as his beard?" I asked. "Yeah, I can see that."

"But what about his alibi," she asked, flipping down the visor mirror to blot the warm summer shininess from her forehead with a tissue. "Or should I say his *non* alibi?"

"You picked up on that, too, huh?" I asked.

She nodded. "It sounds like he could have easily strangled Gia while Jada was changing then met up with her at the cabana without anyone being the wiser."

"And it sounds like he had plenty of reason to want Gia dead too," I mused, wondering how Jada had felt in all this— being kept a secret in Costello's life, having to hide their relationship. And all the while having to work in Gia's shadow. "But then, why would Costello steal the emerald?" I added.

Ava pulled a tube of lip gloss from her purse, reapplying in the mirror. "Well, he did say Gia had been bleeding him dry. Maybe he needed the cash?"

I nodded, giving my own reflection a once-over in the rearview. "I suppose it's possible," I agreed, swiping at a little eyeliner that had migrated in the heat. "But it would have had to have been a spur of the moment thing. I mean, it seems unlikely to me that he knew about Gia's theft scheme ahead of time. If he had, then *he* would have something to hold over *her* head."

"That's a good point," Ava conceded, capping her lip gloss and sitting back in her seat to soak up more of the AC's cool relief. "I doubt he would have paid up if he'd had something that good on her."

"If any designer had figured out what Gia was up to, it feels like Daisy Dot would have been the one in the better position."

"You mean because of her ruby earrings?"

I nodded. "We know Gia was substituting a fake emerald made of glass for the real one. The way that the rubies disappeared and reappeared, it's safe to assume she did the same thing there."

"So you think maybe Daisy Dot eventually realized she had red glass earrings and not ruby earrings?"

"I do. I mean, maybe it wasn't right away. Maybe it took a little while, but when she did, she put it together that Gia had been wearing them. Gia had her private dressing room…the most likely culprit was Gia."

"So we're back to Daisy Dot killing her and taking the emerald out of revenge?"

"Or some sort of reparation. Maybe she confronted Gia in her dressing room about the rubies, they fought, things got out of hand, and Daisy killed her. Then maybe she took the emerald as a way to recoup her losses on the rubies that she clearly was not getting back now."

Ava nodded. "Daisy said she saw Fabio at the reception, but it could have been later—after she'd killed Gia."

"Or before. And then she told *me* she suspected Costello stole her rubies as a way of throwing suspicion away from herself."

Ava shook her head. "It would be pretty low to steal something from *me* just to make up for what Gia stole from her."

"Sorry, hon," I said, putting a hand on her shoulder. "But we're going to get it back."

"Thanks." She sent me a smile that said she didn't fully believe that.

Honestly, it was feeling less and less like a reality as time went on, but I had to hope. At least for her sake.

"But Daisy was backstage after the police arrived," Ava continued. "Which means they must have searched her for the emerald before she left."

I frowned. "Right. Costello was there too. I remember seeing officers take statements from him and Jada."

"But you know who wasn't there after the police arrived?"

I turned to face her. "Who?"

"Hughie Smart."

I nodded. "I noticed that too. Okay, so maybe it was Hughie after all, trying to save face and cover up the fact that his model was stealing from the jobs he booked her on."

"Maybe Costello was right about the call he overheard," Ava continued. "Maybe Gia was making so much with her *side business* that she called Hughie and fired him. Figuring out what she was up to, Hughie showed up at the Links, confronted her, things got out of hand, and she ended up dead."

I could see it all happening that way. "But in that case, why take the emerald?"

Ava seemed to think about that a beat. "Maybe a misdirect, like we originally thought. Send the police looking at burglary gone wrong rather than into Gia's personal affairs, where they'd find out what she'd been up to?" She paused. "Then again, I guess that could go for any of our suspects, huh?"

It could. And if that had been the killer's intention, it had worked like a charm.

"You know," I said, thinking out loud, "in all of these scenarios, it seems like the killer would want some way to get rid of the emerald."

Ava's face took on a slightly pained look.

"Sorry," I said again.

"No, it's okay. You're right. I mean, the longer they hold on to it, the better chance someone might find it on them and they'd be implicated in the murder, right?"

I nodded. "Even if monetary gain was any part of the motive, the killer would still want somewhere to unload it fast."

"Like a pawnshop maybe?" Ava asked, perking up in her seat.

I nodded. "Right." I paused. "Only, with the notoriety of the 'murder necklace'—"

Ava's face pinched again.

"Sorry." I was starting to sound like a broken record.

"No, you're right. The press would make it harder to unload the emerald."

"They'd need somewhere that doesn't ask a lot of questions."

And one such place practically leapt to mind. I turned in my seat to face her.

"Remember that guy Joe Trask?" I asked Ava. "At the Fast Money Pawnshop?"

The way she scrunched up her nose told me she remembered him well. In addition to owning Fast Money, Trask ran a money lending business on the side that sometimes charged slightly more than the national average in interest and often took kneecaps in lieu of prompt payments. Our paths had crossed once before when we'd been looking into the bad habits of David Allen's family after his stepfather's death.

"You think someone might have tried to unload the gem on Trask?" she asked.

"Or someone like him," I added. "It's possible he could at least steer us in the direction of where someone might ditch a gem with ambiguous ownership."

She nodded as she put on her seat belt. "If anyone would know where to unload hot merchandise, it's Trask. Let's go check it out."

* * *

Forty-five minutes later we were parked in front of the Fast Money Pawnshop, located in an ill-maintained historical building near the city center of Vallejo. The neighborhood could be described as "up and coming" by an overly optimistic real estate agent, but to the rest of us the buildings looked old enough to predate central heating, the windows all had bars on them, and the only plants brave enough to grow in the area were weeds pushing through the cracked cement of the sidewalk. Fast Money was a bright spot in the otherwise bleak block—bright only due to the oversize neon sign in the barred window flashing out the notice that they were open 24 hours.

I parked my Jeep at the curb two doors down and beeped it locked, saying a little prayer to the parking gods that it—and my stereo—would still be intact when I returned. I tried to feed a couple of quarters into the parking meter, but it looked like someone had stuck bubblegum in it, so I gave up, adding a prayer that meter monitors steered as clear of this neighborhood as street sweepers apparently did.

Ava and I pushed through the glass front doors of the shop, finding the interior pretty much matched the way it looked on the outside—dark, cramped, and somewhere I did not want to be caught after dark. Smudged glass cases full of jewelry and collectible knickknacks of all kinds ran the length of the store, and the walls were covered in musical instruments, expensive-looking artwork in ornate frames, and a fuzzy velvet wall covering of Elvis. Furniture and used electronics covered the main floor in a seemingly random pattern, looking a lot like a sad swap meet.

A tall guy dressed all in black stood by the door as security, tattoos crawling menacingly up his arms, and we seemed to be in luck, as the owner himself was manning the shop today.

Joe Trask was behind a glass case full of gold chains, arranging his wares. He was short, stocky, and had a nose that was at least a size too big for his face and a protruding belly to match, straining against his cheap, olive colored suit. His bushy eyebrows hunkered down over a pair of beady eyes that turned our way as we approached.

"You here to pawn or sell?" he asked, straightening to his full less-than-impressive height and locking the jewelry case from the other side of the counter.

"Uh, actually neither," I said.

The permafrown etched on his face pulled even tighter. "Then whaddaya doin' here?"

"Uh, I don't suppose you remember us from the last time we were in here?" Ava gave him a charming smile.

His frown didn't budge. Yeah, I didn't suppose he remembered us either.

"Anyway, we're looking for an item that we believe may have been sold recently. To, uh, an establishment like yours."

"What kind of establishment would that be?" he asked, suspicion still in his dark eyes.

"One that doesn't ask a lot of questions," I told him plainly.

That earned me a small grin. "What can I say? I respect my customers' privacy."

"Exactly," Ava continued. "Uh, which is why we believe someone may have come to you looking to sell this particular item."

"Okay, what kinda item we talking 'bout?" He crossed his arms over his chest, displaying the carpet of fur that covered the back of his hands. I shuddered to think how much hair we couldn't see.

"It's an emerald," Ava said, eyes cutting to me. "About this big." She held her fingers a few inches apart. "Princess cut."

Trask's bushy eyebrows rose. "That sounds like quite the item."

"It is." Ava pulled out her phone and quickly found a picture of the gem, showing the screen to Trask. "Have you seen it come through here?"

He squinted and stared at the screen. He used his fingers to enlarge the picture and took another look. "And may I ask, what's you twos' interest in this emerald?"

Ava shot me a look, like she wasn't quite sure how much to level with the pawnbroker.

I shrugged. What could it hurt at this point?

"Actually," she told him, "it belongs to me. It was stolen."

Trask put both hands up in an innocent gesture. "Hey, I don't deal in stolen goods."

"Of course you don't," I said. Though I was pretty sure none of us believed that.

"Look, I'm not interested how it might have *accidentally* changed hands," Ava assured him. "I just want to get it back."

His gaze went from me to Ava. Finally he returned to his arms-crossed position and shrugged. "Yeah, sorry, I can't help you with that."

Ava's face fell. "Please? It's really important to me."

"Hey, I didn't say I didn't want to help you. But I ain't seen this thing." He glanced down at the phone once more. "Trust me, I'd remember a gem like that."

Ava put her phone away with a sigh.

"Maybe you could tell us where else someone might try to take a gem like this to sell it?" I suggested.

"What do I look like, a phone book?"

No. But he did look like someone who'd had a lifetime to make all manner of nefarious connections.

"Maybe you could just *ask around* for us?" I tried. "You know, see if anyone you know might have seen someone trying to sell the gem? Maybe other pawnbrokers in the area?"

Trask shot me a look. "Sure. I'll do that while we're all braiding each other's hair at the next pawnbrokers' slumber party."

I resisted the urge to roll my eyes. Mostly because I was pretty attached to my kneecaps.

"What if we offered you a finder's fee?" Ava piped up.

"Finder's fee?" Trask asked, grinning.

"Finder's fee?" I asked, frowning.

I knew Ava could barely afford the fee for the broken parking meter without that emerald, let alone a bounty to Trask.

But Ava steeled her shoulders, ignoring my frown as she turned to Trask. "Yes, a finder's fee. If you can get a lead on someone who might have been trying to sell this emerald, *and* it pans out, I'll pay you."

Trask nodded, uncrossing his arms and rubbing his hairy little hands together. "Yeah. Sure. I'd be happy to help out a coupla nice gals like yourselves." He paused. "For say, oh, I dunno. How much did you say that emerald is worth?"

"We didn't," I told him pointedly.

He shrugged. "No matter. I'm gonna say it's at least seventy-five K on the open market."

Ava's eyes cut to me again, but neither of us said anything.

"I'll take 10%."

"Seventy-five hundred dollars?" Ava choked out.

He shrugged. "Hey, how hard you want me to look?"

"Fine," Ava said through tight lips. "10%."

Trask grinned widely enough to show off a shiny gold incisor.

If we ever found the emerald, I could see any profit Ava had hoped to make off of it slipping slowly away. Then again, if we didn't find it, things could be worse—her whole store could slip away.

"What about rubies?" I asked, trying a different tactic before my friend went into debt to the loan shark herself.

"Rubies?" Trask frowned again. "You lose some rubies too?"

"Uh, no," I hedged. "Not exactly. Someone we know might have been trying to pawn a pair of rubies recently also. From a pair of earrings. They were heart shaped."

"You got a picture of those gems too?" he asked.

I shook my head. "No," I admitted. "But I have a picture of the woman who might have brought them in." I pulled out my phone, quickly bringing up Gia's social media page and flipping through to a photo of her.

He leaned forward, squinting again, and I had the distinct impression he needed glasses.

Finally he took a step back. "Sorry, ain't never seen her."

"You're sure?" I asked, feeling deflated. "Her name's Gia."

"Yeah, I'm sure. She don't look like our regular crowd."

On that point I had to agree with him. Even among a crowd that was slightly less rough around the edges than regularly frequented Fast Money, Gia's model looks would have stood out.

"But, that guy"—Trask stabbed a hairy finger at the screen—"now that guy, I know."

I pulled my phone back to see who he'd been pointing at. The photo I'd pulled up had featured Gia and Jada at some local red carpet event…standing next to their agent.

"You know Hughie Smart?" Ava asked, perking up.

He nodded. "Sure. He's in here all the time."

"Selling jewelry?" she asked.

His bushy eyebrows drew down in a frown again. "No. What's with you two broads and the jewelry?"

I shook my head. "Nothing. You said Hughie's in here a lot?" I prompted.

He nodded. "He is. We do a brisk business off that guy."

"What does he sell?"

Trask flashed us that gold tooth again. "Honey, not everyone who comes to Joe Trask got something to sell. Sometimes they just need a little loan to float them through some hard times."

"Wait—are you saying Hughie Smart borrowed money from you?" I asked. While I didn't begrudge Hugh needing a little infusion of cash, the fact that he'd gone to Trask for it instead of a legitimate bank was not a good sign that the infusion was for an aboveboard purpose.

"He most certainly did." Trask rocked back on his heels. "You surprised?"

Very. But I tried to hide it. "What did he need money for?"

"You think I do a brisk business by grilling my customers?" he asked with a cackle.

"But I'm guessing it was not a business loan for Smart Models?" Ava said.

Trask shook his head. "No, I guess you would call it more of a personal loan."

"How much of a loan are we talking?" I asked.

Trask looked from me to Ava. "You know, you two ask a lot of questions."

"Humor us," I offered.

"Sure. I got a lot of humor." He paused. "For an *11%* finder's fee."

I narrowed my eyes at him and thought a lot of words my kneecaps and I didn't dare voice out loud.

By the way Ava's nostrils flared, I could tell that her thoughts were running along the same lines as mine.

"Fine. 11," she finally said. "Now what do you know about Hughie Smart?"

Trask put his hands on the glass case, leaning in as if to tell us a secret. "I know Hughie likes to gamble. A lot. And, lucky for me, he also loses. A lot." He smiled, and I swear he looked every bit the predatory fish his profession was named after. "His loss, my gain."

"How much are we talking?" I asked.

"Forty."

"Thousand?" I clarified.

Trask nodded. "This month."

I felt my mouth gape open like some sort of cartoon character. "Just this month?"

"What can I say? The man didn't know when to fold 'em."

Or, apparently, when to walk away.

* * *

Once we were safely tucked back into my Wrangler (which I was happy to report did still have a working stereo and, bonus, all four tires upon our return), Ava blasted the AC as I pulled away from the curb and headed back toward the freeway.

"Forty thousand in one month. Can you imagine?" she asked, her hair flying on either side of her face.

I shook my head. "Honestly, I cannot. Especially if Hughie really was only making a small percentage off every job his models went on."

"Let's see…if he was making 15% off of every $1000 Gia booked…" Ava trailed off, scrunching her nose up as she did some mental math. "That's over 250 shows he'd have to book to make up those gambling losses."

"Each *month*," I added.

"I can't imagine how he thought he was going to get out of that kind of debt."

I let my eyes leave the road for a moment, glancing her way. "Unless he had a plan to steal an emerald worth at least twice that."

Ava shook her head. "So, maybe Gia's death really was about the gem after all. Maybe it really has been a robbery gone wrong all along."

I nodded. "If we're right, what do you think Hughie did with the emerald?"

Ava shrugged. "I dunno. Maybe he didn't want to take it to Trask and sold it somewhere else."

"I could see that. If I were in his shoes, I doubt I'd trust Trask to give me a fair price."

"I wouldn't trust Trask to give me the time of day," Ava said, shifting in her seat to face me. "What was I thinking, offering a finder's fee?"

"I wondered the same thing." I grinned at her. "But it seemed to work."

"I just hope it doesn't come to that." She sighed, looking out the window. "You know, if Hughie really was this hard up for cash, maybe he—"

Unfortunately, she never got to finish that thought.

Seemingly from nowhere, our entire car lurched forward, the sound of metal crunching on metal filling the interior. My body jerked toward the windshield before my seat belt tightened painfully across my chest, causing my head to whip back and forth.

"Uhn!" I heard Ava grunt beside me, her body looking sickeningly like a rag doll as she whipped forward and back again the same way.

Adrenaline surged, every muscle in my body tensing from the impact.

Ava panted beside me. "What was that?!" she managed to get out.

My eyes immediately went to the rearview mirror, where I could see a gray sedan behind us.

Close behind us.

So close he was kissing our bumper.

"There's someone back there," I said.

Though as that someone surged forward, slamming into my Jeep again with a force hard enough to jar my teeth together, that statement seemed painfully obvious.

"What the heck!" Ava said, trying to twist around to see. Though, her seat belt held her firmly, causing her to flail more than turn.

"You okay?" My heart was pounding so loud, I wasn't sure she could even hear me. I flicked my gaze upward to look in the rearview mirror again.

And watched in horror as the car surged forward again.

This time coming in for much more than a little bumper kiss.

CHAPTER FOURTEEN

———

"Hang on!" I yelled, swerving to the right to avoid being rammed a third time.

Ava did—her knuckles white as she braced herself on the dashboard.

Though, the swerve only served to deflect the hit, not avoid it altogether. We jolted to the right, the side of my head slamming painfully against the window. My Jeep fishtailed right then left, the impact of the collisions causing me to strain to hold the wheel tightly and maintain any control of the car. I eased off the accelerator, braking as we narrowly missed colliding with a minivan in the next lane over. My heart beat so hard against my ribs I feared they might break.

"Is he trying to kill us?" Ava asked, her voice rising into panic territory.

I prayed we didn't find out.

I pulled hard to the right, swerving into the emergency lane, and braked amidst a cloud of dust and screeching tires. As we came to an abrupt halt, the sedan surged past us on the left, and I caught a glimpse of the driver.

Male. Dark hair. Giants baseball cap. Chevy Chase chin.

"Stalker Guy!" I heard Ava yell from the passenger seat. She let go of the dash with her left hand, pointing to the offending car as it disappeared into traffic ahead of us. "That was Stalker Guy, right?"

I nodded, not trusting myself to form words yet. My hands were still glued to the wheel, my foot pressing the brake to the floor. We sat there a full minute, cars whizzing past us, before I felt confident enough to ease us toward the off-ramp and into the Walmart parking lot that was situated conveniently beside the freeway exit.

"He was trying to run us off the road. He was trying to kill us. Stalker Guy could have killed us!" Ava said. The adrenaline that had left me mute was causing words to flow nonstop from her mouth.

I found a spot in the parking lot under a spindly tree that at least created partial shade, and I shut off the engine. I had to concentrate on peeling my hands off the wheel, though when I did they were wet with perspiration. I rubbed my palms on my skirt.

"You think he followed us?" Ava asked, still talking. "Maybe he saw us go into the pawnshop. Maybe he followed us all the way from Sonoma. Maybe he knew we were—" She paused finally. "Hey, are you okay?"

I let out a shaky breath. "Yep."

"Liar." Ava unclicked her seat belt and leaned over to put an arm around me.

I took another deep, shuddering breath in, slowly letting it out. "Thanks. Sorry. Just…shaken."

"Ditto," she said, sitting back in her seat. "Should we check out the damage?"

I nodded, though I took a couple of deep breaths first, trying to get my heart to stop pounding before I dared to try standing on my legs that felt like jelly.

Fortunately, it looked like my bumper had taken the brunt of the damage, bearing streaks of gray paint and dents along the left side. One of my taillights had been crushed, and the license plate was hanging askew, but it looked like at the least the body of the car was free of major damage. Which was good. Hopefully the repair job would only be in the hundreds and not thousands.

"You want to call Grant?" Ava asked, standing beside me as I ran a hand over the scratched paint.

"No," I said. "But we probably should."

My hands were still trembling as I pulled my phone from my purse, and I closed my eyes, trying to calm the shakiness out of my voice as I listened to the phone ring on the other end.

Twice. Three times. Honestly, after the way we'd left things the night before, I wasn't sure he'd even pick up.

Finally, four rings in, his voice came across the line. "Hey."

Not the most enthusiastic of greetings, but at least he hadn't screened me.

"Hey," I said back. "I, uh, am in a bit of a situation." I looked to Ava, who had crouched down to inspect the underside of my Jeep.

"What's wrong?" Grant asked, the tone in his voice changing.

"We were hit. Ava and me. By a car." I licked my lips. "We're okay, but...I think I should probably file a police report or something..." I trailed off, hoping he'd fill in what that or something should be.

"Are you hurt?" I could hear rustling in the background, like he was suddenly on the move.

My hand went to the goose egg I could feel forming on the side of my head. "No," I lied. "We're fine." I looked to Ava for confirmation.

She nodded.

"Where are you?"

"In the East Bay. We're in a Walmart parking lot." I glanced at the street sign on the corner and rattled off the name to him.

"Stay there," he commanded. "I'm about half an hour out, but I'll have someone from the local PD meet you there."

I was about to protest that he didn't have to come down personally—I knew we were out of his jurisdiction, and I was sure he had more pressing matters to attend to than a fender bender.

But I didn't get the chance as he disconnected.

"What did he say?" Ava asked.

"He said he's sending someone out."

She nodded, eyes cutting to the Walmart. "How long?"

I shrugged.

"Think I have enough to time run in there and go pee?" she asked. She sent me an apologetic smile. "I have to go when I'm nervous."

Being almost run off the road was enough to make me nervous too, so I nodded my understanding. "Go. I'll wait here."

I watched her jog off in her heels, then sat back down in my Jeep to wait for the cavalry. It wasn't long before a black and white police car pulled in next to us and a young, clean cut officer approached. By the time Ava came back, I'd given him pretty much all the details I could—which, sadly, was not a whole lot.

The car had been a gray sedan, though neither Ava nor I had noted the make or model. I hadn't had to time to read the license plate number. And as far as the driver went, our description wasn't stellar—tall, dark hair, male. Likes hats and sunglasses. Which could apply to half the male population of the Bay Area, where gray sedans were not an anomaly either.

I could tell the officer had much the same thoughts on our description, as he didn't sound too hopeful about finding whoever had rammed us. In fact, if I had to guess, he wasn't even 100% believing our story that the ramming had been intentional.

He was just taking down my insurance information when Grant's black SUV pulled into the parking lot behind us.

As soon as he got out of his car, he immediately stalked toward me, eyes going to the knot at my temple. "You called EMTs?" he asked the officer.

Officer Clean Cut shook his head. "They said they were fine."

"Well, they're clearly not," Grant barked back.

"*They* can hear you, you know," I said.

Grant shot me a look but continued addressing the officer. "Get medical personnel out here."

"Yes, sir," the officer said, ducking his head as he quickly walked back to his black and white.

"That's not necessary," I protested.

He ignored me, taking a step closer, his gaze roving the rest of me as if doing his own visual medical assessment. "You hurt anywhere else?"

"No. And this is just a little bump."

"Little?" He shook his head, his hand going to the spot at my left temple and ever so gently brushing my hair away.

At the unexpectedly tender gesture, I felt tears back up in my throat. Between the car chase, the narrow escape, the pain in my head, and Grant's soft touch, it was hard to keep it all together. A girl can only be so strong. "It only hurts a little."

He sucked in a breath, tearing his eyes from the injury to meet mine. "What happened?"

"Someone hit my car."

"Someone?" he asked. I could tell he knew there was clearly more to the story than that.

"I'm pretty sure it was Stalker Guy."

He frowned. "You mean the person you thought was following Gia?"

I nodded. "He was driving a gray sedan. I gave the description to the officer." I gestured to the guy, who had Ava corralled near the black and white, taking her info down on a tablet.

Grant pulled in a deep breath. "Okay, let's start at the beginning. What were you doing in the East Bay in the first place?"

I was afraid he'd ask that. "Uh...shopping?" Kinda. I mean, we had been to a shop.

"Shopping." His eyes cut to the Walmart behind me. "Really?"

"Really. Ish."

He tilted his head to the side and narrowed his eyes. "Emmy." The one word carried with it all sorts of threats.

Threats that, in my current state of heightened emotion, I was useless against. "Fine! We were at Joe Trask's pawnshop looking for the emerald."

If Grant's eyes narrowed any further he wouldn't be able to see out of them. "Tell me everything." Not a suggestion but a command. And considering he carried a gun, one I complied with.

I broke down and told him everything, from Gia being a jewel thief, to our theory about the killer trying to unload the gem, to being run off the road. I might have slightly skimmed over the part where I'd broken into his crime scene and found the fake emerald, but I figured that little bit didn't do either of us any good. Least of all me, being pinned beneath Grant's Cop Face glare as I finished with telling him how we'd narrowly escaped Stalker Guy by pulling into the Walmart parking lot.

"And then I called you," I finished lamely, giving him a small smile.

One he did not return. Instead he stared at me a beat, his expression never changing. Though the gold flecks in his eyes were dancing in an angry frenzy that warned this was just the calm before the storm.

"If you think about it, it's really kind of funny," I said, trying to defuse the bomb before it went off.

"Funny." Monotone, no expression, no hint of humor.

"You know, everyone's thinking this was a robbery gone wrong. When it turns out the victim was the robber, right?"

Only he wasn't laughing. He sucked in another big breath, as if fortifying his lungs for the lecture to come.

"And you thought it was a good idea to ask a known money lender if he had made any illegal transactions involving stolen goods?"

Well, when he put it that way...

"Trask hasn't seen the emerald," I told him. "No illegal transactions."

"So he says."

"I'm inclined to believe him."

"Because?"

"Well, because if he had, he'd be getting the finder's fee."

"Finder's fee?"

I shook my head. "Not important. Look, what's important is that you need to find this Stalker Guy."

"Oh trust me. I will." The menace in his voice suddenly had me worried about what he'd do when he did find him.

"He's got to be involved in Gia's death somehow," I continued. "I mean, why else would he try to run us off the road?"

"Maybe he's not a fan of nosey blondes."

My turn to narrow my eyes. "Ha. Ha. Very Funny."

"No, Emmy, nothing about this is funny," he said, his voice rising in both volume and intensity. "You could have been seriously injured. Or worse."

I shuddered at the thought of "or worse."

He took a step forward.

I tried to take one back.

Unfortunately, I had nowhere to go and came up against the side of my Jeep. I steeled myself as he moved in closer. So close I could smell the mingling scents of his subtly woodsy aftershave and the leather of his gun holster.

He reached a hand out and surprised me again by gently tucking a strand of hair behind my ear. "I can't have anything happen to you," he said softly.

Those tears jumped up into my throat again, and I blinked hard trying to keep them in check.

"Just promise me you'll be more careful." His voice was low, concern having replaced the former anger in his eyes.

I found myself nodding. What else could I do? Another second of that, and he'd turn me into an emotional puddle of goo. As it was, my heart felt like it was swelling so big that it might burst out of my pink cami any second.

He opened his mouth and seemed like he was going to say more, when the sound of an ambulance cut in on our scene, killing the moment.

After the EMTs had looked over both Ava and me—both of us having sustained minor cuts and mild whiplash but nothing serious enough that it required a trip to the ER—and Officer Clean Cut had taken all our personal info down, we were cleared to go home. Grant said the first thing he'd be doing when he got back to Sonoma was looking for our gray sedan, which gave me a little hope that at least he'd taken our Stalker Guy theory seriously. He offered to give us a ride home, but I didn't want to abandon my Jeep in its current state. Even though as he drove away and I forced myself back behind the wheel, I had to tamp down nerves at getting back on the freeway.

I drove slowly, hugging the right lane the entire ride back to Wine Country, and it was midafternoon by the time I finally pulled up to Oak Valley, the old growth trees lining the drive greeting me with their gentle swaying in the breeze. Warm sunlight filtered through their leaves, casting beams of light across the winding drive, and the comforting scent of ripening grapes filled the air as I parked next to Ava's GTO.

My limbs were trembling with post adrenaline fatigue as I got out and stretched.

"Ohmigod, everything hurts," Ava said, mirroring my thoughts. I looked over to see her rubbing the back of her neck.

"Maybe we should have gone to the ER after all," I said, second guessing myself as the soreness set in.

Ava shook her head. "I'm sure it's nothing a heating pad and a couple painkillers can't fix."

"Or a glass of wine," I added.

Ava grinned. "Is that an offer?"

"You know my cellar is always open to you."

She glanced at the winery, then over to her car. "I feel like I should at least check in on the shop," she said, hesitating. "You know, make sure there's not a line of true crime enthusiasts outside the door."

I nodded my understanding. "Tell you what—go check in on Silver Girl, then come back for dinner. We can order in, and I'll open a bottle of our 2003 Reserve Petite Sirah."

Ava's eyebrows went up into her hairline. "Now that's an offer I can't refuse." She gave me a quick hug before hopping into her GTO and heading back to town.

CHAPTER FIFTEEN

I allowed myself a slow walk into the winery, my legs feeling like I'd run a marathon that day. My destination was a long hot bath followed by a large late lunch of comfort food.

But both indulgences were put on hold as I passed the tasting room and saw two familiar occupants at the bar.

David Allen was sipping a glass of Pinot Noir, a charming smile on his features as he casually brushed his too long hair from his eyes. The recipient of his charms had her back to me, but even from that angle I recognized the long, elegant neck of Jada Devereux.

I paused only long enough to set my purse down behind the bar before approaching the pair.

David was first to look up, his smile breaking into a wide grin as he spotted me. "Well, there's our Emmy now," he said, gesturing toward me with his half-full glass.

Jada pivoted on her wooden barstool to face me.

"David." I nodded his way. "Jada—nice to see you again."

"We were just talking about you," David offered.

"Oh?" I gave him a questioning look.

"Your uh, bar manager said were out." She gestured toward Jean Luc, whose mustache twitched at the "bar manager" moniker. Luckily he was practiced enough at dealing with customers that he covered it quickly and moved on to a couple with empty glasses.

"Yes, I just got back. I was, uh, running some errands," I hedged, covering the lump on the side of my head with my hair. "I hope you're enjoying our Pinot Noir."

"I found Jada, here, on your back terrace, taking in the view. I gave her the full winery tour then offered to buy her a drink." David gave her a wink. "It's not every day I run into a model."

Was he flirting with her? I wasn't sure why my stomach clenched at the thought, but I was pretty sure it had more to do with the fact I'd skipped lunch and not that I cared who David flirted with. Because I didn't. Not even if the recipient of such flirting looked like she might even be enjoying it.

"And did you?" I asked David, clearing those thoughts from my head. "*Buy* her a drink?"

David grinned, waving off the semantics. "I know you wouldn't dream of taking money from friends."

"Gee, with friends like you, who needs customers," I mumbled.

"What was that?" David asked.

"Nothing. What are you doing here, again, David?"

"Thought I'd pop in and see how everything went last night with Grant." He gave me a meaningful look, and I knew he meant about the fake emerald confession I'd meant to make and not the tenuous hold I currently had on our relationship status.

"Fine. Peachy. Great."

David cocked his head to the side, like he knew there was a lot more to that story, but thankfully he dropped it, sipping his red wine.

"I hope I didn't come at a bad time," Jada said, her gaze going from me to David. "But I, uh, wanted to apologize for earlier."

"Apologize?" I asked, turning my full attention to her.

"For lying to you." She set her glass down on the bar before clasping both hands in her lap. "Carl called me. He said you were at his studio this morning."

"I was," I said, nodding.

"He said you know."

"Know what?" David asked, clearly not enjoying being left out of the loop.

Jada cleared her throat, eyes flitting to David. My guess was she'd not envisioned an audience for this particular apology. "About our relationship. Mine and Carl's." Jada turned back to address me. "I'm sorry I couldn't say anything before, but Carl had to keep things quiet."

"Yes, he mentioned that," I said.

"You and Carl Costello?" David asked. "Really?" He looked like he was waiting for the punch line of a joke. "*You two are an item?*"

Jada nodded. "You have no idea how hard it's been hiding this."

"How long have you been seeing him?" I asked, leaning an elbow on the bar.

"A few months," she said. "I know he can seem a little over the top sometimes, but Carl is so sweet. So devoted. He's just really the kindest man I've ever met." She paused. Her eyes imploring as they turned to mine. "Which is why you have to believe he had nothing to do with Gia's death."

That was an interesting statement, considering I hadn't mentioned believing any such thing. I wondered if Costello had primed her to come plead his case.

"Costello said he was waiting for you in a poolside cabana after the show," I said carefully. "How long was he alone before you joined him?"

Jada averted her eyes, gaze going down into her wineglass. "Not long."

But long enough.

"Did anyone else know about your relationship?" I asked. Like, say, the dead woman. Who had blackmailed Costello over it.

But that must not have been something Carl had shared with his secret lover, as Jada shook her head in the negative. "No. Of course not. Carl said we had to keep it strictly secret." She sighed. "Which has not been easy. So many times I've wanted to spend holidays with him or go out to dinner or even just hold his hand." Her eyes got a faraway look in them, and as much as she and Costello seemed like an odd couple to me, I felt for her. She seemed truly in love with him, and it couldn't be easy to play along with Fabio being the love of *his* life.

Jada shook her head, pulling herself out of her fantasy. "Look, Carl would never hurt a fly. He just doesn't have it in him. You have to believe me."

While I had the feeling the conviction behind her words was true, I wasn't quite as convinced as she was about the designer's innocence.

However, after the day I'd had, there were other people higher up on my suspect list.

"Jada, I'm curious—you didn't happen to see your agent as you were backstage changing after the Links show, did you?"

"Hughie?" A tiny little crease formed between her eyebrows. "No. Why?"

I shrugged. "Just curious."

David raised an eyebrow at me, and I could feel him mentally wondering what I'd been up to all day.

"Do you know how Smart Models is doing?" I asked, changing tactics. "I mean, financially?"

"I-I don't know," Jada stammered, clearly caught off guard by the question. "I've always been paid on time, if that's what you mean." She looked from me to David. "Why do you ask?"

"I was just wondering how stable Hughie's financial situation is," I said vaguely, trying not to tip too much of my hand.

She frowned again. "I don't know. I mean, my check for the charity show cleared," she offered, raising her eyebrows as if asking if that tidbit was helpful.

"Speaking of the charity show," David cut in, "I assume you both heard about the memorial at the Links?"

I shook my head. "No. A memorial for Gia?"

David nodded. "Not an official service or anything. But I guess the club felt they needed to do something for her. They're planning a cocktail party tomorrow night to honor her."

Jada's eyes went down to stare into her wineglass again. "That's very thoughtful," she said quietly.

"I hope you'll come as my guest," David added.

I wasn't sure if he was talking to Jada or to me, but then he added, "Ava too."

"Uh, sure," I agreed.

Jada nodded. "Carl mentioned going."

Again David had a look on his face like he was having a hard time wrapping his head around Jada and Costello as a couple, but he quickly covered it. "Well, then, I'll look forward to seeing you both there."

"Uh, if you'll excuse me, I should be getting back to the City," Jada said, her gaze still downcast. Not that I blamed her. I was sure the death of her friend was weighing as heavily on her as the possibility of Costello's secret slipping out.

"Let me walk you out," David offered, downing the last of his wine and slipping off his barstool. He gave me a wink before putting an arm around Jada and steering her toward the front doors.

I had to hand it to David—he didn't give up easily. Then again, if I had to pit David's Bad Boy charm against Costello's artistic flamboyance, I'd bet on David every time.

I paused, watching the couple slip outside.

Bad Boy charm? Since when had I ever thought David Allen charming?

I shook my head. Must be posttraumatic stress from the car wreck.

As a surefire remedy, I made a detour to the kitchen to grab a pint of Ben & Jerry's before making my way to my cottage for that long hot bath.

Though, as soon as I got there, I realized the bathtub was all the way upstairs and the TV was right there in the living room. And since I was already several mouthfuls into my Cherry Garcia, I plunked onto the sofa and grabbed the remote, putting a hot bath on the back burner. I cued up *While You Were Sleeping* and let the nineties rom-com take me away to a place of meet-cutes, implausible misunderstandings, and inevitable happy endings.

After half a pint and a dozen adorable smiles from Bill Pullman, I could feel the stress of the day starting to ease. I contemplated adding a glass of wine to the mix, but that would require getting up. And my kitchen was at least ten steps away. So, I contemplated it for a while longer while I finished off my Cherry Garcia instead. By the time the movie and my ice cream were done, I had enough fortification to pour myself a small glass of Pinot Grigio and drag myself upstairs for that long awaited bath.

After a good long soak, I threw on a pair of black yoga pants and an oversize T-shirt with a picture of Minnie Mouse on it. I left my hair to air-dry and slipped a pair of flip-flops on before venturing outside and down the pathway to the cellar to grab the promised bottle of Petite Sirah for Ava.

My grandmother and namesake, Emmeline, had long ago dubbed our wine cellar The Cave. As a child, I'd had a fear-fascination relationship with The Cave, sometimes enjoying the cool hideaway on hot summer days where I could be alone with my dolls or books—or later journals filled with teenage angst. But at other times its deep, dark depths had been fuel for my childhood imagination, filling it with monsters, dragons, and all manner of creepy crawly things.

While age had faded those visions of monsters and dragons, I knew the creepy crawlies were real. Add to that mix the fact that not only had David Allen's stepfather died in The Cave, but also on a separate occasion I'd been tied up and threatened by a killer, and as an adult I still had mixed feelings about the place.

I flipped on the lights, quickly padding through the welcomed cooler temperatures until I found the rack that held my quarry. I didn't linger, grabbing a bottle and locking the doors behind me before taking the wine to the back terrace where the setting sun and cool breeze were perfect for a dinner al fresco.

An hour later, Ava had arrived, we'd ordered delivery from one of our favorite Mexican restaurants, and we'd just settled at the large tiled table on the patio to dig in.

I poured Ava a glass of our vintage Sirah and couldn't help watching with a lift of pride as she rolled the first sip around on her tongue, smiling contentedly. "Oh, that is nice."

"Mellow, right?" I asked, pouring a glass for myself.

"Very. Smooth, but it still has that hint of a deep plum flavor."

"If only every year were like this." My gaze traveled out over the fields. "Our harvest is going to be a little short this year."

"No!" Ava set her glass down, frowning. "Are you sure?"

I shrugged. "Hector said not to worry about it, but—"

"But of course you're going to worry anyway." She shot me a grin.

I couldn't help returning it. It was comforting having a friend who knew me so well—and hung out with me anyway.

"Well, if Hector says not to worry, then I don't think you should. After all, *he's* the expert."

"Are you trying to say I don't know what I'm talking about?" I teased.

She gave a look of mock innocence as she scooped a chicken enchilada smothered in Authentic Mole Sauce onto her plate. "Not me. I like free wine."

I laughed. The Sirah was definitely kicking in. Plus the glass of Pinot Grigio from earlier. Plus the ice cream sugar rush. "Well, I'll just be happy if we can make payroll and enough to cover the cost of a new fence."

"Deer breaking in again?" Ava asked. Having grown up in Wine Country, Ava knew as well as I did what a constant problem they were.

I nodded. "Set off the motion sensors the other night. Hopefully Hector can fend them off long enough to harvest and get some better barricades up before planting season."

"We could always call my dad," Ava offered. "He's got a twelve gauge."

"Ava!" I shot her a look. "I am not shooting Bambi's mom."

She laughed. "I was kidding! Come on, you know I cry at Disney movies too." She glanced at my T-shirt. "Nice outfit by the way."

I shrugged. "I'm going casual chic."

"Well, you've got the casual at any rate." She shot me another joking grin before shoving a bite of enchilada into her mouth.

We chewed in silence for a moment, each of us enjoying the mingling sweet spices and warm chilies mixed with the deep, rich chocolate flavor that created a complicated mole. Finally Ava broke it, putting down her fork and grabbing her wineglass again. "You know, I've been thinking about something that Costello said."

"Oh?" I licked dark, rich sauce off my fork. "About what?"

"About Daisy Dot." She sipped from her wineglass. "When he accused her of stealing his design for those cutouts in her dresses."

"I'm not sure we should take anything he says about Daisy too seriously. The man clearly hates her."

Ava nodded. "Right. And her him. But, I'm wondering, what if it was true?"

I dabbed at the corner of my mouth with a napkin. "What are you thinking?"

"Well, Daisy was right that someone *did* steal her rubies. It wasn't Costello, but it *was* one of his models, so she wasn't too far off the mark."

I nodded. "True."

"What if Costello was right, too?" she asked. "What if Daisy actually did get ahold of some of his early sketches and go public with the design first?"

"But how would she get the sketches?" I asked. "I mean, it's not like Costello would invite Daisy over to his workroom."

"Noooo," Ava said, drawing out the word. "But as his lead model, Gia was in there all the time."

I paused, bite of enchilada midway to my mouth. "You think Gia stole the design?"

Ava shrugged. "We've learned she'd do just about anything for money. She stole jewelry, and she blackmailed Costello."

"And she had no loyalty to Costello," I said, thinking it through as I shoved the bite into my mouth and chewed. "Actually, I totally see Gia doing it."

Ava nodded, leaning forward in her chair. "She could have easily taken photos of his sketches with her phone and then approached Daisy with them, saying she had a great way to get back at Costello. You know, for a fee."

"You think Daisy would have gone for it?" I asked.

"You tell me. How much *does* Daisy hate Costello?"

I sipped my wine, thinking back to my conversation with her. "A lot."

"There you have it." Ava shot me a triumphant grin and sat back in her seat.

"Okay, so what does this have to do with Gia's murder?" I asked.

"Well, maybe Daisy was afraid Gia would spill that her design was stolen. Maybe something about showcasing them for the public at the Links show was the catalyst. Maybe she even visited Gia in her dressing room to make sure she kept her mouth shut and Gia demanded more money."

"Now that *does* sound like the Gia we're getting to know."

"Anyway, I think it's worth not discounting Daisy as a possibility."

I thought so too. And I was about to say as much, when the sound of glass shattering ripped through the air, causing me to freeze in place.

Ava heard it too, her mouth dropping open in a surprised *O*. "What was that?" she asked, gaze whipping back and forth, scanning the fields behind us.

"I don't know." Thanks to the mellow wine haze hitting my brain, realization was slow to dawn. "But I think it came from the direction of my cottage."

CHAPTER SIXTEEN

———

On pure instinct, I stood, abandoned my meal, and ran down the pathway. I vaguely heard Ava call out my name, her chair scraping against the stone patio as she got up as well, but I didn't hit pause long enough to look back. If someone was trying to break into my home, I was not going to let them get away with it.

I wrestled with my flip-flops as I pumped my legs, my heart suddenly beating at such a frantic pace that I was sure I wouldn't need any cardio for a month. Luckily it was a short jaunt from the terrace to my cottage, and while it felt like it took a month, in reality it was probably only seconds before my small cottage came into view.

Along with the shadowed figure slipping out my front door.

My heart leapt up into my throat at the sight, my fears confirmed. Someone had been in my home. The person was dressed all in black, wearing a puffy black jacket that obscured any shape. Male, female, thin, thick, alien, human—it was anybody's guess.

"Hey!" I shouted, catching up to them.

The figure turned their head my way. Unfortunately the black ski mask covering their face prevented me from seeing any features. Not that I had more than a second to look before they sprang into action. The figure charged at me full force, plowing into me before bolting toward the tree line.

I didn't have time to react. One second I was trying to see past their mask and the next the full weight of their body was shoving me backward, slamming me onto the hard packed earth beside the pathway.

My teeth clashed together, and I bit my tongue, the force stunning me just long enough for the person in black to run past me, up into the thicket of oak trees to our left and effectively disappearing from sight by the time I got my bearings again.

"Emmy!" Ava came pounding down the pathway, her blonde hair flying behind her as a look of concern settled on her features. She stopped when she saw me, crouching down. "Are you okay?"

I nodded, tasting blood in my mouth. "I 'ink oh."

The concern on her face intensified. "You don't sound okay."

I sucked in a breath, ignoring the pain in my mouth. "I bit my tongue," I enunciated very slowly.

Ava's eyes cut to the grove of oak trees. "Well, it could have been a lot worse. Why didn't you wait for me?"

She was right. It had been foolish to run after an intruder alone. I blamed the wine and the fact that my home sometimes felt like the only connection I had left to my family. The thought of someone violating that...

"Oh, honey," Ava said.

I realized I was crying.

"They came running out of my front door." I pointed lamely, trying to sniff back the tears.

Ava helped me up, and together we walked the couple of paces to my door, still standing slightly ajar. I used the corner of my T-shirt to cover my hand, careful not to obscure any prints the intruder might have left, and pushed it open.

And had to stifle a new wave of tears at the sight that greeted me.

While I couldn't pretend that the contents of my cottage were anywhere in the priceless range, they were mine. And at current they were in shambles. Coffee table upended, lamps on the floor—one Tiffany style one shattered against the back wall, which must have been the breaking glass we'd heard. My sofa cushions were scattered to the four corners of the room, and even my poor, innocent Mr. Coffee hadn't escaped the intruder's hand, lying on the kitchen floor amidst a pile of coffee grounds. I wasn't sure what the person in black's objective had been, but chaos was the result.

"Is anything missing?" Ava asked, holding my hand tightly. For which I was eternally grateful.

I sniffed, trying to suck up some strength and focus not on the extreme sense of vulnerability washing over me, but instead on the logical task of inventorying my possessions.

"I-I don't know. It's hard to tell."

"TV is still here," she noted, gesturing to the item, which was lying on its side. "So is your laptop."

She was right. It sat on top of an antique writing desk shoved into the corner under the stairs. Apparently the intruder either hadn't seen it or had been interrupted before they'd gotten a chance to nab it.

"I don't really see anything missing," I admitted.

"Maybe we caught him before he could take anything?" Ava said hopefully. Then she added, "Was it a he?"

My breath quivered as I let out a sigh. "Honestly? I really don't know. They were wearing a mask. And baggy clothes."

Her hope morphed into a sympathetic smile. "Maybe we should call Grant."

As much as I hated calling on him to come rescue me for a second time that day, she was right. This was way out of our league.

We backtracked to the terrace, where we'd both left our phones along with our abandoned food, and Ava poured more wine with a shaky hand as I dialed Grant's number. This time he picked up on the first ring.

"You okay?"

One of these days I wanted our relationship to be in a place where he didn't feel compelled to ask me that kind of question. And, I also hoped that one day my answer wouldn't be, "No, not really."

"What's wrong?" His voice immediately took on an edge.

"I, uh, had a break-in."

"A what?"

I gave a nervous laugh. "I know, right? What are the chances of a car accident and a break-in on the same day?"

"Where are you?" he asked, not even attempting a laugh at my lame humor.

"Oak Valley."

"Are you alone?" I could hear keys jingling on the other end.

"No, Ava's here. The intruder ran away."

"Don't move. Don't touch anything. I'll be right there."

"Okay, but I don't know what the guy was after, because it seems like—" I stopped abruptly, realizing I was talking to no one. I looked up at Ava. "I think he hung up on me."

Ava shrugged. "You are kind of a handful." She sent me a grin.

Normally I loved that her brand of humor could lighten any mood, but there was a little too much truth in that statement for my comfort.

"I am, aren't I," I said, sinking back down into my wicker chair.

"Oh, honey," Ava said for the second time that night. She walked around the table and put her arms around me from behind. "And we love you that way," she said, giving me a kiss on the cheek.

"Thanks," I said. Though my voice came out more like Eeyore than my usual self.

"Don't worry. Grant will be here soon, and he'll know what to do."

I nodded, grabbing my wineglass again. Only, the smooth, aged Sirah seemed to stick in my throat with the thought that even Oak Valley wasn't safe anymore.

Both of us were feeling antsy and neither of us had an appetite anymore, so we took our glasses to the front of the winery, waiting in silence on the steps for help to arrive. It was only a few minutes before we heard the sound of Grant's car coming up the drive and the black SUV pulled into the gravel lot with a crunch of earth beneath his big tires.

Ava patted my knee and sent me a smile.

I tried to return it, but I was pretty sure it didn't reach my eyes. I wondered if it was normal to feel numb after enduring this kind of violation. Maybe by not feeling anything, it would magically disappear. It was either numbness or anger. And, honestly, I worried anger would be entirely too exhausting.

I stood as Grant approached. It only took him a second to close the distance between us, pulling me tightly into his arms. For just a moment, I let myself exist in the warmth of his body, the heat radiating from his chest melting away some of the numbness. I'm not sure how long we stood like that, but eventually I heard Ava awkwardly clear her throat beside us.

I reluctantly pulled back. "Thanks," I managed, looking up into his dark eyes.

He nodded before his gaze cut to Ava and he took a small step back from me. "Can you tell me what happened?"

I relayed the events of the evening, Ava jumping in now and then to add her perspective on them. I tried to give him as much detail as I could, which, I realized as I got to the end, was precious little.

"And you didn't see this person's face?" Grant clarified.

I shook my head. "It all happened so fast."

"No idea if they were male or female?"

"They were wearing a puffy jacket," Ava offered. "I saw that much as they took off into the trees."

"Which way did they go?" Grant asked, his eyes scanning the grounds as if the foliage could bear witness.

"Around the back," I said. "Toward the north field."

He nodded. "Probably long gone by now."

I wasn't sure if he was saying that for my benefit or if he'd been contemplating going after them.

"Once they hit the trees, it would have been hard to follow them," Ava reasoned.

Grant's gaze went to her. "And a terrible idea," he said hotly.

Ava crossed her arms over her chest. "I didn't say we *tried* to follow them—I just said it wouldn't have been easy."

"I know." Grant's features softened some. "You did the right thing calling me." He paused. "Let's go take a look," he said, leading the way to the cottage.

Ava and I followed, though the closer I got, the more I wished for another dose of that numbness to cover the anxiety I felt building in my stomach. I had to force my foot over the threshold again, gingerly stepping into the living room so as not to disturb anything.

"Anything taken that you can tell?" Grant asked.

I shook my head. "No. I mean, it's not like there's much of value to take."

"Except your peace of mind," Ava said, running a hand up and down my back.

Well, yeah, there was that.

But I hated feeling like a victim. I'd already allowed myself to feel that way long enough that day. "Do you think maybe this wasn't a robbery but a warning?" I asked.

"A warning?" Grant asked slowly.

"To back off Gia's murder," Ava said.

I nodded. Then turned to Grant. "It could have been Stalker Guy. He already tried to run us off the road today. Maybe he came back here tonight to scare me or..."

"Or let's not let our imaginations get the better of us," Grant said, shooting me a hard look. Though I could tell it wasn't me his anger was directed at.

"Any leads on the car that rammed us?" Ava asked. "Or its owner?"

Grant sighed and shook his head. "We're working on it."

"I take it that means no?" I asked, hating the hint of fear in my voice.

"No," he confirmed. "We've pulled up traffic cam footage from the area near the attack, but there are a lot of gray sedans out there. Without more to go on, it could be a while before we weed through it all."

I was pretty sure that my disappointment at that statement was clear on my face, as Grant added, "Don't worry. We'll find him." His eyes roved my cottage. "And whoever did this too."

I bit my lower lip and nodded, not trusting my voice.

"I'm going to call CSI. It's possible your intruder left something behind."

"Like fingerprints?" Ava asked.

Grant nodded before turning to me. "They'll probably want to secure the premises for the night."

Meaning my home was now a crime scene.

I felt hot tears build up behind my eyelids.

"Emmy can come stay with me tonight," Ava offered quickly, her hand at my back again.

I sent her a grateful smile.

Grant followed me as I carefully picked my way up the stairs to pack a quick overnight bag. Luckily, it seemed we'd interrupted the intruder before they'd gotten to the second floor, as my bedroom looked exactly the way I'd left it—even if the state wasn't as tidy as I might have liked it to be for Grant's eyes. I kicked my camera bag under the bed and quickly scooped the pile of clothes on my bed into the hamper. If he noticed, he was polite enough not to say anything.

I threw a few necessities into a large tote bag, and we joined Ava back downstairs.

By the time Ava and I arrived at her loft apartment above Silver Girl, I was beyond exhausted and fell gratefully onto her futon in the small living room with a pile of pillows and spare blankets she'd dug out of her linen closet.

As quickly as sleep took me, it was a tentative hold, as I tossed and turned most of the night. Not only because the futon was considerably more lumpy than my own soft bed, but also due to dreams of a gray sedan barreling toward me and an intruder in black playing a sinister game of peek-a-boo with me from behind my favorite oak tree. All overlaid with the sickening image of Gia's sightless brown eyes staring up at me, asking over and over again the simple word, "Why?"

By the time I finally awoke, I felt almost more tired than I had when I'd fallen asleep. Not to mention every muscle in my body was stiff and sore from the impact of Stalker Guy's sedan. I carefully stretched each limb, testing it out before swinging my legs over the side of the futon and padding into the kitchen in search of caffeine.

I found a Post-it stuck to the fridge, telling me that Ava was next door at the Half Calf—a cute little coffee shop whose logo featured a cow drinking a latte on the moon. I knew they made the best caramel flan lattes on the planet, which prompted me to quickly throw on a pair of jeans and a clean T-shirt and meet her there.

Though, as I pushed through the glass doors, I realized she was not alone. Ava was dressed in a gauzy floral printed jumper paired with Grecian sandals and was seated at a table near the back next to David Allen—in his usually head to toe black, broody artist uniform.

I paused, self-consciously smoothing my hair down before quickly ordering my latte and joining them.

"Hey there, sleepyhead," David said as I pulled a third chair up to their table.

"It's only nine," I told him. Maybe slightly more irritably than normal. "What dragged you out of bed before noon?"

If he heard the sarcasm in my voice, he chose to ignore it. "I was worried about you. I heard about the little break-in at the winery last night."

"You heard?" I asked, though I managed to eradicate the sarcasm this time. It was nice to be worried about. Even if that worry was coming from David's camp.

"I called him," Ava admitted.

I sipped my drink, trying not to read too much into the fact that Ava and David were on a calling-each-other-first-thing-in-the-morning basis.

"You okay?" David asked, his dark eyebrows drawing down in genuine concern.

I nodded. "Thanks. I'm fine."

He tilted his head, eyes going to my left temple. "You don't look fine. That's a nasty bruise."

My hand automatically shot up to the lump I'd sustained in the car wreck. Which apparently was bruising now too. "It looks worse than it is," I mumbled, pulling my hair forward to cover it.

"What happened last night?" he pressed. "Ava said you caught some guy coming out of your cottage?"

"Or girl," I said. "I honestly didn't get a good look at them." I quickly filled him in on the events of the previous evening, ending with Grant calling CSI and me displaced to Ava's sofa.

"I don't suppose you've heard from Grant yet?" Ava asked when I was done.

I shook my head. I'd checked my phone while standing in the latte line. No texts or voice mails. Though, considering how things had been between us lately, I wasn't totally certain I'd be his first call if he *had* found something.

"But you think it was Gia's stalker in your cottage?" David asked, looking from me to Ava. "The same one who ran you off the road yesterday too?"

I sipped from my cup. "I think it's a possibility."

"Why?" he asked. "What do you think he was after?"

I shrugged. "Need more coffee before I can answer that one."

"Well, maybe it's not so much something he was after, but something he was delivering. Like a warning," Ava said ominously.

That thought caused David's frown to deepen. I had to admit, I felt much the same way.

"I had that thought last night, too," I said. "But I don't know why he'd warn us twice. I mean, it's not like we did anything after he ran us off the road. The first warning worked."

Ava pursed her lips. "Maybe he's overly paranoid? Maybe he knows we're on to him."

"But we're not!" I protested. "I mean, yeah, maybe he was stalking Gia, but that's all we know. I don't even know the guy's name!"

"But he doesn't know that," Ava pointed out.

David sipped his coffee and sat back in his chair. "So, your theory with this guy is that he stalked Gia, killed her in some crazed fan moment, and now he's going after Emmy?"

Ava sighed deeply. "I don't know. It seems the more we find out about Gia, the less anything makes any sense." She set her paper cup down on the table in front of her. "I mean, *all* the people she worked with had a reason to want her dead, *no one* has a solid alibi, and *everyone* seems to be hiding something."

She was right. The more we found out about Gia, the less it narrowed down who could have killed her. And who had possession of the emerald now.

We all sipped in silence, contemplating that thought, until my phone trilled from my purse. I immediately pulled it out, hoping it was Grant with some news.

Only, a number I didn't recognize came up on the screen instead.

"Hello?" I asked tentatively.

"Is this Emmy Oak?"

"Yes," I hedged, expecting him to try to sell me car insurance or Canadian pharmaceuticals next.

"This is Joe Trask."

"Trask?" I said. Ava perked up in her seat, leaning closer as I put the phone on speaker.

"Yeah, listen, I made some calls to some associates on you two's behalf."

"And?" I prompted. "Has someone seen the emerald?"

"No."

I felt my heart sink. "Oh."

"But," he went on, "I did talk to a friend of mine who owns a shop in Oakland. Al."

"Did someone try to sell Al the emerald?"

"No. I told you, no emerald."

I rolled my eyes. "Okay, so what did this Al say?"

"Well, I told Al about you and your friend and the emerald. I also happened to mention you was asking about heart-shaped rubies. And Al said someone did come into the shop trying to sell a pair like that recently."

My eyes cut to Ava's. "When was this?"

"A few weeks ago. Now, I dunno if they are the same ones you was looking for, but I figured you might wanna talk to Al."

He figured right. "How can I get ahold of your friend?" I asked. I tried to contain my enthusiasm, but I'm certain I didn't succeed. There was a reason I didn't play poker.

"Al runs the Cash Exchange in Oakland. I'll text you the address."

"Thanks," I told him.

"Uh, but you know, if anything comes of this, don't forget I'm entitled to that finder's fee. Eleven percent."

David raised a silent eyebrow at Ava, but she just shrugged.

"Sure. Yep. Eleven percent," I told him, mentally crossing my fingers behind my back. As much as I hoped this lead panned out, I also hoped it didn't come to ponying up a finder's fee. Because without that emerald, Ava might be forced to make a hard decision between seventy-five hundred dollars and her kneecaps.

CHAPTER SEVENTEEN

———

An hour later, David, Ava, and I were in Ava's GTO, pulling up to a strip mall in East Oakland near Piedmont.

While Joe Trask's Fast Money looked like the type of place you didn't want to linger at after dark, the Cash Exchange was a bright, modern storefront sandwiched between a GAP and a dog groomer in a strip mall anchored by a kids' play gym. No bars on the windows, no neon signs, no tattooed thugs at the door. In the front window there was a poster of a happy family on a beach with an advertisement below saying *Finance your next family vacation.* Clearly they catered to a different type of clientele than Trask.

"Is this what they call an upscale pawnshop?" I asked as we parked and got out of the car.

"Why did you look at me when you asked that?" David asked. "I've never pawned anything in my life."

"No, people just have to pawn their valuables when they lose to *you*," Ava pointed out.

David shrugged. But he couldn't very well deny it, since that had been the very way we'd originally met Trask. "Hey, if you can't pay, don't play."

"You should have that printed on a T-shirt," I mumbled as we navigated around a couple of minivans parked near the entrance to the Cash Exchange.

"I just might," he told me with a wink.

A bell jingled as we pushed inside the shop, and soft jazz music greeted us along with cool air conditioning. In contrast to Trask's place, the interior of the store was light, open, and airy, the wares for sale arranged in artful collections in well-lit glass cases or modern shelving units along the walls. A couple of old merry-go-round horses near the far wall and several antique toys gave the place a cheery, family friendly vibe.

"Welcome to the Cash Exchange," a woman behind the glass case greeted us. Her hair was curly and graying, her smile pleasant, and her frame ample, giving off a grandmotherly vibe. She wore a navy, nautical striped dress that hugged against her middle and a small gold cross around her neck. "May I help you?"

"Hi," Ava said, stepping forward. "Uh, we're here to see someone named Al."

"Well, you're in the right place. I'm Al," the woman told us.

She must have seen my shocked expression, as she laughed. "Short for Alecia, but all of my friends call me Al. Was there something I could help you all with?"

"Uh, yes. Joe Trask sent us," I said, having a hard time picturing Granny being "friends" with the likes of Trask.

"He said you might be able to help us locate an item," Ava added, looking as skeptical as I was.

"Oh, yes, Little Joey said he was trying to track down some jewelry for a customer."

Little Joey? I had to bite my lip to keep from snickering. I'm sure Trask loved that nickname.

"I'm happy to help if I can," Al went on. "It was a pair of heart shaped rubies, right?"

Ava nodded. "Trask said someone came trying to sell them to you?"

She nodded. "Yes, a few weeks ago. We don't get a lot of loose gems like that coming in here, so it stuck with me."

"Did you buy them?" David piped up.

"No, no, actually we couldn't agree on a price. You see, without any paperwork or information on them, I felt the asking price was a little high."

I opened Gia's picture on my phone. "Is this the women who brought them in?" I asked, turning the screen so she could see it.

She pulled a pair of reading glasses from her pocket and slipped them on, leaning against the glass case to inspect the photo. "Oh my, isn't she pretty."

"She was a model," David informed her.

"*Was?*" Al looked up, eyes going from me to David. While she looked the part of the innocent little granny, I suddenly had a feeling not much got past her.

"She passed away recently," Ava said, not elaborating on the how.

"That's a shame." Al's eyes held a note of suspicion still, but she let it go, pulling her reading glasses off and shaking her head. "But I'm sorry, that's not the person who brought in the rubies. For one thing, it was a he."

"He?" I asked. I looked to Ava. That was a surprise. While both Hughie and Costello were two *he's* we'd possibly envisioned taking the emerald, I couldn't imagine why either would have had the rubies. Gia had been alive and well when they'd been stolen.

"What did he look like?" Ava asked Al. "Can you describe him?"

Al laughed and nodded. "I can do you one better." She pointed up toward the ceiling, and I noticed for the first time we were standing under a small, round black camera with a little red blinking light. "Would you like to see the security footage?"

I could have kissed her.

"Yes please," Ava said eagerly, giving Al a wide smile.

"I cued it up after Joey called me. He said you'd want to see it."

I almost could have kissed Trask too.

Al grabbed a laptop from behind a counter and opened it, clicking around a little before she found the video in question. Then she swiveled the computer so that we could see the screen and let it play.

We watched as a black and white version of the shop came into view. A time stamp in the corner was dated just over three weeks ago. From the angle of the camera, we could see the top of Al's head as she helped a couple who were looking at rings at the next case over. A beat later, a new person walked into the frame. He was wearing nondescript jeans and a dark hooded sweatshirt, but other than that, it was impossible to see much from the camera's angle. Honestly, it could have been either Costello or Hughie. Or the Unabomber.

"We can't see his face," Ava said, tilting her head to the side as if that might help.

"Sorry, this is the only angle I have of that spot," Al told her.

The bell over the door jingled as a new customer walked in, and Al excused herself to wait on them. I vaguely heard her repeating the same pleasant "May I help you?" that she'd given us, but my focus was on the man in the video, still angled away from us.

We watched as the Al on the screen moved from the couple looking at rings to the newcomer, and they exchanged a few words. There was no sound, so I had no idea what they were saying. But a moment later, he pulled something from his pocket and laid it out on the counter. Wrapped in a piece of black cloth were two beautiful heart-shaped rubies. It was hard to tell how big they were or what they'd be worth, but he and Al seemed to be discussing price—him talking animatedly with his hands as Al picked up the gems and inspected them through a jeweler's loupe.

"Look up, look up, look up," Ava chanted quietly beside me.

After a couple more minutes of watching the silent exchange play out, Al finally shrugged. Then she shook the man's hand and walked away. The man wrapped the gems back up in the cloth and shoved them into his pocket before turning to go.

"There!" Ava cried, stabbing at the screen.

I hit the space bar on Al's computer, pausing the video, as the man turned his body. For that split second, his face was pointed directly at the camera.

Only, it was not the face of Carl Costello or Hughie Smart.

The dark-haired man had a very prominent cleft in his chin.

"Ohmigod, it's Stalker Guy!" Ava said. She turned to me. "That's him, right?"

I nodded, my mind churning over this unexpected development. "But what was Gia's stalker doing with the rubies?"

"That's the guy who ran you off the road?" David asked, leaning in to get a better look at the screen.

"Yes!" Ava said. "And possibly broke into Emmy's cottage."

"And was fencing stolen rubies from Daisy Dot's show." I turned to Ava and David. "Is it possible we've had it all wrong? Gia wasn't the thief after all?"

"But you found the fake emerald in her makeup bag," David reminded me.

"Right. I did." I glanced at the man's face on the screen again.

"Did you get what you needed?" Al asked, coming back over.

"Uh, yes, thank you," I told her. "Is there any way I could get a copy of this footage?" I asked, thinking that a picture of this guy's face could help Grant in his search for a name.

"Of course," Al said, spinning her laptop back around to face her. "I'd be happy to email you a copy."

"We just need the last couple of minutes," I told her. "Where his face is visible."

She nodded, though the way her eyes flickered up toward us, I could tell she was curious what we wanted with the guy. Luckily, she was a savvy enough pawn broker not to ask. Even if her shop was "family friendly."

I quickly gave her my email address, and with a few keystrokes, she sent the last minute of the video to us.

"Now, is there anything else I can help you all with today?" she asked, closing her laptop and stowing it back behind the counter again.

"No, thank you. You've been very helpful," Ava told her.

"Well, I'm always happy to help out a friend of a friend," she said. Then added, "Especially when there's a finder's fee involved." She gave us a wink.

* * *

"Okay, so Stalker Guy has the rubies," Ava said once we were back in her car and heading toward home.

"Or he *had* them a few weeks ago," David noted.

"Right," Ava agreed. "But how did *he* get them? Did he steal them from Daisy's show, or did he steal them from Gia?"

"Well, it feels unlikely he'd be in a position to steal them from Daisy's show himself. I mean, I suppose it's possible, but Gia would have had more access," I said.

"And she had a fake emerald," David pointed out again. "Which means she at least intended to steal the emerald."

"Right," I said. "It would be too coincidental if two different people stole the rubies and emerald."

"Okay, so let's still assume it was Gia who took the rubies and replaced them with fake glass ones," Ava said as she signaled and merged lanes. "Then, how did Stalker Guy get them from Gia? You think he stole them from her?"

"Or maybe," I said, a theory forming as I spoke. "Maybe she gave them to him."

Ava's eyes left the road just long enough to glance my way. "Why would she do that?"

"This guy has shown up in the background of a lot of photos where Gia is working. Fashion shows, photo shoots, even that car show."

"Right," Ava agreed, nodding.

"Well, maybe he wasn't actually stalking her. Maybe he was there for another reason?"

"Like what?" David asked from the back seat. "You think he was on to her theft?"

"Or maybe he was *in* on the theft."

I swiveled in my seat to see David's face break into a wicked grin as the implication set in. "Her partner in crime."

I nodded. "Exactly. I mean, where did Gia get those fake glass gems to swap for the real one?"

"I never thought of that," Ava mused.

"She had to have had someone make at least passable copies. Heck, we were all fooled by the emerald."

"So you think this guy is the one who made the fakes?" Ava asked.

"It's possible. Let's say Gia takes photos of the gems at fittings. She sends them to this guy. He creates a copy made of glass and gets it to Gia to make the swap."

"Which Gia does at the fashion show or photo shoot where she's slated to wear the jewelry," David added.

"Gia makes the swap in her insisted-upon private dressing room," I continued. "Then she hands the real gems off to Stalker Guy—"

Ava gasped. "Which is why he's always hanging around! He's waiting for her to have an opportunity to hand it off!"

"—and Stalker Guy then sells the gems at pawnshops or wherever he can unload the stolen goods, and splits the profits with Gia," I finished.

"So, does this mean Stalker Guy is our killer?" Ava asked.

I sucked in a breath. "Maybe?" I paused, thinking. "But it could explain that phone call Costello overheard."

"Oh?" David asked. "Do tell. What was this?"

"He said he heard Gia firing someone over the phone." I quickly filled him in. "At the time he thought it was her agent, Hughie Smart, but Hughie denies ever calling Gia. Costello said he heard Gia tell the person on the other end that she didn't need him anymore and she could do the job on her own."

"Ohmigosh, she didn't mean a modeling job," Ava said. "She meant the thefts. She was cutting her partner out!"

David nodded, digesting that idea. "I can see where he might not like that."

"Might not like it enough to go backstage after the show and hash it out in person," I added.

"Where he kills her," Ava said, "and takes the emerald all for himself."

"But he didn't swap in the fake he made," David pointed out, playing devil's advocate.

Ava shrugged. "Maybe he didn't know where Gia had it hidden. Or maybe he didn't have time. Maybe he panicked and just fled."

I nodded. All of those scenarios seemed plausible.

"So what was this guy doing following you from Trask's?" David asked, still playing the skeptic. "And why break into your cottage?"

He had me there. The only reason I could think of was Ava's idea that it had been a warning of some sort. Maybe by us going to Trask's and asking about the emerald, he thought we were getting too close. I mean, it had eventually led us to Al and the footage of him trying to offload the rubies. Of course, he was giving us a lot more credit than we deserved if he thought we had any proof that he'd killed Gia. In fact, as we approached Sonoma County again, I realized that while we had a fantastic new theory, we had zero real evidence of anything except the fact that some guy with dark hair and Chevy Chase's chin had tried to sell a pair of rubies. We didn't even really know for sure that they were the same ones Daisy was missing. Heck, to be perfectly honest, we didn't even really know if Daisy's rubies *were* missing.

I tried not to dwell on that depressing thought as Ava pulled up to Oak Valley.

While I wasn't filled with super happy feelings at the thought of returning to the scene of my break-in, the cocktail reception honoring Gia at the Links was that evening, and no way were my T-shirt and jeans going to make the cut. Plus, I had to go home sometime. So, I put my big girl panties on as I hoisted my overnight bag out of her trunk, thanked Ava for the impromptu sleepover the night before, and bravely waved good-bye to her and David as the taillights of her GTO disappeared back down the oak lined drive.

I made my way into the main winery buildings, stopping in the tasting room first. While it was still early for the happy hour crowd, I found Eddie and Jean Luc standing at the bar, heads bent over Eddie's phone. They both looked up when I walked in, and Eddie pounced first.

"Oh, Emmy, my lovey, are you okaaaeeeee?" His voice went up like a middle schooler, that last syllable drawing out into a whine as he crushed me to him in a hug.

"Ive fie," I mumbled against his seersucker vest.

"What was that?"

I pulled back with little effort. "I said I'm fine."

"Zee policia have been 'ere all morning," Jean Luc jumped in, his mustache twitching with concern. "Zay say there was a break-in?"

I nodded, quickly filling the two of them in. I may have glossed over a few details, trying to make light of it all—though whether it was for my benefit or theirs, I'd be hard-pressed to say. However, I must not have been as successful as I'd hoped, as Eddie grabbed me in another tight squeeze when I was done.

"You could have been hurt! Maimed! Killed!" he cried into my hair.

"I'm fine," I protested again, wiggling free of his grasp. "But go easy on the maimed thing when you tell Conchita, okay?" Which I had no doubt he would. As soon as humanly possible. Not that I totally minded in that moment—the fewer people I had to retell the story to, the better. I was feeling that same vulnerability creep up on me again each time I had to relive it.

"Well, eet eez lucky you scared him away," Jean Luc said, nodding in my direction.

"Yeah. Lucky," I mumbled. I glanced at Eddie's phone. "What were you looking at when I walked in?" I asked, hoping to change the subject.

Eddie's pudgy features immediately morphed into a wide smile. "None other than Aurora Dawn's posty list."

"He means her feed." Jean Luc rolled his eyes. "You cannot be on zee internets if you cannot get zee words right!"

"List, feed, page—they're all the same." Eddie waved him off, unfazed. "Anyway, look what she posted this morning." He pushed the phone my way, pointing to the screen.

I did, seeing a picture of a woman with platinum hair and lots of eye makeup holding a glass of red wine up to the camera as she took a selfie. She'd added a hashtag to it that read: #undertheinfluenceofoakvalleyvineyards. While it was a tad long, I had to admit the phrase was kind of catchy. "That's cute." I made a mental note of the slogan, thinking it could be fun to have printed up on wine totes for the holiday buyers.

"Isn't she fab!" Eddie squealed. "Look, the post already has ten thousand likes. And she just put it up an hour ago!"

Glossing over the influencer's day drinking, I had to admit, that was a lot more eyes on our brand than I'd be able to get in one morning. "Wow. I'm impressed," I told him.

Eddie beamed. Jean Luc snorted.

I couldn't help but grin. "Maybe you should see what other influencers you can reach out to," I suggested to Eddie. "You might be on to something here."

"You got it, boss lady!" Eddie said, giving me an exaggerated salute.

Jean Luc's eyes rolled so far back in his head I feared he could see his brain. "When we start to see zee followers come to buy our wine—then we will know if zee *influence* is real."

"Oh, they'll come," Eddie said, nodding sagely. "If Aurora does it, they'll do it too."

I decided to step out of that particular debate and left them both to hash it out before the afternoon tasting crowd arrived. Instead, I pushed outside and took a couple of deep, fortifying breaths before navigating around the back of the winery to my cottage.

Like the rest of the winery buildings, the small cottage was done in a beige stucco and terra cotta roof in the Spanish revival style that was so common in the Valley. Ivy grew up one side, and morning glories clung to the chimney on the other, making it feel almost as if the building had organically sprung from the earth, having sprouted there alongside the oaks and vines. No crime scene tape covered the door. No fingerprint dust. No proverbial or literal black cloud hovering above. In fact, it looked just as charming and inviting as it always had.

At least, that's what I tried to tell my pounding heart as I reached the front door and inserted my key.

Luckily, as I stepped inside and surveyed the room, some of the pounding subsided. While I was sure Grant's CSI crew had done a thorough job of cataloging just where the thief had tossed all my belongings, someone had then put everything right back where it was supposed to be. Minus the shattered lamp, which was just a memory now.

As I walked through the room and set my tote bag down, I knew that *someone* had to have been Grant. Who else would have known which shelf that photo of my mom and me at Christmas had originally sat on or that the afghan my grandmother had crocheted belonged over the arm of my easy chair? I felt tears of gratitude prick the back of my eyelids.

Feeling relatively safe that the boogey man wasn't going to jump out at me from any closets, I sat on the sofa and texted Grant.

Thanks

A beat later, his response came in.

For?

Putting my house back together again.

You're welcome :)

I never would have pegged Grant for a smiley face kind of guy, but I felt my heart warming at the little icon.

I'm sending you something, I told him. I switched screens and found the video that Al had sent me of Stalker Guy, then forwarded it to Grant, along with a brief explanation of where we'd gotten it. Very brief.

I wasn't sure if visiting a pawnshop in a strip mall violated my promise to him to be more careful, but I didn't really want to find out.

Luckily, the short version seemed to suffice, as he sent back a one liner: *I'll see what I can find.*

Feeling like I'd done all I could on that front, I dragged myself upstairs and into a shower to get ready for Gia's memorial cocktail party.

CHAPTER EIGHTEEN

———

While I'd been to the Links on several occasions for other events, I was always impressed by the club's level of attention to detail and decadence. Since the weather was mild that evening, the sunset having chased the heat away, the cocktail party was being held on the outdoor terrace, where flowering trellises, potted plants, and twinkling fairy lights had been erected to create an elegant ambiance. Soft music played from a string quartet set apart from a large outdoor bar, manned with ample staff to make sure no guest had to wait for their glass of champagne or aged malt whiskey. The party spilled out onto the south lawn, empty of golfers at this hour. Several men in suits stood chatting in amiable groups, while women in cocktail dresses and smart pantsuits mingled among the wait staff circulating trays of canapés. The only thing to delineate this occasion as a somber gathering rather than a celebration was a life-sized poster artfully placed near the entrance with a publicity photo of Gia and the words *In Memoriam*.

I was glad I'd erred on the side of overdressed as, apparently, my idea of "over" was different than the majority of the Links ladies. While my budget wasn't nearly in the same realm, I was happy to report that my go-to little black dress still fit, even if the hips were a bit snug. I'd paired it with simple silver stud earrings and a necklace with a pearl teardrop pendant that had been my grandmother's. Since I'd kept the palate simple and classic, I'd decided to add a little pop of flair with red lipstick and pair of red stiletto heels to match. Though, I was second guessing the stiletto part as I caught a three inch heel in the limestone tiles while I scanned the crowd for familiar faces.

I spotted Ava and David right away, heads bent together over a couple glasses of white wine beneath an arched trellis covered in flowering jasmine. I caught their attention and gave a small wave, carefully picking my way toward them through the growing crowd.

"Quite a turnout," I said as I approached.

"Very," Ava agreed.

"Especially considering the majority of these people never even met Gia," David said with a cynical grin.

"Glad you made it." Ava leaned in to give me a hello hug. She'd gone with a subdued knee length, strapless dress in a pale lavender that contrasted beautifully with her flowing blonde hair, kept loose. A silver shawl hung over her shoulders, complementing the silver hoop earrings that I recognized from her shop.

"You look lovely," I told her, meaning it.

"You don't look so bad yourself," she countered with a smile.

"Is the lipstick to distract from the lump on your head?" David Allen added, eyes going to my left temple again.

I fluffed my hair in an attempt to cover it. "It's not that noticeable," I mumbled.

"It's turning purple." He took a step closer, and I could smell his expensive aftershave. I had to admit, he had cleaned up well. While he was still in jeans, he'd traded in the band T-shirt for a button-up and blazer that, instead of looking overly casual, just looked like he was too cool to try that hard. "You sure you don't need to get this checked out?"

"I'm fine," I told him, taking a step back. "It's just a bruise." And a lump. And maybe some minor whiplash.

"Well, you missed some excitement," Ava told me.

"Oh?" I asked, glad for the change of subject.

David nodded. "Hughie Smart just got into it with the manager."

I frowned. "Over what?"

"Hughie said no one had compensated him for the use of Gia's likeness." Ava gestured toward the large *In Memoriam* poster.

"You're kidding?" I had to laugh. "He wanted the club to pay to use her picture at a memorial?"

Ava nodded. "He must be very hard up."

"If Trask is to be believed, he is." My eyes scanned the crowd, looking for the agent, and found him scowling into a glass of Scotch near the musicians. He was dressed in black slacks and a blazer paired with white loafers and no socks, showing off his unnaturally orange ankles.

"I think I missed something," David said, gaze going from me to Hughie. "What's Trask's connection to Hughie Smart?"

"Hughie owes him money," I said. "A lot of it." I hesitated to say exactly how Hughie had amassed those debts, as knowing David's penchant for card sharking, he was liable to take advantage of it.

David gave me an assessing stare. "You're holding something back, Ems." He shook his head and *tsked* his tongue.

Ava laughed, the sound light and airy. "Hughie is a gambler."

I shot her a look.

"What? He was going to find out eventually," she reasoned.

"I'm assuming not only does Hughie gamble but he's not very good at it, then?" David asked.

Ava nodded. "Forty-K a month not-good-at-it."

David's eyebrows went up into his dark hair. "I may have to invite Mr. Smart over for a friendly game of five card stud."

"Don't you dare," I told him.

He gave me a shark-like grin that said he totally dared.

"Anyway," Ava cut in, "it's possible Hughie found out what Gia was up to and decided to take the emerald for himself to help alleviate his debt."

"What did you say the emerald was worth—a hundred grand?" David asked Ava.

She nodded.

"I don't know." He cocked his head to the side, assessing Hughie's spray tan, white veneers, and leather loafers. "You really think a guy like Hughie would kill for that amount of money?"

"I think it depends on how much pressure Trask was putting on him and how much he likes his kneecaps," I said.

David laughed. "Good point."

"Speaking of bodily harm," I said. "I don't suppose either of you have seen any sign of Stalker Guy–slash–Partner in Crime?"

Ava shook her head, and I felt a small lift of relief. As much as I'd like to see Grant arrest him, I wasn't sure I could take many more run-ins with him.

"But the rest of your gang's all here," David noted, nodding toward the bar where Costello stood, a champagne flute in one hand and his "boyfriend" Fabio's arm in the other.

It might have been my imagination, but as Costello leaned in close to Fabio, giggling in his ear, it seemed like he was laying the lovey-dovey act on extra thick that night.

I spotted Jada standing beside a potted palm with a couple of the other models I recognized from the hotel pool. If the frown on her perfect features was any indication, she'd noticed Costello's over-flirting as well. While her tall, slim companion talked to her, Jada's eyes seemed to be rooted on Costello. Or, more accurately, on Costello's lips as he kissed Fabio on the cheek and nuzzled closer.

"Daisy just walked in, too," Ava said, pulling my attention away from the love triangle. She gestured toward the glass doors where the woman with the multicolored hair was making a grand entrance in a form-fitting, cheetah-printed jumpsuit beneath a white feathered cape. She'd capped the outfit off with a pair of green snakeskin boots and peacock feather earrings. It looked as if she was wearing half of the Amazon rain forest.

I thought I heard a woman in a tasteful navy suit sneeze as Daisy flounced past, and I had to stifle a grin.

"Hello, Silver Girl!" Daisy said, spotting Ava and making her way toward our little group. She paused to give air kisses. "Don't you look scrumptious tonight?"

"Thank you," Ava said. "You look...lovely too." She even said it with a straight face. Points for her. "Uh, you remember Emmy?"

"Oh, yes, yes. Miss Wine & Dine." Her gaze moved to David. "And who, may I ask, is this dashing young man?"

David raised an amused eyebrow my way. "Dashing?"

"Uh, this is my...friend. David Allen," Ava said, making the introductions.

"Delighted to meet you," David said, giving an exaggerated bow and kissing Daisy Dot's hand.

She giggled, molting a few feathers onto the terrace. "Oh, a charmer, huh? I'll have to keep my eye on this one."

David grinned. If I didn't know better, I'd say he was enjoying the attention. "Can I get you ladies something to drink?" he asked, eyes going from Daisy to me.

"I'd kill for a glass of rosé." Daisy Dot paused, seeming to realize what she'd said. "Oh. Poor taste?"

David shook his head. "Simple slip of the tongue," he assured her, waving it off. "Emmy?"

"Rosé is fine for me too," I decided.

"I'll help," Ava added, taking David's arm as he turned toward the bar.

"Well, aren't they a cute couple," Daisy Dot said, watching them walk away.

"They're not a couple," I said quickly.

Maybe a little too quickly, as Daisy's pink eyebrows rose in response. "Oh?"

I shook my head. "I meant to say, they're just friends."

"Yes, well, isn't it nice to have such charming friends." The way she was still staring after David, I feared that maybe I should have let her believe he was taken.

"You know, I hadn't realized when we talked last that you and Gia knew each other so well," I said, trying to draw her attention away from the fit of David's jeans.

"Hmm?" She turned a distracted gaze on me.

"You and Gia. I didn't know you worked together so closely."

She blinked at me. "Well, the fashion community is small. We all work together."

"I heard that Gia even walked in your spring show," I said, watching for a reaction.

But if she had any, it was expertly covered. "Gia was a lovely creature, and I'm sure she'll be missed," she said flatly. "But all of this is all so morbid," she went on, gesturing around her to the not-so-grief stricken. "This dwelling on death. It's not good for one's creative psyche."

"Your look tonight is very creative," I noted, hoping that came off as a compliment.

She smiled. "Thank you. I shall never be accused of being mundane."

Of all the things I'd mentally accused her of, she was right. That was not on the list. There were other things, however...

"You know, I always wondered where designers like you get their creative inspiration," I said carefully.

"Oh, you know. Here. There. Everywhere, really," Daisy said, flapping her arms again like wings.

"I'm curious...where did your inspiration come from for the line you showed here this past weekend? Those dresses with the cutout backs?" I asked, hoping to jar a reaction out of her this time.

"Hmm?" She blinked at me. "Oh, uh, yes. Well, things like that just seem to come to me."

"Really?" I asked. "You didn't see anything or hear of anything similar that, maybe, put the idea into your head?"

"No." Daisy's eyes narrowed. "I'm not sure what you're getting at."

By the way her posture had become defensive, arms crossing over her chest in a flurry of feathers, I thought maybe she did.

"Carl Costello says *his* original designs for his fall line featured cutouts. Very similar to yours."

I could see her working out several possible answers to that in her head before she finally settled on one. "Well, *my* models were the ones wearing them down the runway, weren't they?"

"Are you saying you knew he had the idea?"

She waved her arms in a blur of cheetah spots. "I'm saying I have no idea what Costello's pea brain might have come up with. How would I even know what goes on in his stifled little studio?"

"Gia would have known," I pointed out. "She worked with him all the time. I'm sure she could have seen his early sketches."

"Yes, I'm sure she could have," Daisy Dot said, frowning.

"Did she?"

"What?"

"Did she see them and share them with you?" I paused, realizing I was flat out accusing her at this point and figured I might as well go all in. "For a fee?"

Daisy Dot paled to just one shade above a ghost. "I'm sorry, I haven't the faintest idea what you're talking about. Now, if you'll please excuse me." She maneuvered her body around mine and stalked across the terrace toward the lawn.

"Where's she going?" Ava asked, coming up behind me.

"Away from me," I mumbled, turning to find David with two glasses of pink colored wine in hand. I gratefully took one and filled them in on what Daisy Dot *hadn't* said.

"Doesn't sound like the actions of an innocent party to me," David said when I'd finished. Then he took a sip of rosé from the glass previously procured for Daisy.

"No," I agreed. "But not innocent of what—stealing fashion designs or killing Gia?"

"And stealing my emerald," Ava added, her eyes tracking Daisy as she made her way through the crowd, greeting guests.

"Well, why don't I see what kind of *dashing* charms I can work on Mizz Dot," David said. "Maybe I can flatter her into unburdening her soul a bit."

"You're not that charming," I mumbled.

"Oh, ye of little faith." He raised the glass of rosé and sent me a wink.

"Good luck," Ava told him before he made his way over to the human zoo.

"He's gonna need it," I added. "She's looking at him like he's dessert."

"David can handle himself," Ava said.

I didn't want to know how she knew that.

"Emmy?"

I turned to find Jada approaching us. She was dressed in a simple white sheath dress that might have looked plain on anyone else, but the way it fell over her elegant shoulders and slim hips made her look like a Grecian goddess.

"Jada," Ava said, stepping forward. "How are you holding up?"

She glanced past us to where Costello was still glued to Fabio's side. "As well as can be expected," she answered.

I was pretty sure Ava had been talking about the fact that we were at her friend's memorial, but I could see how deeply the display Costello was putting on was affecting her.

I leaned in, lowering my voice. "He's a little overzealous this evening, isn't he? It must be tough to watch."

She nodded. "Some days are definitely harder than others." She blinked some emotion away, tearing her gaze away from the fake couple. "Anyway, I'm glad I found you. I saw that police detective…the one you're friends with?"

"Grant?" I asked, my eyes immediately going to the glass doors. I hadn't known he'd be there, but considering it was a memorial for the victim of an ongoing investigation, I suppose it stood to reason.

She nodded. "I guess so. Anyway, I just ran into him outside. He said he was looking for you. He asked me to tell you to meet him in Gia's dressing room."

I felt my heart kick up a notch. This could be either very good or very bad. It was possible he'd found out about our breaking and entering to nab Gia's fake glass emerald and he was calling me to the scene of the crime to pry a confession out of me. Then again, it was also entirely possible he'd found something on Stalker Guy's identity that he wanted to share.

I glanced to Ava, a question in my eyes.

She shrugged. "Go. How bad can it be?"

I gave her a rueful grin. "I guess I'm about to find out."

Jada looked from Ava to me, like she was left out of some inside joke.

"Thanks for relaying the message," I told her.

"Sure." She gave me a quick smile and nod before turning and melting back into the well-dressed crowd.

"I hate to leave you alone here," I told Ava.

She shook her head, sipping her wine. "I'm fine. I'll mingle. Maybe go save David Allen from being devoured by the Cheetah-Bird-Snake."

I let out a snort before I could stifle it. "I'll be right back," I promised, setting my half empty glass of rosé down on a side table before threading my way toward the glass doors.

The din of the party was less once inside the club, though I could still hear the soft music playing and the mild chatter of voices. I passed by the lounge, which looked like it was serving as a secondary party room, a lively crowd of men in expensive suits and Italian leather shoes downing shots at the bar. Though, as I moved down the hallway and into the Grand Ballroom, all the party sounds faded, replaced only by the echoing of my own footsteps as I crossed the cavernous room.

The police tape was gone from the door to the storeroom that Gia had used, and any evidence that a horrific crime had been committed there had been whisked away by the efficient Links staff. The former dressing room's door was closed, but as I turned the handle, I realized it was not locked.

"Hello?" I said, stepping into the room. "Grant?"

It was dark, and I figured maybe I'd beaten him there. I leaned to the right to flip on the light switch, illuminating the room. It was much the same as I'd seen it before—minus Gia's personal effects. The bags and suitcase were gone, and the makeup table had been moved out. But the dusty filing cabinets still sat against the wall, along with the built-ins, and a couple of wooden chairs. I wasn't sure if it was the still silence in the air or the fact that a woman had died there, but a round of goose bumps erupted on my arms as I shifted from foot to foot, hoping Grant arrived soon.

Luckily, the sound of another pair of footsteps echoing off the polished floors of the ballroom alerted me that someone was approaching. I shook off the creepy vibe as they approached the dressing room door.

"I'm glad you're here," I started, turning toward the figure entering the doorway. "I was just starting to get a little creeped out—"

But the rest of that thought died on my lips as I saw the figure was not my favorite tall, dark, and imposing member of law enforcement, but the Grecian goddess–clad Jada.

With a shiny black gun in her hand.

Pointed right at me.

CHAPTER NINETEEN

———

Dozens of thoughts ran through my head at a rapid pace as the barrel of the gun stared back at me. Not the least of which was that I'd been a fool to jump at Jada's bait and walk blindly to an isolated, dark corner of the club. One where a woman had already died. I licked my lips, not wanting to think that the presence of a gun was about to up that body count.

"Wh-what are you doing?" I asked, hearing my voice come out shaky and confused.

Jada shook her head. "I'm so sorry it's come to this, Emmy."

That made two of us.

"Come to what?" I hesitated to ask.

Jada let out a sigh. "If you'd just left it alone, I had everything under control. Everything was going to get better with her gone."

"Her? You mean Gia?" I asked. I took a tentative step backward, trying to create some distance between the weapon and me. Sadly, in the confined space of the dressing room, there wasn't much of anywhere to go. I felt my back come up against the built-in cabinets.

"Gia." Jada said the name on a sneer. "She was poison! Ruined everyone she touched. Hurt everyone around her!"

"So you killed her?" I asked. While the fact she had me at gunpoint was a pretty good clue that I was on the right track there, I was still drawing a blank when it came to why.

"I had to," Jada said, shaking her head again. "She had to be stopped." She sucked in a breath, her nostrils flaring. "She was evil. She deserved it."

From all I'd learned about Gia over the past few days, I had to agree that she hadn't been the most innocent of people. Or scrupulous either. But I wasn't sure anyone deserved to be strangled to death.

However, I had a strict policy never to argue with people with guns. So I kept that opinion to myself.

"What happened?" I asked instead.

Jada shook her head, as if replaying the scene in her mind. "It was all my fault, really. I mean, I never should have trusted her. I should have known better, but I...I was weak." Her face lifted to meet mine, her eyes imploring, as if begging me to understand. "A person can only take so much, you know?"

No, I didn't know. In fact, I was having a hard time piecing together what she was saying. "Take so much of Gia?" I asked.

But she shook her head. "Of being cast aside. Ignored. Of him pretending I don't exist."

"Him? You mean Costello?" I guessed.

She nodded vigorously, tears forming at the corners of her eyes. "Do you have any idea how hard it is to be someone's dirty little secret? What it feels like to live that way? To be in love and have to hide it? To pretend you're happy the man of your dreams is fawning all over someone else?"

"That must be very difficult," I said, trying at sympathy. Which wasn't too hard to fake. I had, in fact, been sympathetic of Jada's plight. Of course, that was before I'd known she'd murdered her friend.

"Difficult doesn't begin to describe it," she responded. "Every time I have to watch Carl play up to that idiot Fabio, it's like a piece of my heart dies. You understand, right? I was dying inside, and I had no one to turn to!"

"Except Gia," I said, finally putting it together. "That's how she found out about your relationship. You told her?"

The tears spilled over Jada's eyelids, making wet tracks down her cheeks as she nodded. "I-I thought she was my friend. I thought I could confide in her. She pretended to care."

"Maybe she did?" I offered.

Jada sniffed loudly. "Gia only cared about one thing—Gia. She used me. Used what I told her to..." She paused as a sob escaped her.

"To blackmail Costello," I finished for her.

She pursed her lips together to stave off more sobbing and nodded. "You see, it was all my fault?"

"Did Gia tell you she was blackmailing Costello?" I asked. While I was honestly curious how it had all played out, I was also hoping to keep her talking. To distract her long enough to think of some way to get away from the gun in her hand. Which, by the way, looked about as unsteady as her emotions. I couldn't help my eyes tracking its every movement as it bobbed up and down in her hands.

"No," Jada answered. "Gia didn't tell me a thing. She had me fooled. And Carl...he didn't want to worry me. He thought he was protecting me. I didn't know anything about the money he'd been paying her until...until the day of the runway show here."

"What happened?" I asked again. I moved my hands behind me, carefully feeling along the cabinets for anything I might be able to use as a weapon. Unfortunately, no stray letter openers or handy baseball bats had been left sitting around for just such an occasion. Unless I could distract Jada long enough to open a cupboard and throw spare paper towels at her, I was out of luck.

And with her standing between me and the only door out, the walls were suddenly feeling very close, claustrophobia kicking in. Or maybe that was my gun-aphobia.

"What happened?" Jada repeated. "What happened was Gia was greedy! A heartless, greedy woman who was bleeding Carl dry!" The weapon in her hands moved precariously close to me as she waved her arms in the air.

I tried to take another step backwards, but I was out of places to go.

"Gia was demanding more money," Jada went on. "Carl broke down right before we were set to go on stage. The stress—he just couldn't take it anymore. He was so distraught that I knew something was wrong. That's when he finally told me."

"That Gia had been exploiting your friendship for her own gain."

"Exactly!" Jada said, throwing her hands up and nodding as if I finally saw her side. "Poor Carl. I could see the strain of it all crushing him. And, I couldn't stand it." She shook her head. "I couldn't stand that I'd been the cause of it!"

"Gia was blackmailing him, not you," I said softly, trying to calm her. I wasn't a big fan of the way the gun continued to wave wildly. "What she was doing was not your fault."

"But I'd given her the fuel!" Jada argued. "So, I had to fix it. I had to make her stop."

"By killing her," I said.

"I didn't plan to! I-I just went to her dressing room to talk. I thought maybe if I told her how much damage she was doing, how the financial strain was killing Carl's creativity, that she'd see reason. She'd leave us alone, and we could just be happy."

"But she didn't."

"No." Jada almost sounded sad. "No. She laughed." She lifted her eyes to meet mine again, shimmering with tears. "She laughed at me. Said I was a fool. Said she'd take every penny Carl had and he'd have me to thank for it."

That couldn't have gone over well.

"So what did you do?" I asked, even though the answer was painfully obvious at that point. But the longer I kept her talking, the better the chance someone would come looking for me.

Though, how, I wasn't sure. For all Ava knew, I was safely tucked away somewhere having a private moment with Grant—not something a good friend would interrupt. David was probably fully engrossed with Daisy Dot. And Grant...

I swallowed down a lump of emotion when I thought of Grant. He'd been right. I should have left this all to him. I should have minded my own business, kept to wine making, let Grant figure out who had killed Gia and taken Ava's emerald. He would have. I had doubts that Jada had been on his radar any more than she'd been on mine, but at least if I'd listened to him, I'd be sitting at home right now with a pint of Chunky Monkey, watching Sandra Bullock fall in love, and not facing down a highly emotional killer.

"What did I do?" Jada said, repeating my question. "I stopped her. I had to. I couldn't let her destroy Carl that way. I love him!"

"So you strangled her."

Jada nodded and began to take deep breaths. So many that I feared she might be hyperventilating. "I-I didn't plan it. You know? I just…she just had to be stopped. She was wearing that chain. It looked so strong and heavy, and I just…I just pulled it. Tightly. And didn't let go."

Until her friend was dead.

I shuddered, trying not to picture the aftermath of Jada's actions that I had been the unlucky person to find. "And the emerald?" I asked. "Why did you take it?"

Jaded blinked back a fresh round of tears. "It was just sitting there. On her vanity. I-I don't know how it got out of the pendant, but it was on her makeup table." She licked her lips. "Once I realized she was…realized what I'd done, I panicked. I wasn't sure if anyone had seen me go into her dressing room. So I grabbed the gem. I figured it would make everyone think Gia had been killed by a thief and not…not someone like me."

Which they had. At least, almost everyone. It was little comfort in that moment that Ava and I had been right—the theft had been secondary all along and Gia had been the killer's real target.

"So you took the emerald then met up with Costello at the cabanas by the pool," I said, picturing it in my mind.

She nodded. "I almost told him everything. I was shaking so badly, I was sure he'd notice."

"But he didn't?" I asked, trying to keep her talking as my eyes scanned the four corners of the room, desperately searching for some magical portal out of this situation. I could feel the moments slipping away, Jada's narrative running down. And I knew I was almost out of time before she did something with that gun.

"No, he didn't." Jada shook her head. "I said I'd just had some nerves left over from the show, and he believed it." Her eyes misted again. "I hated lying to him, but I'd already caused him so much pain. I didn't want to add more."

"That was very thoughtful of you," I lied, trying to keep her calm and delay the whole *now you know too much, and I'm going to have to kill you* scenario that I knew was coming.

Jada sniffed and nodded. "Anyway, we weren't there very long before we heard the police sirens, and I knew someone had found her." She paused, her eyes meeting mine again, this time a new emotion behind them. One that was far less imploring and much more accusatory. "I didn't know that someone was *you.*"

"Sorry?" I croaked out.

She shook her head. "And why you couldn't just leave it alone, I don't know. It had nothing to do with you!" she yelled, the sound echoing through the open door behind her and out into the cavernous ballroom.

"Except that you took my best friend's emerald," I pointed out.

"She would have gotten it back eventually," Jada said, shrugging off what appeared to be a minor detail in her mind.

"But you were backstage after the police arrived," I said. "I saw you there. And the police searched everyone before they left the fashion show. What did you do with the gem?"

Jada's face broke into a slow, wicked smile, and I suddenly glimpsed the slightly deranged murderer who had been lurking behind the role of the beautiful victim she'd been playing thus far. "So you haven't figured it out?" She let out a laugh. "I wasn't sure how long it would take you, but I guess I overestimated your intelligence."

I wasn't sure if I should be glad or insulted. Though I was having a hard time summoning up any emotion other than fear as she kept that gun trained on me.

"No," I admitted. "I didn't figure it out. How did you get the emerald out of the Links?"

She shrugged. "Easy. I gave it to the one person I knew the police would never suspect and wouldn't search." She paused, sending me a smirk as her wide, crazed eyes met mine. "You."

"Me?" I said, genuinely surprised.

Jada threw her head back and laughed again. "Clever, right? I noticed immediately the way that detective acted with you. It was clear you two were close. So, I figured you'd never be suspected of taking the gem."

"B-but I don't have it," I sputtered, my mind trying to play catch-up.

"Don't you?" Jada grinned at me again, as if she was enjoying playing this little mind game with me. "I was afraid you'd found it when you showed me those photos you took backstage. The ones with that guy you thought was stalking Gia?"

"The photos..." I still wasn't getting it.

"That you took on your camera? The same one you had backstage? In that camera bag of yours that you left unattended while you cried into the arms of your detective friend?"

"My camera bag." Mental forehead smack. "You put the emerald in my bag?"

Jada nodded. "Stuffed it in the inside pocket. I figured it would get the gem out of the building at least."

"But then what?" I asked. "I mean, like you said, the police weren't going to think *I* stole it and killed Gia. As soon as I found it, they'd have known someone put it there and that the gem wasn't the real objective."

"Sure," Jada agreed. "You're right. But I figured it would be a lot easier to retrieve the gem later from you than from a sealed crime scene."

Good point. I knew firsthand it took some skills to break into a locked crime scene.

"Wait—retrieve it. You're the one who broke into my cottage last night!"

Jada nodded. "Took me some time to find it. The first night I visited your winery, I realized I had no idea where to look."

"The first night..." I thought back to the night after Gia had been found. "The motion detectors," I said, putting it together. "Hector said something set them off. He thought it was deer, but it was you."

Jada shrugged. "I don't know who Hector is, but yeah, I guess I did set something off. Lights flooded the place. I had to leave before I could even really look around."

"But you came back," I said, pieces falling into place. "David said he found you wandering around on my terrace the next day."

She laughed. "That *was* lucky I ran into him, wasn't it? After the sensor fiasco, I figured I'd come back during the day and play lost tourist to scope out the building for where you might have that bag of yours tucked away. Of course, after running into David, he graciously gave me a full tour of the winery, including pointing out where your private cottage was."

I resisted the urge to curse David's name. Clearly he hadn't known he was mapping out the road to my front door for a killer. To be honest, nothing about Jada had felt menacing to me at the time either. Proving just how deceiving her good looks had been.

"So you came back that night and broke into my cottage to get the emerald."

Jada nodded. "Only, I broke that ugly lamp—"

"That was my mother's!" I protested.

"—and I heard you come running up, so I had to get out quickly."

"And you shoved me on your way out." I shook my head. "I thought you were Stalker Guy." So had Ava. So did Grant, who was currently trying to run down his identity, going full tilt in the wrong direction. The direction I'd led him in.

Which meant I was totally on my own here. Just me, Jada, and that nasty little gun of hers.

I tamped down a whimper of fear as she took a step closer to me.

"So the emerald," I said, desperate to keep her talking. "Where is it now?"

Jada shrugged. "Still in your camera bag, I guess."

I could almost laugh at the irony. Ava and I had been running all over Northern California trying to find that emerald, and it had been tucked away in my own home the entire time.

"At least, that's where it is for now," she added.

"For now?" I almost hesitated to ask what her plans were. Because as long as the gun was pointed at my head, I had a pretty good idea what her first step was.

"You're going to tell me exactly where you put that stupid camera bag." She took a step closer to me.

"I am?" I squeaked out.

"Yes." She nodded slowly. "That emerald is the key to keeping the police looking for a thief. I need it."

"They'll find it sooner or later, you know," I said. "Too many people are looking for it."

"Oh, I know they will," she said, her creepy smile growing again. "And they're going to find it right where I put it."

"Which is?" I asked, feeling distinctly like I was on borrowed time. My eyes flitted around the room, still seeing the same useless file cabinets, dusty corners, and blocked escape route.

"They're going to find the emerald on Hughie Smart."

I blinked at her. "Hughie?"

"Hey, it was your idea," she said. "Hughie is in financial trouble, right? He was at the show that day. Carl even told me he overheard Gia firing Hughie on the phone."

I figured now was not the time to point out how wrong Carl had been about who had been on the other end of that phone call.

"It would have been the easiest thing in the world for Hughie to slip into Gia's dressing room, kill her, and take the emerald. Sounds like he needs the money. At least, that was how it sounded at your winery when you asked me all about his financial situation."

"So you're going to frame him?"

Jada sighed. "It's my only choice. Look, I can't have the police looking my way. And you so nicely laid the groundwork for Hughie being guilty."

I had done that, hadn't I?

"And," Jada went on. "I'm sure the fact that *you* exposed his debts was the catalyst for Hughie killing you."

I felt a cold fear wash over my body. "Killing me?" I repeated, my voice little more than a whisper. While I wasn't totally naïve about the reason she'd been pointing that gun at me, hearing her say the words out loud was terrifying.

Jada nodded, taking another step closer until we were practically touching. "I'm sorry, Emmy, but you were getting too close. Asking too many questions. So Hughie had to kill you."

I swallowed hard. I couldn't seem to tear my eyes from the gun barrel, just inches from me. This was it—there was nowhere left for me to hide, nowhere to go. I was pinned, and the scenario she was weaving was all too plausible. Grant knew we'd been looking at Hughie. Ava had been with me when Hughie had gotten defensive and angry. Even Trask could testify to the fact that Ava and I had been asking questions about Hughie Smart.

I felt tears prick the back of my eyelids as I realized just how neatly I'd dug my own grave. "You don't have to do this," I pleaded with her. "It doesn't have to end this way."

"I'm so sorry, Emmy," Jada said, and for a brief moment something human flickered behind her eyes, as if some part of her truly *was* sorry.

But just as quickly it was gone, as she added, "But you need to die now."

I felt time stop. The room stilled. All sound blurred into one indistinguishable hum. My heart even seemed to stop beating as Jada lifted the gun, aiming at my head, tensing her jaw, her dark, soulless eyes staring right at me.

"Good-bye, Emmy," she whispered.

Her last word echoed in my head. "Emmy. Emmy. Emmy."

Only I realized it was not in my head.

Someone was calling my name.

Jada heard it too, as she paused just long enough to turn her gaze toward the doorway...

Before something metallic sliced through the air and collided with her head.

Jada made a sort of grunting sound before her eyes rolled back, revealing only whites, and she crumpled into a pile, the gun clattering unceremoniously to the wood floor.

It took me a second before I dared to breathe.

When I finally did, I looked up to find the most beautiful sight I had ever seen.

Ava stood in the doorway of the dressing room with a golf club in her hand, looking like she'd just landed the hole in one of her life.

CHAPTER TWENTY

———

I collapsed into Ava's arms, the two of us dissolving into a mess of tears, *I love you*s, and incoherent babbling as we both at once tried to fill each other in on the events of the last hour.

Ava said that after I'd left the cocktail party, she'd had the thought that it seemed weird Grant would send Jada to come get me instead of just calling or texting me himself. In fact, it felt weirder and weirder as more time passed and I didn't return to the party. She'd finally decided to just have a peek in on Grant and me, even if only to reassure herself that he wasn't hauling me off to jail for breaking into the dressing room when it had been a sealed crime scene. She'd arrived just in time to hear the tail end of Jada's confessions.

Luckily, there was a lost-and-found closet right next to the Grand Ballroom, where Ava had found a stray nine iron and come to surprise Jada with it just in the nick of time. Something I would forever be grateful to her for. Which I'd told her over and over in blubbering, teary hugs that only ceased when we'd heard Jada moan from the floor.

Finally some of the shock had started to wear off, and we'd had the mental wherewithal to get help. Ava had grabbed the gun from the floor and kept it trained on Jada's inert form while I'd dialed 9-1-1. It hadn't taken long before the entire club had been swarming with police officers and emergency personnel.

Ava and I had watched EMTs wheel an unconscious Jada away before officers corralled us to separate corners of the ballroom to give our statements. At some point in the evening, David Allen had even braved his innate fear of authority and joined us, sitting with his arm around Ava as she gave her statement to one officer after another of apparently escalating ranks.

I did much the same, probably mostly incoherently to the first woman who asked me what happened. Though, by the time I was with the third person up the food chain, the adrenaline was ebbing enough that I was beginning to make actual sense.

I'd just about gotten through one coherent narrative of all that Jada had confessed to me, when I heard a deep voice behind me.

"I can take it from here, Officer."

I turned to find Grant striding across the room, his jaw tense, eyebrows drawn down over a pair of dark eyes that gave zero emotion away.

The officer nodded, clearly sensing he was outranked, and quickly scuttled away to join the other guys in blue uniforms a few paces away.

I cleared my throat, trying not to do a repeat of the blubbering mess thing at the comforting sight of him.

"Hey," he said once we were alone. He sat down on the wooden chair beside mine so he was at my eye level. "You okay?"

I swallowed down tears. "Fabulous."

The corner of his mouth hitched up. "Good." His eyes moved to the growing bruise at my temple, and his right hand followed a beat later, fingers gently brushing my hair away. "You're one tough cookie," he said.

That was it. I lost it. The tears burst out of me on a messy sob, and once they were free, I couldn't hope to hold them back.

"I-I-I'm not a tough c-c-cookie. I'm a m-m-marshmallow!" I cried.

Grant chuckled, though his eyes were full of more sympathy than humor. "Oh, Emmy." His arms were suddenly around me, shielding me from everything the big bad world might have thrown at me over the last twenty-four hours. They were strong, warm, and I never wanted to leave. I burrowed deep into his chest, creating wet spots on his shirt as I bawled like a baby.

I had no idea how much time passed before I ran out of tears, but when I did, I finally pulled back and managed to get ahold of myself.

"You really okay now?" he asked, his thumb wiping wetness from my cheek in an intimate gesture that made me feel like we were the only two people in the world and not sitting smack in the middle of a crowded crime scene. Again.

I nodded. "Sorta."

"Can you tell me what happened?" he asked softly, taking one of my hands in his.

I took a deep breath. "I think so." And I did. This time spilling everything, including all of my not-so-shining moments that I'd previously glossed over. I told him about the glass emerald, the fact that the real one was apparently in my camera bag, and that we might very well owe not one but two pawnbrokers money now. By the time I was done, the little gold flecks in his eyes were moving in a frenzy, but his expression was still not giving anything away. I wasn't sure if he was about to arrest me or kiss me.

But if I had to guess, I'd lean more toward handcuffs.

"I'm sorry," I finished, swiping at those pesky tears again. "I'm so sorry I didn't just tell you everything sooner."

He nodded slowly. "You should have," he said, his voice thick with unexpressed emotion.

"I'm sorry," I repeated again, hoping that if I said it enough times, he might believe it.

He gave my hand, still cocooned in his, a squeeze. "I know," he said softly.

I opened my mouth to expound on my apology, but he continued right over me.

"And I know I don't always make it the easiest for you to come to me with these things."

I shut my mouth with a click. Well, that was unexpected.

He gave me a sheepish grin. "What I'm trying to say is I'm sorry for blowing up at you the other night. And after you baked me pie, too."

I couldn't help an answering smile. "Well, Conchita baked it."

He shrugged. "Okay, then I don't feel quite so bad."

I laughed in earnest. "But I'm sorry I blew up too," I added. "I guess we were both kind of tense."

He nodded and sighed deeply, his gaze going around the room. "You tend to bring out the tense side in me."

I wasn't sure if that was an insult or a compliment.

Before I could figure it out, he leaned forward, cupping my chin in his hands. "You scared the crap out of me, Oak," he said, rubbing his thumb over my lower lip.

I shivered, the sensation suddenly taking all of my focus. I watched his mouth move closer to me, slowly, until it was softly brushing against mine. His breath was warm and smelled of coffee, his touch tender and creating a tingle that started at my lips and quickly spread throughout my body.

It was over much too quickly, but even as he pulled away, my head felt light and giddy.

I heard him draw in a deep breath, as if trying to pull himself back to reality too. His eyes went to the dozen or more officers and EMTs still mingling in the ballroom.

"It looks like they're going to be a while here, documenting the scene of the assault."

I willed myself to come back down to earth at the word *assault*. "Is Ava going to be okay?" I asked, glancing toward my best friend. "Legally speaking. I mean, it's clear she acted in self-defense, right?"

Grant nodded. "We won't be charging her with anything. In fact, Officer Green said as soon he's finished with her statement, she can go home."

I nodded. "Good. She saved my life, you know?"

His gaze moved to my hand still ensconced in his, and I could see his shoulders tense. "I'm glad she was here," he said, his voice thick with emotion again.

"That makes two of us," I mumbled, trying to lighten the mood. "I think I owe her at least another bottle of vintage Sirah after this."

"Yeah, well, not tonight," he said, raising his eyes to meet mine. They were dark, hooded, and filled with all manner of unfulfilled promises. "Tonight, you're all mine."

For the second time that night, I thought I felt my heart stop.

Oh boy.

*   *   *

"I could get used to this lifestyle," Ava said, stretching her long, tanned legs out in front of her as she sipped her Bloody Mary on the terrace of the Links club.

It had been just over a week since Jada had held me at gunpoint and Ava had saved the day, and our lives were finally starting to go back to some semblance of normal. Jada had been treated for a mild concussion, thanks to Ava's excellent golf swing, and had been transferred from the local hospital to the county women's correctional facility to await trial. She'd pleaded not guilty at her arraignment, though the insanity plea she was offering up was going to be a tough sell, considering how neatly she'd laid out all her plans to me in detail. Not that her high-price lawyer wasn't going to give it an expensive try. Word was Carl Costello had put his House of Costello up for auction, using the proceeds to pay for Jada's legal defense.

Once the truth had played out in every gossip column in America, Costello had bravely faced the criticism he'd been so terrified of and stood by Jada's side. In a way, she'd finally gotten what she'd wanted—a *very* public acknowledgement of their love. While the backlash on all fronts was as sharp tongued as Costello had feared, the "dark place" he told the press that this scandal had taken him to emotionally had inspired him to start a whole new fashion line—an emo-chic, all-black collection he'd dubbed the "death of beauty," which fashion critics were already hailing as the most fresh and innovative thing Costello had done in decades.

To celebrate the return of the gem, and me not being Jada's second victim, David Allen had invited Ava, Eddie, and me to the Links for Sunday brunch, which we were currently enjoying—on his dime—to the fullest. We'd already made our way through eggs Benedict, spinach quiche, and freshly baked blueberry muffins and were currently leisurely sipping our cocktails in the sun as we watched the golfers on the freshly mowed expanse of lawn in front of us.

"Well, if this lifestyle suits you, my dear," David said to Ava, leaning back under the shade of an oversize umbrella, "I dare say you could afford a membership here now."

"Now that is tempting." Ava winked at him.

After the emerald had been recovered from my camera bag, Grant and his team had taken it into evidence as part of their case against Jada for Gia's murder. As grateful as Ava had been to see it recovered, Grant had explained that it would likely be several more months to possibly even years before Jada's trial would conclude and the gem could be released to her. An explanation that had nearly brought Ava to tears at the time. However, after Bradley Wu had published his sensationalized account of her heroic rescue in the *Sonoma Index-Tribune*, the line to get into her shop had been around the block the next day. And, while some had been the previous brand of curiosity seekers, several had actually purchased items from the "Daring Designer," as Bradley had dubbed her. Including one woman who turned out to be a collector of nefarious jewelry, including a collection of Borgia rings, and had offered Ava a very tidy sum up front in order to secure the ownership of the notorious necklace as soon as it was released from police custody.

An offer Ava had jumped at—using the funds to not only pay back the loan on the shop but also funnel 11% to Trask plus a small sum to Al in finder's fees, leaving her shop secure, her financial future looking bright, and her kneecaps totally intact. Plus more profit than she'd been expecting to pad her own bank account.

"Oh, if you do buy a membership here, you totally have to bring me to the spa," Eddie jumped in, sucking his mimosa noisily through a straw. "My husband Curtis told me that they do a mango cucumber brown sugar facial that is to die for!"

"Sounds tasty," I said, unable to keep a giggle in. I blamed the fact that I was currently on my second morning cocktail, a summer watermelon Bellini.

"Well, don't go spending all my money yet," Ava said, wagging a finger at us. "The reason I got into this whole mess was for funds to expand Silver Girl's hours."

"You think you will now?" David asked, dropping a pair of dark sunglasses over his eyes.

Ava nodded. "I think I'm going to need to. Did I tell you I had orders for two custom pieces this week?"

"Wow, that's great," I said.

"It is, but it's going to keep me busy working on them. I'll definitely be hiring someone to help look after the shop. Heck, if it works out, I may be able to work full time designing and let employees run the shop."

I could see the wistful look in her eyes and knew that the creative side of the job was the one she relished. I hoped things did work out so she could indulge in it more.

"I guess that means if I want an Ava Barnett original, I should put my order in soon," David said with a grin.

I shot him a look. I'd never pegged David as the man-jewelry type.

"Well, what I want to know is, whatever happened to your Stalker Guy?" Eddie asked, swirling liquid in his glass.

"The police actually picked him up a couple of days ago," I said, setting my Bellini down. "Grant said they finally did get a hit from a traffic cam. With our photo of the guy from Al's security footage, they were able to place him in a gray sedan that came up on a camera just down the highway from the Walmart parking lot we pulled into."

"And they could get a name from that?" David asked.

I nodded. "They followed the footage to a traffic cam that picked up the plate number, and it came back as registered to a guy named Bradley Squires. Aka Stalker Guy."

"Aka Gia's partner in crime," Ava added.

"So he *was* working with Gia?" Eddie asked.

"He was," I confirmed. "When Grant charged him for the hit and run, Squires agreed to take a plea deal in exchange for confessing to his part in the jewel thefts."

"Which we were totally right about," Ava said, picking up the story. She knew because she and I had been enjoying a well-earned night of wine, chocolate, and rom-coms when Grant had stopped by to fill me in. "This Squires guy was a friend of Gia's from high school who worked at an art glass studio. When Gia cooked up her theft scheme, she contacted him to see if he could make glass replicas of gems. He did, and even went one further, agreeing to fence them for her for a cut of the profits."

"He confessed that the two of them had pulled this scam at least half a dozen times," I added.

David raised an eyebrow my way. "Wow. I can imagine designers all over San Francisco are inspecting the authenticity of their gems right about now."

I nodded. "Grant estimated they stole at least half a million in precious gems over the last year."

"But even that wasn't enough for Gia," Ava jumped in. "According to Squires, she got greedy, just like we'd thought, and figured she could find someone else to make the replicas for less and fence the gems herself."

"So it *was* the partner that Costello overheard her firing?" David said.

"Sounds like it," I agreed. "Squires said he was at the show, waiting for Gia to have a chance to make the swap and hand the emerald off to him. Only Gia called him just before she took the runway and told him it was off. That she didn't need him."

"He must not have been happy about that," Eddie said.

"No, he wasn't. In fact, he says he went backstage to talk to Gia about it, but before he had a chance, he saw someone leaving her dressing room in a hurry."

"Jada!" Eddie said.

I nodded. "Jada had been right to be worried about someone seeing her. Someone had—Gia's partner. When he peeked into the room after Jada left and saw that Gia was dead, he immediately took off, afraid someone was on to their theft scheme."

"Which is why the police didn't question him when they arrived. He was already gone," Ava added.

"So why was he trying to run *you* off the road after you left Trask's place?" Eddie asked.

"He was after the gem," I said. "When Squires heard that the gem was missing, he was just as keen to get his hands on it as we were. He guessed that the woman he saw exiting Gia's dressing room had taken it, which is why we saw him at the hotel that day. He'd been tracking down Jada."

"Only he saw Emmy and me, recognized us from the fashion show, and got spooked when we apparently recognized him as well," Ava said.

"He was afraid we might be getting close to figuring out the truth about him and Gia," I added.

"Which, we actually kind of were," Ava noted with a small hint of pride.

"So, he decided to follow us the next day. The fact that we went to Trask's and started asking about gems made him nervous enough that he tried to warn us off by ramming my Jeep." I paused. "Which, by the way, is still in the shop," I said, trying not to sulk about it.

"Don't suppose Mr. Squires' insurance will be covering that?" Ava asked.

I shrugged. "I put in a claim, but we'll see."

"So, did Squires still have Daisy Dot's rubies?" Eddie asked, signaling a passing server in a blue polo shirt for another mimosa.

I shook my head. "Sadly, no. At least, not that he gave up to Grant."

"Poor Daisy Dot," Ava mused, picking up another blueberry muffin and peeling the wrapper off. "I hope she's not out too much."

"Oh, I wouldn't worry about her," David said.

"Oh?" I asked.

"I happen to know Daisy has something new up her sleeve, so to speak," David said, grinning at his own pun.

As he'd filled us in after the memorial cocktail party, David had spent the better part of that evening chatting up the eccentric designer, right up until the police sirens had alerted the partygoers that something other than champagne and caviar was afoot. As David had plied her with rosé, he had gleaned that we'd been right about her stealing Costello's designs. My accusation had shaken her, and she'd felt the need to unburden her soul to an understanding ear who might see the situation her way. It hadn't hurt that the ear had been attached to a young and charmingly attentive man either. As Daisy had told it, she'd paid Gia to send her photos of other designers' work in order to "inspire her to be more creative" with her own designs.

Which made me wonder what her latest endeavor was. "And what sort of new thing would this be?" I asked.

"She's set to begin filming the next season of *On the Runway* in the fall," David told us.

"As a contestant?" Ava asked, scrunching up her nose as she took a bite of muffin.

David shook his head, his too long hair falling across his shoulders. "Nope. This time she's signing on as a mentor. She told me she can't wait to be 'inspired,'" he said, doing air quotes around the word, "by a whole new generation of designers."

Ava laughed out loud. "Well, that sounds like a dramatic season. Those newbies better watch their backs."

"I can only imagine how many of those inspirations will end up in her collection next season," I mused.

"'Imitation is the sincerest form of flattery that mediocrity can pay to greatness,'" David quoted.

"'It is better to fail in originality than to succeed in imitation,'" I countered with a quote of my own.

David raised an eyebrow. "Melville, Ems? Shocking. Who knew you were well-read."

I stuck my tongue out at him.

He chuckled behind his sunglasses.

"Well, speaking of new endeavors, I assume you all heard about Hughie Smart?" Eddie said, nodding a silent thank-you to the server who arrived with his drink.

I shook my head. "No. What happened to Hughie?"

"Well," Eddie started, "I read yesterday in Aurora Dawn's instabloggy thing—"

Ava snorted at the mangled term.

"—that Smart Models is filing for bankruptcy."

"I can't say I'm surprised," I said, lifting my Bellini to my lips for a quick sip. "I mean, one of his top models is dead and the other one is in jail."

"Plus his debt to Trask," Ava added.

"Well, I have a feeling Hughie will be bouncing back from all of that soon," Eddie interjected, shaking his head.

"How do you figure?" Ava asked, licking crumbs off her fingers.

"Well now, honey, that was the best part of the article. Hughie's put out a call for new talent for his brand new *male* modeling agency he's starting, Smarter Models."

Ava rolled her eyes. "Oh brother."

"Oh, you jest, but male modeling is big business. Hughie said he's already booked his first model with a *national* jeans campaign. In fact, the model is someone you ladies might know." Eddie's eyes twinkled.

Mine narrowed. "Who?"

"Well, he's hot, toned, and tanned in the way only a delicious Puerto Rican man can be…"

"Fabio!" Ava said, stabbing a painted nail in Eddie's direction.

"Bingo!" Eddie bounced in his seat.

"National campaign, huh?" I shrugged. "Maybe he'll be able to pay Trask back after all."

"Oh, with Fabio as his new star, Hughie's going to be swimming in offers," Ava said. I could see her eyes get a far off look, as if she were mentally picturing the boy toy now.

"I saw a picture of him," Eddie said. "*Muy caliente*, if you know what I mean." He turned to Ava. "You weren't kidding about those abs, honey."

"What is it with girls and abs?" David said, the frown below his sunglasses registering mild annoyance.

I couldn't help but laugh. "Don't worry. A hot Latin guy isn't *every* girl's type." But I couldn't help ribbing him a little by adding, "Just most."

"Oh really," he countered, crossing his arms over his chest. "Is that your type too, Emmy?"

"Oh, we all know Emmy's type," Eddie jumped in. "Tall, dark, handsome, carries a gun, and likes to arrest people."

I felt myself blush. "How did this all of a sudden get to be about me?"

"Speaking of which…" Ava leaned her elbow on the glass table. "You never did tell me what happened that night after Jada's arrest. When Grant took you home."

"Oh, I have a guess," Eddie said in a sing-song voice, face once again alight with the knowledge of good gossip.

"Eddie," I warned.

"What?" He blinked wide, totally-not-innocent eyes at me. "Can I help it if I just happened to see your delicious little detective walking away from your cottage?" He paused for dramatic effect. "The next morning."

David raised an eyebrow my way, the look on his face hard to read behind his glasses. "The walk of shame, huh, Ems?"

I shook my head. "There was nothing shameful about our evening."

"Oh, do tell," Ava said, leaning in so closely that she was almost off the edge of her seat. "I want to hear everything about your not-shameful evening." She waggled her eyebrows at me in a way that said she'd probably had enough Bloody Marys for the day.

I shook my head. "Sorry. I don't kiss and tell."

"So there *was* some kissing," David said, raising his sunglasses to let me see the teasing glint in his eyes.

Eddie let out a giggle.

I shot him a look. "Grant and I are mature adults. What I do with him in the privacy of my own home is my business."

"And this *business* that's just yours and Grant's," Ava said, "was it done in the *privacy* of your bedroom, by any chance?"

Eddie giggled again like a little girl.

I rolled my eyes, but the smile at the memory of what I was most certainly *not* kissing and telling about was too strong to hold back.

"Oh, that grin says it all," Eddie decided, sitting back in his seat and slurping up the rest of his second mimosa.

"What? What grin?" I said, trying my darndest to wipe it from my face.

"The one that's causing you to blush brighter than my drink," Ava said, giggling now too. "He didn't spend the night on the sofa, did he?"

"You people are relentless," I told them.

"Just tell us this," Eddie said, grinning at me. "Was it everything you could have hoped for?"

I looked from his eager face to Ava's shining eyes to David's mocking smile half hidden by his hair.

I shrugged. "Sorry, kids. My lips are sealed."

Eddie *tsked* disappointedly between his teeth.

Ava scrunched up her nose at me.

David dropped his sunglasses back down over his eyes with a shrug.

"But…" I told them.

All three leaned forward just a scootch.

"I'm meeting him for dinner again tonight." I paused, pulling a move from Eddie's dramatic playbook.

"And?" asked Eddie.

"And," I said with a wink, "I don't think you should wait up."

RECIPES

Flourless Chocolate Cake with Mocha Whipped Cream

Ingredients for Cake:
½ cup unsalted butter
6 ounces semisweet baking chocolate, finely chopped
⅔ cup granulated sugar
2 teaspoons espresso powder
1 ½ teaspoons vanilla extract
4 large eggs, at room temperature
⅓ cup unsweetened cocoa powder
⅛ teaspoon salt
½ teaspoon baking powder

Ingredients for Whipped Cream:
1 teaspoon espresso powder
1 teaspoon warm water
1 cup heavy cream
3 tablespoons confectioners' sugar
1 tablespoon unsweetened cocoa powder

Preheat oven to 350°F. Be sure that you have a bottom oven rack and a center rack in place.

Cut the butter into pieces then place in a large bowl with the baking chocolate. You can melt in the microwave, heating in 20 second increments, or in a double boiler, but make sure chocolate is completely melted and mixture is smooth.

Into the chocolate mixture, whisk the sugar, espresso powder, and vanilla extract. Whisk in the eggs until smooth and heavy, with a consistency like brownie batter. Then whisk in the cocoa powder, salt, and baking powder.

Grease an 8-inch round cake pan, line it with a parchment paper round, and then grease the parchment paper. Pour and spread batter into prepared cake pan.

In your heated oven, place a large roasting pan or baking dish on the bottom oven rack. Boil water (on the stove or in a kettle or microwave) and add to the pan until it's roughly 2 inches up the sides of the pan. Then quickly place the cake on the center rack and shut the oven door to trap the steam inside the oven.

Bake for 30 minutes or until the edges are set. To test doneness, insert toothpick in the center of the cake. It should come out clean.

Remove cake from the oven and place on a cooling rack for 10 minutes. Run a knife around the edges of the cake to help release it, then invert onto a cake plate to completely cool.

For the Mocha Whipped Cream:

Mix espresso powder and warm water together in a small bowl.

Using a hand or a stand mixer, whip the heavy cream, sugar, cocoa powder, and espresso mixture about 4 minutes or until medium peaks form.

Spoon over cooled cake or pipe onto top for a more decorative look. Additionally you can add fresh fruit, such as raspberries, or a dusting of confectioners' sugar.

Tips!
Espresso powder can be left out of the cake if you're sensitive to caffeine or have children who are picky eaters. It helps deepen the chocolate flavor, though, and can be found in the coffee aisle sometimes labeled as instant espresso. Parchment paper and generous greasing helps the cake seamlessly release from the pan. This cake dries out quickly, so do not overbake!

Wine Pairings

Best served paired with red wine with a dark berry or fruit notes like a Cabernet Sauvignon or a port-style wine like a Petite Sirah to compliment the coffee flavors. Some of Emmy's other suggestions: Bogle Petite Sirah Port, Rabble Cabernet Sauvignon, Vanderpump Cabernet Sauvignon

Roasted Tomato Frittata

Ingredients:
16 ounces cherry tomatoes, halved
3 tablespoons olive oil
10 large egg whites
5 large egg yolks
salt and pepper to taste
1 cup chopped baby spinach
2 scallions or green onions, finely chopped
2 tablespoons chopped fresh dill
2 tablespoons feta

Preheat the oven to 400°F.
Place the halved cherry tomatoes in a single layer on the sheet pan and drizzle with 2 tablespoons of olive oil and salt and pepper to taste. Bake for 25–30 minutes then remove from oven and set aside.

Place a rack in upper third of the oven and preheat broiler.

Beat egg whites and yolks in a medium bowl and add salt and pepper.
In a large ovenproof cast-iron or nonstick skillet, heat 1 tablespoon of olive oil over medium heat. Add spinach and scallions and cook just until spinach is wilted, about 2 minutes. Pour eggs evenly over the spinach mixture and cook until the edges and bottom are just set, about 30 seconds. Add dill, roasted tomatoes, and feta. Transfer skillet carefully to the oven.

Broil until frittata is golden brown and center is set, about 4 minutes. Enjoy!

Tips!

You can use any type of tomatoes in this recipe, though cherry or grape make for easy, bite sized pieces. Leftover frittata keeps well in the refrigerator for up to seven days and can be served chilled, room temperature, or warmed.

Wine Pairings
Best served paired with sparkling acidic wines to cut through the richness of the eggs, like Champagne, or a light fruity Rosé or crisp Sauvignon Blanc. Some of Emmy's other suggestions: Yes Way Rosé Wine, Francis Coppola Diamond Collection Sauvignon, Mumm Napa Brut Prestige

Sea Bass with Lemon Herb Sauce

Ingredients:
1 ½ lbs. sea bass
¼ cup all purpose flour
1 teaspoon salt
½ teaspoon black pepper
3 tablespoons butter, divided
1 tablespoon extra virgin olive oil
2 cloves garlic, minced
¼ cup dry white wine such as Sauvignon Blanc
½ cup chicken stock
2 tablespoons fresh lemon juice
1 tablespoon fresh oregano, roughly chopped
1 tablespoon fresh thyme, roughly chopped
1 tablespoon fresh parsley, roughly chopped

Rinse the fish and pat it dry, making sure it's free of bones. In a shallow dish, mix together the flour, salt, and pepper. Dredge each piece of fish in the flour mixture until the entire surface is coated.

In a large skillet, melt 1 tablespoon of the butter with olive oil over medium high heat. Add the fish to the skillet and cook for about 4 minutes on each side or until golden brown and cooked through. Remove fish from the skillet and set aside.

Turn the heat under the skillet to low and add the white wine to deglaze and unstick any browned bits. Add 1 tablespoon of butter, garlic, and fresh herbs. Sauté only about 1 minute or until fragrant. Then add the chicken broth and bring to a low simmer. Once it simmers, remove from heat and add remaining butter and lemon juice.

Plate fish and spoon lemon herb sauce on top of it. Enjoy!

Tips!

A stainless steel, well-seasoned cast iron, or nonstick skillet works best. When browning your fish, try not to move it too much, so it has a chance to brown evenly and not stick to the pan. To make this dairy-free, you can substitute more olive oil or ghee for butter, or for gluten-free use almond flour. If you can't find sea bass at your local grocery store, any type of mild white fish will substitute nicely, like pollock or cod.

Wine Pairings
Best served paired with crisp, un-oaked wines to compliment the delicate flavor of the fish like a Sauvignon Blanc, Pinot Grigio, or an Italian white like Vermentino. Some of Emmy's other suggestions: The Pinot Project Pinot Grigio, Palmalias Vermentino, SeaGlass Sauvignon Blanc

Crepes with Bacon Onion Jam

For the Bacon Onion Jam:

Ingredients:
1 lb. thick cut bacon
2 extra large sweet onions, sliced
½ cup brown sugar
⅓ cup strong brewed coffee
½ cup water
1 tablespoon balsamic vinegar

Chop the bacon into small slices and add them to a large frying pan. Cook over medium heat for about 10 minutes, until the fat is rendered from the bacon but the pieces are not too crispy. Remove bacon from the pan and set aside.

Drain the majority of the bacon drippings from the pan, leaving just the bottom lightly coated. Add the onions and cook for about 9–10 minutes until they are translucent. Reduce heat to low and add the sugar, stirring continuously. Cook until the onions have caramelized, about 15 minutes. To the pan, add the coffee, water, and the cooked bacon pieces. Continue to cook, stirring often, for about 25 minutes or until the onions take on a jam-like texture.

Remove from heat and stir in the balsamic vinegar.

Jam can be used immediately or will keep in the refrigerator for up to a week.

Tips!
When the jam is cold, you will see little spots of white bacon fat in the jam. Bring the jam up to at least room temperature to melt these down and they will disappear.

For the Crepes:

Ingredients:

2 eggs
½ cup milk
½ cup water
½ teaspoon vanilla
1 cup all purpose flour
¼ teaspoon salt
2 tablespoons butter, melted
oil or butter

In a large mixing bowl, whisk together the eggs, milk, water, and vanilla. Gradually sift in the flour. Add the salt and butter and then beat the batter until smooth. Chill batter for at least 30 minutes in refrigerator.

Heat a lightly oiled frying pan over medium high heat. Scoop out about 1/4 cup of the batter and pour evenly over the pan. Tilt the pan with a circular motion to ensure that batter evenly coats the surface. Cook until the bottom is very lightly browned, about 2 minutes, and then loosen with a spatula and gently flip crepe over to brown the other side.

Fill crepes with filling of your choice and fold or roll. Enjoy!

Tips!
If you're having a hard time getting your batter smooth, try mixing in a blender or with an electric mixer. If you're making a large batch of crepes, you can tent the finished ones with foil to keep them warm while you cook the rest.

Wine Pairings
Best served paired with a white wine, like a Chardonnay or a light bodied red, like a Pinot Noir. Some of Emmy's suggestions: Butter Chardonnay, La Crema - Chardonnay Sonoma Coast, Werewolf Pinot Noir

Mama Halliday's Apple Pie

For the Crust:
Ingredients:
4 cups unbleached white flour, organic preferred
2 teaspoons sea salt
1 cup walnut oil
6 tablespoons water, very cold to almost freezing
Mix flour and salt with a fork in a medium bowl. Stir in oil until well blended. Add water and knead with hands until absorbed, but no longer. Divide dough in half and roll one half out between waxed paper into a pie-sized round. Carefully place into a 10-inch deep-dish pie plate and trim the edges to about 1 inch from the top of the dish. Reserve the other half of the dough for after the filling is placed into the bottom crust. It's a good idea to cover it with waxed paper or plastic wrap so that it doesn't dry out.

For the Filling:
10 medium Granny Smith apples
½ cup sugar
3 tablespoons white flour
2 teaspoons cinnamon
2 tablespoons butter (optional)

Core, skin, and thinly slice apples, either by hand, apple corer, or spiralizer. Place cored apples into a large bowl and add sugar, flour, and cinnamon. Then gently mix, arrange into pie plate over the crust, and dot with butter.
Roll out the reserved dough, and make 3 slits in it for steam to escape. Place over the apple filling and seal the edges with the under crust by pressing together. Cover pie with aluminum foil, also with slits for steam to escape. Bake 60 minutes at 425°F. Remove foil and bake for 10 more minutes or until crust is slightly golden brown. Remove from oven and sprinkle with 1 teaspoon of sugar if desired. Cool before slicing. Enjoy with vanilla ice cream or without!

Tips!

Sugar may be eliminated for a very tart, appley flavor (Mama Halliday's favorite!) or increased for more sweetness. Simple fingerprints make a nice decorative edging for the crust. Rather than slits, Mama Halliday often likes to cut out designs into her upper piecrust using small cookie cutters. A little heart is nice!

Wine Pairings
Best served paired with sweet wines that complement the tart apples, like a Moscato or caramelly tawny port. Some of Emmy's suggestions: Porto Valdouro Tawny Port, Stella Rosa Moscato D'Asti, Primo Amore Moscato Champagne

Authentic Mole Sauce

¼ cup sesame seeds
5 whole cloves
1 cinnamon stick
1 cup chopped white onion
½ teaspoon anise seeds
¼ teaspoon coriander seeds
6 dried guajillo chile peppers
4 dried ancho chile peppers
6 tablespoons corn or canola oil
¼ cup raisins
¼ cup whole blanched almonds
¼ cup hulled pumpkin seeds
2 6-inch corn tortillas, torn into pieces
6 cups chicken broth
1 2.7-ounce disk Mexican chocolate, broken into pieces
Pinch of sugar

Toast the sesame seeds in a dry skillet over medium heat. Toss until golden, about 5 minutes, and then transfer to a blender.

In the same dry skillet, toast the cloves, cinnamon stick, and anise and coriander seeds until fragrant, about 3 minutes. Add to the blender.

Remove the stems and seeds from the dried chile peppers. Heat 4 tablespoons oil in the same skillet over medium heat. Add the chiles and fry until lightly toasted and fragrant, about 1–2 minutes. Transfer the chiles to a bowl and cover them with hot water. Set aside to soak until pliable, for about 30 minutes.

Meanwhile, add the raisins, almonds, pumpkin seeds, and tortilla pieces to the oil in the skillet. Stir continuously and cook until the seeds and tortillas are golden brown. Add to the blender, along with any oil left in the skillet, the softened chiles, and the onion.
Puree, slowly adding 2 cups of broth to make a thick, smooth sauce.

Transfer the sauce to a large pot over medium heat. Add in 4 cups of broth and simmer until the sauce starts to thicken, about 20 minutes. Add the chocolate, stirring frequently, and simmer until the chocolate melts and the sauce reduces, about 20 more minutes. Add the sugar and season with salt.

Add cooked meat to the pot or pour over enchiladas, rice, and any cooked meat!

Tips!
There are as many versions of mole as there are ingredients, so don't be afraid to experiment and improve with your own additions. Some versions can be sped up using a pressure cooker or cooking low and slow in a slow cooker.

Wine Pairings
Best served paired with a full bodied red like a Petite Sirah with high tannins. Some of Emmy's suggestions: Stags' Leap Petite Sirah, Spellbound Petite Sirah, Line 39 Petite Sirah

ABOUT THE AUTHOR

Gemma Halliday is the #1 Amazon, *New York Times & USA Today* bestselling author of several mystery and suspense series. Gemma's books have received numerous awards, including a Golden Heart, two National Reader's Choice awards, a RONE Award for best mystery, and three RITA nominations. She currently lives in the San Francisco Bay Area with her large, loud, and loving family.

To learn more about Gemma, visit her online at
www.GemmaHalliday.com

The Wine & Dine Mysteries

www.GemmaHalliday.com

Made in United States
North Haven, CT
06 April 2022

17946476R00150